NO GOOD LIKE IT IS

McKendree R. Long III

No Good Like It Is

No Good Like It Is is a hard-ridin', fast-shootin' adventure tale of Texas Rangers in the Civil War. McKendree Long knows his history, his weapons, and puts you right in the middle.

> — Dac Crossley, award-winning author of *Return of the Texas R anger.*

A fresh, compelling voice with a strong grasp of our colorful historical heritage. I highly recommend this novel to fans of the true western saga.

> — John W. Huffman, author of *A Wayward Wind*, *The Baron of Clayhill,* and *Tiger Woman.*

In *No Good Like It Is*, Mike Long has given readers a page-turner with a believable plot, realistic characters, and a reading experience that will linger in the reader's mind long after the events unfold.

Every reader who enjoys a good story that will hold his interest from first page to last should mark *No Good Like It Is* as a must-read.

> — Kenneth E. Hamburger, Ph.D. Colonel, U.S. Army, Retired.

Author of *Why America Is Free* [1998] and *Leadership in the Crucible: The Korean War Battles of Twin Tunnels and Chipyong-ni* [2003]

Prologue

There was a large adobe building, a lean-to shed on each end, a barn, outhouse, and corrals. A small garden and cornfield, all brown and withered from the heat. No cook smoke. No dogs or chickens. No horses or milk cows. No people.

Well, not exactly. There were five people on the ground around the adobe and the barn. Even from this distance it was apparent that they were dead. They wore little or no clothing. Several had long black hair and the bodies were sun-darkened, as though they'd lain there for some time. It wouldn't need to be long in this heat. Not yet noon, it was already scalding hot.

Dobey couldn't hear the flies yet nor pick up the smell of death, but he knew it was there, waiting for him to come a little closer. He was in no hurry now.

Dobey's throat constricted. He hadn't seen his family in years. Years of fighting, and years of school before that, and finally this long trip 'home'. For most of that time, he hadn't even known where his family was. And now this. He couldn't breathe.

There'd been some movement down by the river, which was half a mile further downhill to the right, past the barn. As he rode slowly down past the outhouse, Dobey could see the barn doors were standing open. Sergeant Melton and Bear rode with him, pistols drawn, twenty yards out to either side, on full alert. The others waited atop the low ridge with the Cherokee scouts.

Melton and Bear spread out some, walking their horses slowly to check out the bodies. Bear halted and said, "Dead goat here. Three arrows. They ain't Cheyenne."

"Prob'ly Comanche, or Kiowa." Melton stood in the stirrups for a better look around. "Might be better me and Bear look these folks over, Dobey. You go on to the store. You might not want to see this."

Now Dobey fought the rising bile.

BOOK ONE

June 1858

CHAPTER ONE

"You want a chew, Lieutenant Walls?"

"Ah—no. But thank you, Sergeant. I'm still sucking on this pebble."

"Pebble. Yessir." Sergeant Kibler cut himself another slice from his tobacco plug and added it to his already full left cheek.

Second Lieutenant Thomas "Dobey" Walls took off his hat, rubbed sweat from his face with his sleeve, then used the hat to shield his eyes as he strained to see the approaching riders. "A pebble helps when you're thirsty and trying to save water."

Kibler spat. "Yessir. I'spect you learned that at West Point."

Walls put his hat on again and looked sideways at the old sergeant. He knew it was important to maintain 'face' with these old non-coms, especially as a shave-tail, Class of 1858, straight out of the Academy. "Well, no. I learned that out in Colorado Territory, long before I went to school."

"Yessir. We ain't exactly dying of thirst here. There was water in that creek we just crossed. You ain't got a scope to look at them riders?"

"No, not yet. Do you have any idea who they are?"

"Yessir. They's either Jayhawkers, Border Ruffians, or our escort from Fort Smith. You might want to get a scope. It helps to know something afore they's on top of you, though it ain't as interesting as waiting. Least ways, they ain't Indians. Did you really want some water?" He offered his canteen.

The two mounted men were under a tree and behind low scrub on a small hill. They'd seen the dust two miles away, long before they could see or hear the riders. They could now tell that fifteen or twenty men were riding hard toward them from the west, right out of the late sun.

"No, Sergeant. Just forget the water, alright? How do you know they ain't Indians?"

"Well, sir, they'd come on the sneak, at night. Be after our horses, 'stead of looking for a fight. Course, if they had us bad outnumbered, they'd probably want our hair too. But some of these folks is wearing white shirts and black top hats. I can see that much. Want to look?" Grinning, the old sergeant handed Lieutenant Walls his brass telescope.

"Oh. Thanks." Walls focused on the group. "They ain't soldiers, either. How do you know whether they're Jayhawkers or, what did you say, bushwhackers?"

"Border Ruffians, I said. Though they is usually bush-whackers too. Well, Jayhawkers is from Kansas. Free Staters. Loves them darkies. Border Ruffians, now, they's from Missoura. They holds with slavery. Don't care for Jayhawkers nor darkies. Hates 'em."

"But how do you tell 'em apart?"

"Don't know as you can. Doctors, lawyers, merchants, law-men, farmers, schoolboys." Kibler spat again and reached for his scope. "Vicious, murdering, back-stabbing, barn-burning buggers, all of 'em. I have heard that some of the Jayhawkers has taken to sporting red-dyed sheep wool atop their boots. Calls themselves Redlegs. You catch a flash of red there?"

He handed the scope back to Walls, who trained it on the men and nodded. The riders were now less than a mile away.

Sergeant Kibler took his scope back, stuffed it in his saddlebag, and wheeled his horse around. "Let's get back and report, Lieutenant. I think these boys spotted the wagons from that big ridge over there and is heading to cut 'em off."

The two cavalrymen rode directly to the lead wagon, a buckboard, and saluted the captain sitting in the driver's seat. The two trailing wagons were covered Conestogas pulled by oxen. As they ground to a halt, the ten troopers of the escort closed in to hear the report.

Their captain took off his hat and wiped his head with a yellow scarf. Lean, maybe thirty-five and balding, he had impatient eyes. "Let's have it, Sergeant."

"Maybe twenty Jayhawkers, Cap'n Ellison. Less than a mile behind us, coming this way fast. Probably seen us from that hill back there. We made out some red on their boot tops."

Captain Ellison re-tied his scarf. "Free Staters. What are they doing in Arkansas? Anybody chasing them?"

"Nossir." Kibler spat once more, then wiped his chin. "Sorry, ma'am."

A young black-haired woman was seated beside the captain. She smiled. "No need for an apology, Sergeant Kibler."

Turning back to Ellison, Kibler finished his report. "That was it, Captain. Didn't seem to have no prisoners, neither."

"Anything to add, Lieutenant Walls? I hope I didn't slight you by taking the report from the sergeant."

"No, sir. On both counts. Thanks for letting me go with him, and thanks for the use of your horse." He dismounted. He knew he was just baggage here, enroute to his first post, not even issued a horse or weapon yet. "I was getting tired of that wagon seat."

Captain Ellison looked past him. "There they come. You keep the horse for now, Walls. You may need that pistol."

He nodded toward the Dragoon Colt in the pommel holster. Addressing the woman, he said, "Beth, go to the other wagon and try to keep Sissy out of sight. Don't want these scoundrels to think we're keeping a slave."

Hearing her name, a young black girl peered over the shoulder of the trooper driving the first covered wagon.

Beth Ellison gathered her skirts and jumped down from the buckboard. "Yes, master." She gave her husband a worried smile, then shouted, "Hide yourself in there, Sissy. And don't talk."

As the Redlegs lumbered to a halt, Captain Ellison nodded to his sergeant, who shouted, "Draw carbines, boys. Dismount. High Port. Check your primers." Like a drill, two troopers led the horses back toward the big wagons, while the other eight troopers stepped into line holding their weapons across their chests.

A harsh ripple of murmurs ran through the eighteen Redlegs as they noticed the weapons. Colt revolving carbines. Forty-fours. Six-shooters. Goddamit, anyways.

Walls, Kibler, and the trumpeter, an immigrant named Migliore, remained mounted beside the captain's buckboard. Captain Ellison set the butt of his shotgun on the seat between his legs, smiled, and said, "What can we do for you?"

A squat man in full beard and top hat replied, "I'm Doctor Jennison. We're from Kansas, and we're looking for scum transporting slaves into the territories." His horse danced a little. He wore a short sword and, like most of the others, had a muzzle-loading rifle across his lap.

Ellison's smile widened. "We can't help you. Haven't seen anything like that."

An unkempt fat man with wild eyes rode up beside the Redleg leader. "I'm telling you, Doctor, I seen a nigra woman in that first big wagon as we come up. That bluecoat is lying. Let's search them wagons. We got 'em outnumbered."

Ellison's smile disappeared. "That's not going to happen." He cocked both barrels of the shotgun.

Hearing that, Kibler just said, "Ready, boys." There was the chatter of oiled clicks as the carbines went on full cock.

Lieutenant Walls watched the fat man. The others were nervous, but that one was unafraid. "That fat one's crazy," he whispered to Sergeant Kibler.

"Yessir, I think you're right. Millie, give that fat bastard a toot on your horn."

"Si, Sergeant." The trumpeter dismounted, tucked his bugle under his arm, and quick-stepped towards the big Redleg.

Kibler choked on his tobacco wad. "No, Millie, I didn't mean . . ." It was too late. Migliore marched up to the man's mare, put the bugle to his lips and blew "Recall" right in the mare's nose. The horse reared and tossed the fat man. Unused to bugle calls, the other Redleg horses danced jigs too.

Migliore stood over the stunned fat man and shook his bugle at him. "You no talk my Capitan a liar, you hear me?" He turned, nodded to the captain as he put the bugle under his arm and marched back to his mount. In the saddle again, he turned to Kibler. "Tha's alright, si?"

Kibler was still choking, but on laughter. He nodded a yes. Even some of the Redlegs were laughing as the fat man ran after his horse.

Ellison was still serious. He raised his voice to the doctor. "This is an army re-supply mission to Fort Smith. You don't get to touch us, long as we live. You have us outnumbered, we have you out-gunned. The law is on our side, and this is not Kansas. Just ride on. An escort from Fort Smith is due to meet us at any time. We thought you was them."

Doctor Jennison looked back to the west, then stared at the captain with hate-filled eyes. "Maybe another day, then. Let's go, boys."

As the intruders rode north, Kibler cut another chew. "Let them hammers down easy, boys. Cap'n, why din't you just tell 'em that Sissy girl was already free?"

"None of their business, Bud. Besides, they pissed me off."

✡ ✡ ✡

Lieutentant Walls jerked awake. It was early morning, still dark,and slight rain made the campfire pop and sizzle. The sentry knelt between Walls and Sergeant Kibler, and was nearly frantic.

"They're right there," he whispered, pointing to bushes not twenty yards away. "I ain't seen 'em, but I heard 'em. They's a bunch of 'em, I tell you. Just listen."

Walls picked up the big revolver and rolled onto his stomach, pointing it over the saddle. No longer a pillow, the saddle gave him some protection. He'd had a restless night already, thinking of night-raiding Indians and vengeful Jayhawkers. The Fort Smith escort still hadn't showed, and now he couldn't swallow.

Kibler yanked the sentry down. "Easy, boy. Crawl around and make sure ever' one's awake and ready." The trooper scuttled away.

Walls heard them now, too. He cocked the Dragoon and peered down the barrel. The firelight reflected on the damp leaves, dancing, playing tricks on his eyes, but something was right there where he heard the rustling. The bushes moved, just slightly, and there they were: two mean, golden eyes, staring back at him from the bushes. He fired.

The flash blinded him for a second, but the bushes were obscured by the gunsmoke anyhow. The bang left his ears ringing, but he still heard the squeal, then grunts of pain. The little army camp exploded around him. Walls fired again.

Kibler yelled, "You got one, sir." He went up on his knees and fired three quick rounds from his Colt carbine into the same bushes, drawing more screams. "Hold up, now. Don't shoot 'less you got a real target, boys. I think they's running."

Captain Ellison yelled from across the camp. "Nothing on this side, Kibler. Anybody hurt?"

"I don't know yet, Cap'n. Hang on. Hey, Lieutenant, listen. You hear that?"

Walls nodded. The attackers could clearly be heard racing away through the underbrush.

Kibler shouted, "They's gone, this side. Hey, Millie, grab a firebrand and come with me. Lieutenant, cover us." Trumpeter Migliore brought the torch and Kibler eased up to the bushes carefully, pushing the branches aside with his carbine barrel.

Even from twenty yards away, Walls could see the dark body still twitching, bright blood pulsing in the torchlight.

Kibler looked back at him. "Damn, Lieutenant, that's good shooting for a shave-tail." Migliore touched him and pointed farther back in the bushes. "Hell, there's two more in here."

CHAPTER TWO

Like Fort Smith, Fort Gibson was just off the Arkansas River. The fact that it was forty miles north and upriver didn't make it any cooler. June of 1858 had been a scorcher so far, but the temperature was not the sole reason for the sweat pouring down Lieutenant Dobey Walls' forehead and nose as he waited outside the office of his commanding officer, an officer he had yet to meet, an officer reputed to eat second lieutenants for breakfast. Especially new West Point graduates, as the commander was a crusty old major named Caskey, a "mustang," up from the ranks, with little formal education.

Sergeant Reid, who picked up the new arrival at the dock, filled in Lieutenant Walls on their short wagon ride from the river to Fort Gibson. The more grim possibilities the sergeant outlined, the happier he seemed to become.

As he deposited Dobey here ten minutes earlier, his parting shot was, "No sirree Bob. I wouldn't want to be no shavetail reporting to Major Caskey today, no way. He was madder'n a hornet already this morning."

As he drove away, narrowly missing Dobey with the rear wheels, another sergeant hailed him. "What's doing, Harry?"

"Delivering a baby, so to speak," Reid cackled, in a voice just loud enough for Dobey to hear also.

Dobey decided that Reid was one of that breed of sergeants put on earth to make life miserable for junior officers. They used their age and experience to push to the very edge of insolence, and generally only treated senior officers respectfully out of fear. Dobey now thought of several things he might have said to put the sergeant firmly in his place.

Now I think of them, he thought, then, *his place, hell I don't even know my own place. Though I'm probably about to find out.*

The door opened. The sergeant major came out and smiled. "The major will see you now, sir. I'll bet you know how to report."

Dobey nodded grimly, marched in, stopped three feet from the major's desk, saluted and announced, "Lieutenant Walls reports to the commanding officer as ordered, sir."

The hard leathery face fixed him in a stare. "Walls, Thomas MacDougal?" He didn't return the salute.

"Yessir." Dobey held his salute, and his anxiety level went off the scale. *Is he going to return it? How long do I hold it? This is not a good start.*

"Army brat, son of an enlisted man, right?"

"Yes sir." Sweat was now pouring off the tip of his nose.

The major returned his salute and stood. Lanky. Nice smile. *Jesus*, thought Dobey, *he's laughing at me.* He dropped his salute.

"I'm told you rode to Fort Smith with Captain Ellison and was in that standoff, and in the gunfight the next morning."

Dobey fought to keep his eyes on a nail in the wall behind the major. Sweat ran into his eyes. He tried to blink it away.

"Heard you was a hell of a shot, too. Stayed calm, killed three of 'em, that right?"

Dobey struggled to find his voice. "Nosir. I only got off two shots . . ."

Sergeant-Major McCabe cut in. "Three of 'em, with two shots. Amazing. Sergeant Kibler sent word that it was an entire family, too. Mean old leader of the clan, a fat sow of a mother, and their filthy runt. How you ever gonna top that? You ever hear of starting out slow?"

Dobey tried again. "Sergeant-Major, it was probably Kibler that killed two of 'em. I just . . ."

Major Caskey cut him off. "Not what he said. The big question is, though, did you let the men cook and eat them?"

Dobey hung his head. "Yessir."

Caskey smiled. "Wish you'd saved some. I love razorback hogs. Little vinegar and mustard? Man."

The major walked around the desk and extended his hand. "John Caskey. Welcome. I'm glad to have you. K. E. Hamburger was through here, maybe a year ago, told me about you. Was on his way to Washington. I asked for you. Looks like he was able to swing it."

Dobey shook his hand, numb, thick-tongued, non-believing. "Major Hamburger, sir? From Fort Motte?"

"The one and only. Sit down, son. Sergeant Major, a couple of mugs of coffee—no, make it three. I'll bet you remember this lieutenant's old man. Come on in."

Sergeant Major McCabe brought in the coffee, but wouldn't sit. "So you're 'Big Mac' Walls' boy. I will be damned. I'da thought you'd be six foot tall, at least, Lieutenant."

"So, you knew him?" Dobey held himself erect, but as a slender five and a half footer, he was dwarfed by the older soldiers.

"Oh, yes sir. Served with him as a private and as a sergeant. Hell of a soldier, Mac was."

"I guess you didn't know Mama. She's five foot two." Dobey finally relaxed enough to grin, and the two others had a good laugh.

"Wasn't that Sergeant Reid who brought you in?" Major Caskey got serious again.

"Reid. Yessir."

"And what did you think of our Henry Reid?"

"Well, sir, I guess he had some fun at my expense." Dobey smiled at McCabe. "Probably the same sort of things my father would have said to a new lieutenant."

McCabe shrugged without smiling, but Major Caskey stood suddenly and said, "No, I doubt it. I knew your father too, and he was more like Jack McCabe here. No, Reid's a problem. Probably told you that I'm an asshole. Well, you'll have to judge, Walls, because I can be one."

Sergeant Major McCabe snorted and rolled his eyes.

"Reid's got 'L' Troop, now, with no officer for several months," continued the Major. "We got other troops without officers, but 'L' Troop has morale problems."

"Reid's the problem, Major, and you and I know it, and Lieutenant Walls needs to know it, if you gonna send him there. He's a bully and a backstabber and a cheat, and I'd shoot the sonuvabitch, you just let me."

"And let Corporal Potter run it? 'Cause he's senior to Melton, and he ain't as good as Reid. No, Reid ain't no Mac Walls, nor no Jack McCabe, but he's been around for twelve years, and he don't have much discipline problems, and he's seen some fighting."

"So he says. But you're the boss."

Caskey turned back to Dobey. "Now, tell me how you got a nickname like 'Dobey'. That must have come at West Point. Hamburger didn't mention it."

"Yessir. Weren't many Texans at the Academy, so they pegged me as 'Adobe Walls' right away after those mud houses back home, then just cut it to 'Dobey'."

"Well, despite my sergeant-major's concerns, I'm gonna assign you to 'L' Troop. Reid's your troop sergeant. Potter has one section, Melton the other. Melton's a good man. Let's see can you pick things up down there."

☆ ☆ ☆

Dobey tried to blow the flies away from his sweating nose as he knelt to replace a rat trap. He stood and waved off the flies with his hat as Corporal Melton walked up.

"Afternoon, Corporal Melton. Why so dressed up?"

"Corporal Potter didn't feel good this morning, so Sergeant Reid substituted me as Sergeant of the Guard today. I was just checking 'em over before inspection. You be doing that too?"

"No. Lieutenant Albert's the Officer of the Day."

"Hmm. Well, sir, he's sick too. Thought I heard that you was his replacement. Gotta be you. Lieutenant Adams is at Fort Smith, and Captain Morrison's on patrol, and Lieutenant Boswell had the duty last night. That leaves you." He bit his lip. "Guess you'd better clean up, sir. Only got fifteen minutes 'fore Guard Mount. Major's likely to be there, 'specially with a new officer performing it."

Dobey started walking toward his quarters. "How'd you hear this? How's I supposed to know? Bad enough the major sees me like this, after I've been crawling around in horse manure checking rat traps, but think what the men on guard would think. Jesus. Them cleaned for inspection, and me in shitty stable clothes."

Melton started to answer, then thought better of it. He saluted and said, "Yessir. See you in a few minutes. Front of the guard house."

Eleven minutes later, Dobey rushed out of his quarters with clean fatigue pants, jacket brushed, pistol belt, gloves, and saber in place, and ran squarely into Sergeant Reid.

"Jesus, Lieutenant, where you been? I been looking for you for over an hour. You got Officer of the Day, and you got Guard Mount in about five minutes..." Reid's happy face turned to surprise, then sour, as it became apparent that Dobey was ready.

✧ ✧ ✧

At the completion of the inspection, Dobey turned and saluted Major Caskey, who waited to the side and watched the procedure. "Would you like to address the guard, sir?"

Major Caskey returned the salute. "I would. Thank you, Lieutenant Walls." He strode to the front of the tight formation of sixteen men, hands clasped behind him.

"You all been told how, if you don't stay alert on your posts, wild injuns might slip by you and murder us all." He smiled. So did the men. "Been a while since we was attacked here, so I know it's hard to get excited 'bout walking a guard post here. Out on patrol, hostiles around you, no problem staying alert. But back here? Tough, ain't it?" The men smiled and nodded.

"So let's put it in a different light for you." Same even voice. "Tonight, somebody is gonna be checking on you. Corporal Melton, Corporal McDowell, Lieutenant Walls, maybe me. I find you dozing, or learn that you relaxed, I will have Sergeant Major McCabe whip your ass. To a frazzle. Carry on."

Dobey snapped him another salute. As Major Caskey faced him to return it, he gave Dobey a broad wink and marched away.

＊ ＊ ＊

"Let me guess. Reid was supposed to tell me about the change in duty, right?" Dobey and Melton watched as Corporal McDowell marched the guard formation off to eat.

"I don't know about that, sir. This sort of thing happened before?"

"Once or twice."

"You don't mind, I could tell the sergeant major that his choice of messengers ain't always working where you're concerned. He'll fix it, best he can."

This man knows more than he's telling me, Dobey thought. He couldn't help wishing that Melton was more senior, and could be his troop sergeant. He knew the twenty-six year old man had enlisted here five years earlier, and rose rapidly to corporal because of his size, fighting skills, intelligence, and leadership ability. He was widely believed to have had prior military service, but there must have been a cloud. Why else wouldn't he claim that service, for pay and promotion eligibility?

"'Nother thing, Lieutenant. Why the hell are you mucking around with rat traps in the first place? I can have some of our men do it."

"I feel that I ought to learn these jobs for myself, if I'm gonna order others to do them. You know that's why the junior officers at a post always get these extra duties."

Dobey was the rodent control officer, the venereal disease monitoring officer, and the stable officer. When he gained experience, or when a more junior officer arrived, he might become supply officer, mess officer, marksmanship officer, or morale officer.

"Alls I know is, my daddy was a horse breaker, spent a lot time around barns and stables. Always kept some cats there. Didn't really need no traps, and with the rats gone, didn't see so many snakes neither."

Two days later, Dobey bought two cats off a steamer on the Arkansas, and asked Melton if he had any ideas about getting rid of the whores that lived in the tent city outside the fort.

"Ain't gonna happen, sir. And if it did, the men would go to Fort Smith or to an Indian village."

"How am I expected to cut down the pox, then? I send the men to the medicos, they get dosed, then they go get it again. I've tried scaring them. They say, yessir, yessir, then go right back."

Melton thought a minute. "Was a deserter off a English boat, a marine, come through here a year ago. Heading for

California, gonna get rich. Said the English had whores on the ship, and with their army, and their doctors treated the whores as well as the men. Said it helped. Couldn't hurt. Hell, it ain't no good like it is."

CHAPTER THREE

"Walls, I want you to know that the sergeant major keeps me posted on your doings. Says the cats are helping, and multiplying."

"Yessir."

"Says having the medicos treat the whores has cut way back on sick time for the pox. Says the whores is paying for the dosage?"

"Yessir. We told them we'd run 'em off unless they submitted for treatment and paid. You reckon you could get the commander at Fort Smith to try it? Our men still catch it over there. They say the whores are prettier."

"I've already sent the sergeant major over there to talk to their top sergeant. We'll see. You got any more ideas for me?"

"Major, both those ideas come from Corporal Jimmy Melton. Soon as he can be promoted, he should be. But I do have another idea, maybe two."

"Go ahead. I thought you might." Caskey leaned back and smiled.

"I don't know 'bout the other troops, but my men ain't in good shape. Can't run up a short hill. Some of 'em can't ride worth a tinker's dam. Maybe we could have some contests.

Riding and foot races, boxing, even wrestling. Some short foot marches. Make 'em appreciate those horses?"

"Who in hell would teach 'em boxing or wrestling?"

"I learned some about it at West Point. Lieutenant Boswell knows some too, and Melton says there's a couple of non-coms was prize fighters."

"All right. Was that one idea, or two?"

"No sir. I mean, just one. The other one was on marksmanship."

"Goddammit, you think I don't know that's a problem? Walls, we don't have enough Sharps cartridges for our basic load—not enough to fight with. You think we can burn half of 'em for target practice? 'Cause that's what it would take, to get this cross-eyed outfit halfway ready to qualify with their carbines. And forget about the pistols." He yanked open a drawer, pulled out a flask, took a swallow, and slammed it back into the desk. "No cartridges. No money. That's all I hear from regiment, and district, and dammit, Walls, they ain't lying."

"Yessir. But here's the thing. Melton says..."

"Melton says. Melton says. Jesus Christ. What else does Melton say?"

Dobey took a breath. "Sir, there's this trader, Boissineau, that trades in the Indian Territory. Mostly legitimate. But he also buys a lot of powder and lead off the boats here, and not all of that goes to buffalo hunters and to the peaceful Indians."

"By peaceful, you mean the Five Tribes?" Caskey asked.

Dobey started to let that pass, but couldn't. "The who?"

Major Caskey smiled. "The Five Civilized Tribes. Choctaw, Cherokee, Seminole, Creek, Chickasaw. They was forcibly moved here maybe forty years ago from the southeast. Got their own governments and police forces."

Dobey nodded. "That was the Trail of Tears I heard of."

It was Caskey's turn to nod. "Just so. And now this trader is selling to the Comanche and Kiowa?"

"Yessir. And Cheyenne and Arapahoe. So Melton says. Says we could trail him, trap him, confiscate it. Ought to at least get enough for basic training, and a contest, maybe."

"Another contest," Caskey snorted, but now he was smiling. "What do you and Melton think we should give as prizes? Furlough to Saint Louis for a week? Free whores?"

Sergeant Major McCabe had eased into Caskey's office during his tirade, and now spoke. "Bragging rights, Major. Won't need no rewards. You know, just so's they can say, 'My troop is better'n your'n,' or hear you tell everybody at parade."

"Mmm. All right, I'll cogitate on this. Dismissed."

With Walls gone, Sergeant Major McCabe brought in two cups of coffee, and stood, waiting.

"You know about this? I mean, these ideas?"

"Melton just briefed me this morning, Major. Did the lieutenant take credit for the cats and dosing the whores?"

"Nope. Gave Melton full credit. Matter of fact he gave credit for about everything to Melton."

"Thought he would. He's Big Mac's boy, all right."

Chapter Four

"At ease, Captain Morrison, Lieutenant Walls. Messenger from the colonel says he just sent a wagon train toward us from Fort Smith. Be here tomorrow. Wants us to escort 'em through the Territory to the far end of the Big Bend of the Arkansas, put 'em on the Santa Fe Trail. Eight wagons, plus livestock. I plan to send your two troops. How many you got, Bob?"

Morrison was taller than Caskey, thinner, but almost as old. "Fifty-two, John. Maybe forty-seven can ride."

"Walls?"

"Forty-nine assigned, forty-six for duty, Sir."

"At least until we announce this little ride, huh? Well, you ain't going up the Arkansas River. You're to follow old Nathan Boone's path in reverse."

"Sir, I don't know Nathan Boone or his path." Dobey smiled sheepishly.

Morrison answered, "Daniel Boone's son. One of 'em anyhow. Took a ninety man company of the old First Mounted Rangers sort of northwest from here, up to the Trail, along it a ways west, then straight south to First Fort, then sort of followed the Canadian River back to here. That about right, Major? Twelve, maybe thirteen year ago?"

"Fifteen year, Bob. Summer of '43. Took us two and one-half months. But you'll go and come back the southernmost route, swinging a little farther west here to the far tip of the Big Bend, so's you won't go so far north. And you won't be exploring, as we was." He sketched it with his finger on a wall map.

"Jaysus, Johnnie, that's got to be three hundred, three hundred-fifty mile. It's the fifth of September, for Chrissake."

"It's four hundred, if it's a foot. And I want you back in a month. You got to make twenty-five miles a day, steady. What do you think—two wagons, ten extra horses, each troop?" The major looked at Dobey.

"Sir, I'd have to go with Captain Morrison's judgment, or yours. This'll be my first long patrol."

Morrison knocked the ashes out of his pipe onto the major's floor. "Yeah. That'll do. Walls, let's you and me go talk to my supply corporal. He'll tell us what we need for them wagons. John, is there some special reason for us to be back here in a month? That's pushing it."

"Yeah, Bob. I can't lose two troops in the snow. You're overall in charge. See you in the morning."

✵ ✵ ✵

Morrison suggested they do a joint briefing for their non-coms, which Dobey thought was kind. There would be plenty of questions he couldn't answer, and more that he wouldn't know to ask.

Morrison ran a no-nonsense briefing, leaving room for few questions, and was nice enough to let Dobey field some of the easy ones. As he wrapped it up, he commented that, thanks to some of Lieutenant Walls' health and welfare ideas, each troop was able to field five to ten more men than usual, and they'd have plenty of ammunition. "That won't hurt when it comes to sharing out guard duty, and some of the men can actually hit a damn mule at forty yards now. Let's do it."

As the non-commissioned officers filed out, Dobey thanked Morrison for handling the briefing, and for his comments. "You don't owe me thanks, son. But I'll let you pick any two of my corporals for your Corporal Melton, anytime. Just don't repeat that."

※ ※ ※

As Dobey hurried back to his quarters to pack, he was cut off by Troop Sergeant Reid. Corporals Potter, Melton, and McDowell stood nearby.

"Well, you'll finally get to see what real soldiering is about. Probably have to do some fighting," Reid almost sneered, "Sir."

"Yes. I guess I'm lucky to have good non-coms to look to, if that happens. What time should we inspect the troop?"

"Oh, don't you fret over that, Lieutenant. Me and the other old soldiers will take care of it. We been doing this for years, before you was even in school."

"Nevertheless, I'd like to learn how you do it, so just tell me when you're ready, and I'll watch."

"Sure, sir, we can do that. Thing is, though, there was s'posed to be a fight tonight."

"Jesus, I forgot." Reid had pushed for a boxing match between Potter's section and Melton's, and it was to be that night. Dobey suspected Reid had generated a lot of outside interest in it, for gambling reasons. "Who was supposed to fight?"

"Well, Lieutenant, Corporal Potter is representing his own section, and since Melton don't choose to hurt his hands, Corporal McDowell's representing them."

"Tell them I'm sorry, and we'll reschedule after the patrol."

"What I'm trying to suggest here, sir, is if we gets the men ready, and they meets your approval," Reid turned his head to spit, "we'd like to go ahead with it tonight. What with all the preparation and all."

Dobey looked to Melton, who shrugged. "All right. After the troop is inspected."

☆ ☆ ☆

Both troops were ready to move by dawn the next day. As the wagon train was coming up the far side of the Arkansas and wouldn't arrive until late in the day, Morrison won approval to cross the river immediately. They'd head southeast, meet the wagons and turn west, saving a half-day of backtracking later. He saluted Major Caskey, and they rode out, with Morrison's 'M' Troop leading.

As 'L' Troop started to file out, Major Caskey walked close to Dobey and grabbed his harness. "Pay attention to Morrison. Don't be afraid to ask questions. Officers don't get to carry carbines in the cavalry, and I never liked that. If they's a fight, though, generally they's also carbines laying around. Anyhow, you might need to do some hunting, so I had McCabe put my shotgun in your wagon." He walked along with Dobey as he eased toward the gate. "You ever handle a Paterson shotgun?"

"Yes, sir, I did. Major Hamburger gave us one, when my dad was killed."

"Thought that's what he said. Well, it's there, with all the fixings. Loaded with buck-and-ball, but there's a spare cylinder loaded with birdshot too. Be careful, son." And he was gone.

As Dobey waited to cross the river, Corporal McDowell nodded to him while leading his half section past. Both eyes were black, his nose was crooked, and his jaw swollen.

Melton trotted up beside Dobey, and pointed toward McDowell. "Sorry 'bout that, sir. I bet on him, and I ain't a betting man. Potter, I didn't think he was no pushover, but he beat McDowell like he was a redheaded stepchild. From the first lick. McDowell just failed to quit is why he's so black and blue."

"He's all right?"

"He's embarrassed. He'll eat small bites for a few days. But he's tough as nails." They started across. "I asked him did Potter get something in his eyes or something, and he said, no, just knocked hell out of him."

CHAPTER FIVE

Black Bob Morrison pushed the wagon train hard, but ten days out, they had not made it to First Fort. Rain slowed them. He pushed harder.

Melton's section was on the right flank, rear, and Potter's was off to the left. Captain Morrison's troop was out front.

Dobey rode by the last wagon, near Troop Sergeant Reid. "Can you tell me what's at First Fort?"

"You don't know that, Lieutenant? Ain't no fort, for sure. Old trading post. Some ol' Frenchman run it for years. Don't know who's got it now. You looking to take a rest there?" He sneered, loud enough for others to hear.

"No, Sergeant Reid, I'm doing just fine. Just thought I would take advantage of your amazing knowledge."

"You being sarcastic, Lieutenant?"

"No. Well, maybe. A little." Dobey prodded his horse off to the right to talk to Melton. They were in a vast open area, criss-crossed with gullies, small creeks, and ravines between the Canadian River and the North Fork of the Canadian. There were scattered patches of rocks and hillocks covered with scrub oaks.

"Reid can't tell me much about First Fort. Or won't."

Melton shifted in his saddle. "Ain't much to tell. Old trader name of Chouteau opened it years ago, to trade with the Comanche and Kiowa. Got a corral, stable, 'dobe building. His old dugout in back serves for overnight visitors. Usually an Indian maid or two, case someone needs some sewing done." Melton grinned.

"Yeah. We had seamstresses at Fort Motte, too. Why do they call him Black Bob?" Captain Morrison had thin brown hair, going white.

"Cap'n Morrison? Black-hearted. Nice enough around camp, but don't take no prisoners in a fight."

Dobey's bugler and guidon bearer, a new corporal named Phemister, galloped over to them.

"Sir. Captain Morrison's called you to come up front. Says there's a rider is coming in."

Dobey joined Morrison and their scout, a young Creek named Bent Roof. Born in the Territory twenty-two years ago, the day after a tornado dropped a tree on his family's cabin, he spoke a good bit of all the local languages; Cherokee, Chickasaw, Choctaw, Seminole, and Creek of course, but also Kiowa, Comanche, Cheyenne, and Osage.

The rider had stopped, two ridgelines away. Bent Roof raised his old .44 Sharps with both hands, and the rider waved and galloped to them.

He was an Osage boy of maybe sixteen years, and old Gus Chouteau had sent him to warn anyone downriver that there was a gang of bandits operating in this part of the Territory. There were maybe twenty-five of them, and they had laid siege to Chouteau's store last night. The boy had ridden forty miles at full tilt, not knowing if he was being chased. Another rider went northwest.

Black Bob Morrison wasted no time. "I'll take this boy and 'M' Troop and relieve 'em. You bring the train as quick as you can. Keep Bent Roof near, and keep flankers out all directions. Do they hit you, circle up, fight 'em and send Bent Roof and another well-mounted man to get me. Barring any problems, you'll be there tomorrow night."

☆ ☆ ☆

After Morrison's departure, Dobey held a short briefing with his non-coms and the leaders of the wagon train. He gave them all the information that he had, and suggested that the civilians make sure their shotguns and muskets were loaded with buckshot, or at least buck-and-ball. He sent Melton and a half section under Corporal McDowell out front with Bent Roof, and had Potter split his section out to the rear about a quarter mile off each flank. Melton's other half section of ten men under Corporal Rowe would ride with Dobey, Sergeant Reid, Phemister, and the wagons.

"We'll stop for coffee and food just short of darkness, then push on through the night. We'll rest in the morning when we can see around us, then push on in tomorrow afternoon. Questions?"

Sergeant Reid shook his head. "You think this is a good idea, Lieutenant? Riding through the night? You ask me, I'd say stop at dark, throw out a good perimeter, then go on at light, fresh. I know this is all new to you, but ..."

Dobey cut him off. "That would probably work, as might several other plans. But we're going to use mine, unless we find it's not working. Let's let these folks get to work, and you and I will discuss this by ourselves."

Reid must have noticed the steel in Dobey's voice. He said, "Yes sir."

As the others moved away, Dobey said softly, "If you ever have a question about what I'm doing, I'd expect you to ask me privately, rather than in front of subordinates." Reid started to say something, but Dobey cut him off again. "Unless, of course, you think I'm putting people in immediate danger. Do you think that I am?"

"Well, no, Lieutenant, but ..."

"Then let me explain my thinking. I doubt those bandits are looking to attack us. If they are, it means they've left or been driven away from First Fort, which means Captain Morrison and 'M' Troop will be heading back here. If the bandits are watching us, then when we stop to eat, they'll think we've set up for the night. They'll wait til two in the morning to attack, and we'll be twenty miles west. If they attack us in broad daylight, we can handle them, and we'll be that much closer to reinforcements." Dobey paused. "Now, if you don't have any specific objections, let's get them moving."

Dobey rode to 'L' Troop's wagon and drew the Paterson revolving shotgun. He slung the 'possibles' bag of extra powder, shot, and primers over his shoulder, and laid the gun across his pommel. They moved out and pushed hard til dusk, ate quickly, and moved on again just after dark, keeping the flankers and the lead element tight. A couple of violent storms came close but they hardly got wet. At daybreak, early that time of year, they stopped, put out pickets, and most of them got four hours sleep. By ten o'clock they pressed on, fortified with coffee.

Dobey rotated the assignments for the move. Corporal Potter and a half section went out front with the scout, his other half section with the wagons, and Melton's section was split out to the rear flanks, though Dobey kept Melton with him. As an afterthought, Sergeant Reid was sent out forward with Corporal Potter, with instructions to, "Push, but keep us in sight. Take a twenty minute break on my signal, one gunshot, around one p.m."

After an hour, Dobey turned to Melton and asked, "You see anything basically wrong with my plan?"

"Nossir. Seems to be working just fine. 'Course had it gone bad last night, Reid woulda been on the record as being against it. If any of us lived," Melton smiled.

"I guess I could have asked for his ideas, before I decided."

"Weren't no time, really. I think you thought it through, couldn't see no better way, and give us a plan. I mean, this ain't no committee, sir." He smiled again. "I happen to like it. 'Specially changing our position after dark."

"You don't think I embarrassed Sergeant Reid back there, yesterday?"

"I think what's embarrassing Sergeant Reid is that this seems to be working just fine. Now he's just on record as being not as smart as a dumb-assed shavetail. Beggin' your pardon, sir."

Two hours later, Melton spoke again. "I'm gonna ride out to my flankers, and tell 'em to stay well out there and alert, when we take that break."

At one-fifteen, Dobey had Phemister fire off his carbine, and the train ground to a halt and made coffee.

CHAPTER SIX

Dick Austin led what was left of his band of scoundrels southeast to the Canadian River at dawn, with the arrival of a substantial party of hostile Osage at First Fort. The damned old Frenchman must have sent for help. Either that, or the Osage wanted the trading post themselves, as they had attacked Austin's group at first light. He'd lost three wounded and three more missing, and they'd run like rabbits to keep their hair. With the loss of Little Billy Buddin last night, their fighting strength was down to seventeen.

He had sent Little Billy up to talk to the Frenchman after two buffalo hunters spotted them on the sneak and spoiled the surprise. Billy relayed Austin's simple, fair proposal: give over, no fighting, and no one would be hurt, and they wouldn't burn the place. The old bastard said he had a house full of buffalo hunters and didn't choose to surrender.

"Leastways, not to no cross-eyed raiders from Texas," he shouted. Then he blasted Little Billy with both barrels of buckshot. Little Billy somehow held on as his pony bolted back to Austin's position but died before midnight.

Pride Conyers, who was a little sweet on Little Billy, rode out to cover him, flinging two pistol shots at the Frenchman.

"Why'd you shoot him, you old son of a bitch? He just come out to talk."

"Well, me, I did not," cackled the old man. "Next time, try a white flag. It's tradition. Or just kiss this." He'd slapped his rump and ducked back inside, as Conyers wasted another shot at him.

"We ain't got nothing white," yelled Conyers, which was an accurate statement, as they had been on the prod for over twenty days.

One of the hunters stepped into the doorway, braced against the sill and staggered Conyers' horse with a .52 caliber slug. A second shot from one of the windows dropped the horse dead, and a shot from the other window wounded Buddin's horse twenty yards farther away. By the time the buffalo hunters reloaded, Conyers scampered out of range. Even now, he was riding Buddin's wounded horse. The raiders had kept up some sniper fire through the night, but then the damned Indians had run them off. Four hours ago, Austin had decided that they weren't being pursued and angled back northeast toward the North Fork, hoping to find some pilgrims on the wagon trail. And now this.

The gunshot, straight ahead, snapped them all to full alert. They scrambled to dismount and take cover in the shallow ravine. "Anybody hit? Anybody see 'em?"

Sour Johnson yelled back, "Hell, no. They ain't shooting at us. That shot was prob'ly a mile away."

"Go scout it out."

Johnson was back in ten minutes. "Wagon train, all right. Counted twelve wagons, stopped for a meal. Strung out, too. Ain't even circled. Maybe five or six soldiers mixed in with 'em. There is a little hill with rock cover this side. We could fire on 'em from there, send some riders to charge 'em from the front, stop 'em from getting away."

"We don't want to stop 'em from getting away, least not most of 'em. I wisht somebody in this outfit had some brains besides me." Austin was not only frustrated at his band's incompetence, he was damned hungry. "Ain't you hungry, Sour? We get some of their food in us, we'll do better. No, what we gonna do is, send some men behind 'em to chase 'em, and we'll go in them rocks and shoot the horses pulling the last two or three wagons, let the rest of 'em run away. Now don't that seem smarter to you?"

"What seems smarter to me is, we should'a just rode up there friendly last night, ate some of that Frenchie's food, maybe used his squaws some, afore we let on our intentions of robbing him. But I ain't in charge, Mister I-Know-Ever'-Damn-Thing, am I?"

"This ain't the time to talk, Sour. Hell, maybe these will run and leave some women. Pride, take five men and get on their back trail. Once we open up, y'all charge, make some noise, try to get 'em to run."

"Well, if Little Billy's horse don't fail me. Can't I get a better one, that ain't been shot?"

"Why, sure, Pride. I expect any number of men here would like to trade for your half-assed horse. And it ain't Billy's no more, it's yours. Move, and stay out of sight, til we fire. Git."

Sour led them to the back side of the rocky hillock. They staked out the horses, and crept into the rocks. They could smell the wood smoke and almost taste the coffee. As they crested the hill, Austin looked down and whispered, "Sour, this is gonna work just fine."

Shots broke out to their right rear. "Thought I told Conyers to wait 'til we opened fire." Austin got up on his knees to look back toward the noise. A bullet careened off a rock, then took a chunk out of the left side of his head. He went down.

✲ ✲ ✲

Corporal Hank McDowell was a tough, quick thinking, natural soldier. He was well aware that he and his ten men were in Indian country with a band of raiders nearby. He was still smarting from the beating Pudgy Potter had given him, and Melton had just told him that if he didn't stay alert, Melton would personally give him a real ass-whipping.

These related facts made it a particularly inopportune time for Pride Conyers and his five men to trot up a ravine right into McDowell's position.

Trooper Ed Monteith heard them coming before they came in view. McDowell left two men holding the horses, and two watching their rear as the rest faced the ravine. When Conyers appeared, forty yards away, McDowell centered his carbine on his chest, let him get closer, and shouted, "Hold what you got, and state your business."

✲ ✲ ✲

Conyers was proud of his speed with his Navy Colt. He was very fast. He was still working on the intelligence and accuracy parts of the gunfighting formula. He got off two quick shots toward the voice, then snapped on an empty cylinder. His last thought was, *Durn—I didn't reload.*

✲ ✲ ✲

Corporal McDowell's shot knocked Conyers over and almost off the injured horse. His right foot twisted in the stirrup, and the horse turned and ran from the firing, dragging the dead man back through his startled party.

The troopers' first volley also hit Big John Zepke and his horse in the legs, and Breed Burton's horse was killed, throwing him clear. Zepke and the other raiders bolted, following the dead Conyers. When Breed stood and tried to surrender, three bullets from the second volley dropped him.

McDowell levered open the Sharps and reloaded. "Monteith, ride straight in to Melton, tell him what happened. See does he want us to hold, chase 'em, or come back in."

As Monteith raced off, McDowell turned to Trooper Jones. "Jeff, go down there, see if that one's finished. Rest of y'all cover him."

Jones reloaded, slid down the bank and jogged up to Burton. Burton struggled to sit up.

"Help me. I give up."

"Not today, Aunt Martha." Jones shot him point-blank, then turned and walked back. "He's done."

As the ringing in their ears from their own gunfire abated, they became aware of the firing back toward the wagon train. "Mount up, boys. Birch, watch our backside."

✼ ✼ ✼

At the first pops of pistol fire from McDowell's position, Melton yelled, "Take cover. Face left." He was back by 'L' Troop's open wagon. He dropped his coffee, and laid the Sharps over the wagon box. A man's head appeared in the rocks, sixty yards above their left side. Melton said, "I should'a put a man up there," as he squeezed off at the straw hat. The hat and head were gone when the smoke cleared, but sporadic musket fire came from the other rocks.

Dobey ran to join him, and fired the shotgun over the wagon. "How many, you think?"

"I dunno, maybe ten. That shotgun ain't no good at this range. Save it, in case they charge us." Melton squeezed off another shot. There was a steady cracking of the carbines from Potter's half section, added to the booming of the civilian shotguns. "And tell them civilians the same thing. Reload with buck, and hold fire. Sir."

Dobey nodded and scrambled up the line of wagons, calming the group with information and instructions. "Only maybe ten of 'em, so far. Steady fire, rifles and carbines. Shotguns, reload with buckshot and hold fire. Stay covered." He spotted Phemister.

"Mike, anybody hit yet?"

"I don't think so, Lieutenant. Couple of horses down. You want me to go get Shoo-Fly and his boys? I think McDowell's engaged, off on the left."

"Shoo-Fly?"

"Corporal Rowe and his men, sir. Want to pull them in?"

"Of course I do. Thanks for reminding me. But tell him just to come in closer, and keep five men with him to cover our backside. You bring the other five back with you. Surely Sergeant Reid is moving against these people already."

Phemister gave him a funny look. "Oh, surely." He mounted and raced away north.

Another rider approached the head of the stalled train, carbine held high, a hundred yards away.

"Hold fire. It's Bent Roof." Corporal Amick and Trooper Lumpkin from Potter's section were behind the 'M' Troop wagon at the head of the column. Amick shouted, "Cover him. Let fly, dammit." Potter's men opened rapid fire, and Dobey got up to them just as Bent Roof finished his dash in.

"Where's Reid?" shouted Dobey, as Bent Roof dismounted. "Has he gone behind them?"

"He took your men and rode to get help," Bent Roof spat. "So he said. Told me to lead him there. I told me I'd lead him here, or he could lead himself straight to hell. What are we facing?" He fired uphill at a puff of smoke, and drew a distant "God-Damn!" as a response.

☆ ☆ ☆

The wounded Zepke and the three other survivors of Conyers' group followed their dead leader and his horse on a circuitous half mile ride to the back of the hill, arriving just as Sour Johnson slipped back to the horses with the intention of returning to Texas.

"God almighty, Zepke, what happened to Conyers?" Sour stared at the battered body, as the blown horse thudded to a halt.

"He vas dead when we left there. I doubt he got much better." Zepke dismounted, but collapsed when he put weight on his leg. "There vas an ambush, back there. Where's Austin?"

"Half his head's gone. I tell you what, Zepke, this ain't going well. We might better slip away, while them others cover us."

"Ja. Help me up. I take Red's horse." They mounted, and started southwest.

☆ ☆ ☆

As McDowell's half section crested a low rise two hundred yards from the train, they could see the whole battle scene: some horses and a few men behind a rocky hill, men on the hill firing down at the wagons, with steady return fire from the wagons. Some riders leaving the far end of the train. Charging the hill?

McDowell veered left and led his men on a quick charge to a gully near the hill, dismounted there, and moved forward firing, leaving two men with the horses.

✱ ✱ ✱

Melton mounted and rode to meet Rowe's men and Phemister. "Keep moving, out to the right. You're gonna flank 'em. Swing wide, then come in behind their hill. I'll take some men and go straight at 'em." He swung back to the head of the train, where the lieutenant was mounting up some men.

"I need a couple of you to trade your carbines for shotguns, grab an extra Colt, and come with me," said Dobey. "We're gonna charge right up there, and put the shotguns to work. Finish 'em with pistols." He checked the caps on his Dragoon.

"Me and Rock will go," said Lumpkin as he took a shotgun and Navy Colt from a pilgrim.

"Rock? Who's Rock?"

"Me, sir," said Corporal Amick, a huge humorless man from New York.

Bent Roof took a Dragoon from one of Potter's men, and mounted. "I keep my Sharps," he said, and wheeled around the front of the wagons, straight at the rocks.

Melton arrived just in time to join them. It was a wild, screaming, short ride.

✱ ✱ ✱

Old Carlos Rangel was hunkered behind a boulder, ramming his charge for his eighth shot. Like most of the raiders, he had a .54 cal. Mississippi Rifle, model of 1841, and the barrel was hot enough to burn his hand. As he dug for a primer, a bullet hit the rock beside his head. The back of the rock. He looked to his right and saw some bluecoats moving up that side of their position. "Hey, Amigos. Yanquis on the right." As he shifted to face the new threat, he saw Sour Johnson, Big John Zepke and some others mounting up behind the hill.

He stood and yelled, pointing at McDowell's men. "Hey. They're over there. Ride them down like dogs." Behind him on the forward slope, someone yelled, "Here they come."

Rangel started to face back toward the wagons, but saw a new group of Yanqui cavalry riding around their left side. "Hey," he pointed, but something hit him under the right arm and knocked him down the back slope.

He struggled to sit up, and watched Sour Johnson, Zepke, and three others thunder off the wrong way, into the arms of the Yanqui riders. Some of his own party ran by him downhill. They were all bleeding. Then more bluecoats ran after them, firing pistols. An Indian boy knelt beside him and fired a Sharps at the fleeing raiders. As he reloaded, he smiled at the startled Rangel and said, "You're one of mine," then moved off.

Rangel made it to his feet, leaning on his rifle, but someone said, "Hey. Senorita Maria."

He turned, and said, "¿Quien? Who?"

The bluecoat raised his carbine, and said, "Try this." There was a blinding flash.

✫ ✫ ✫

As they herded the prisoners and horses back to the wagons, Corporal Amick caught up with Dobey and Melton.

"Yo, Lieutenant. You think that Indian was telling the truth about Reid and Potter hanging us out to dry here?"

"We'll see. Why?"

"'Cause I think they did. And I wanna tell you something, all right? Corporal Potter, he didn't win that fight against McDowell fair. No Sir. He had a lot of carbine slugs in his gloves, sewed in the palms."

"Sergeant Reid checked both men's gloves," Dobey said, looking confused.

"Sergeant Reid's the one that fixed the gloves. Had me take 'em to that fat laundry woman. I had Lumpkin put one on, hit me with it. It was like a goddamn hammer, sir."

As McDowell and his men walked back downhill to their horses, he asked Jones, "How come you sometimes call 'em names?"

The skinny private took off his hat and rubbed his curly hair. "They's old women, Mac. They's looking for mercy. I give 'em justice."

Chapter Seven

Black Bob Morrison was positively cheerful. They ran into his 'relief column' two hours after the fight. Reid, with Potter and his men, had been left at First Fort.

"By God, Walls, what a coup. From what Sergeant Reid said, I thought I was coming to recover your bodies. Give me the count again?"

"Them, sir? Seven dead, eight wounded and captured, two missing, thirteen horses taken, ten rifles, three Hall carbines, two shotguns, eight revolvers, three Johnson pistols. Turns out, a lot of them were wounded by buckshot, when the civilians were spraying the hill early in the fight."

"And the butcher's bill?"

"Two civilians and five troopers wounded, one trooper died of wounds. No weapons lost. Four horses killed or destroyed. And we did butcher them. We can have meat tonight."

"How you going to handle Sergeant Reid?"

"He should have supported us. He ran. There's got to be an inquiry. Do I arrest him now, or when we get back?"

"He says you signaled him to go for help."

"You buy that, Captain?"

"Not for a single minute. He should have sent a rider to me, and supported you. Your call, but I'd arrest him. Maybe he'll run, and we can shoot the bastard."

"Well, sir, turns out this ain't all. He sort of rigged that fight between Potter and McDowell."

"McDowell threw that fight?"

"No. No sir. Potter had loaded gloves."

"Any proof?"

"I've got the man who fixed the gloves, on Reid's order. He's kind of upset about Reid and Potter leaving us swinging in the breeze."

"Humph. We'll arrest both of 'em. They'll be lucky to make it to trial. Lot of men lost money on that fight."

☆ ☆ ☆

They closed First Fort before dark, and after posting guards, Dobey and Melton went looking for Reid and Potter. A buffalo hunter said that he thought they were at the stable. Dobey took the stable, and sent Melton to try the main cabin.

The culprits had already left the stable. Dobey hurried to the cabin, and walked in the back door just in time to see Melton hit Potter in the mouth. There was the crunch of metal on bone. As Potter dropped, Melton removed the brass knuckles, stuck them in his shirt pocket, and kicked Potter in the head.

Before Dobey could shout for Melton to stop, Reid stepped behind Melton and hit him with a sap. Melton went down on his hands and knees and Dobey found himself pointing his cocked Dragoon at Reid. "That will be enough. You're under arrest, both of you."

"Me and Melton?"

"You and Potter. Cowardice, abandoning your post, lying to an officer...I could go on ... and I know about the gloves."

"Don't know what you're talking about, Lieutenant, and you got no proof."

Facing Dobey's pistol and stuffing the sap in the back of his belt, Reid didn't notice Captain Morrison and his troop sergeant come in behind him.

"My word against yours, and the word of an experienced sergeant means something out here. Ain't no West Point, no siree Bob. And an inexperienced lieutenant has to be real careful out here . . . look out for accidents and such," Reid sneered.

Captain Morrison nodded to his troop sergeant, a big Swede named Wenstrom, and the Swede swung his carbine barrel. Reid heard movement, started to turn, and took the blow over his right eye. He staggered back three steps, hit the bar, and fell on his face.

"I'll have my money back, Henry Reid," Wenstrom said to the unconscious man.

Black Bob lit his pipe. "Heard him threaten you, Lieutenant Walls. Thought he was going to attack you. We'll get Chouteau to keep 'em now 'til we get back here. Then put them in your wagon for the trip home. Or they can walk behind it. Have your men ready at dawn. We'll have a little ceremony before we hit the trail."

"Ceremony, sir? What's that for?"

"You'll see."

✲ ✲ ✲

One of the raiders died during the night.

Sergeant Wenstrom led the other seven wretches tied together onto the plain, barefoot and in their underclothes, and had them face the rising sun. Their clothing and boots had been sold to Chouteau and the money turned over to Dobey's wounded.

One section from 'M' Troop faced them—nineteen men, carbines at low port. Wenstrom strode to join them as the doomed men shielded their eyes from the sun's fresh glare, trying to see what was happening.

Wenstrom cocked his Sharps and said, "All right, boys, show these 'L' Troop bums that we can shoot, too. On three, now ..."

Zepke fell to his knees, and another raider began screaming, but every one heard the count, and the volley was one to be proud of. Wenstrom had assigned three shooters to each of the standing prisoners, and he and Corporal Shealy shot Zepke.

Two were still squirming as a fresh breeze blew the acrid smoke away. The Osage relief party cheered and started some sort of dance, and Shealy, on a nod from Wenstrom, walked out and finished the two wounded with his pistol.

Reid and Potter stood watching, squirming themselves. "What happens to us, Cap'n?"

Black Bob lit his pipe and let them stew. "Oh, if you make it back to Fort Gibson, there'll be a trial. These men attacked the U.S. Army, without benefit of flag or uniforms, and were not entitled to trial. Nevertheless, I would have made them walk to the Santa Fe Trail and back to Fort Gibson for their execution, 'cept they'd have slowed us down. Reid here will prob'ly be shot too. You, Potter, I'd guess you'll get twenty, maybe thirty years, hard time."

"Cap'n, I'm thirty-nine years old. I doubt that I'll live that long."

"Well, Potter, you'll just have to give it your best effort."

Chapter Eight

"We'll leave your wounded here with Reid and Potter. Chouteau and his squaws can look out for 'em while we hurry these pilgrims on up to the Trail, and we'll pick 'em up on the way back." Captain Morrison poured out the dregs of his coffee and stood up.

Dobey did the same. "Yessir. I gave old Chouteau some money from the dead men's traps to look out for our men, and Melton made it clear that Reid and Potter had better not escape. Chouteau seemed to take Melton serious."

Morrison grinned. "Well, at least you now got Melton for troop sergeant. Let's ride."

✲ ✲ ✲

"Person didn't realize that you was just a dumb ass shavetail, they might think you actually knew something about using a Paterson shotgun," Melton offered. 'L' Troop was riding drag again, behind the wagons.

Dobey smiled. "Why would they think that?"

"I seen how you handled it. You and Amick and Lumpkin fair scoured that hill face with them shotguns. Let us get right in among 'em with our pistols. Hell, it was over, then. Am I right?"

"Yeah. Yes, I did use one before. Back in '53 at Fort Motte. Using it here made me think about that all over again."

✫ ✫ ✫

Fort Motte was typical of many early forts: no palisade, some crude barracks, a guardhouse, headquarters buildings, and the sutler's store and corral. Dobey's father was killed the year before, and the sutler took in Dobey, his mother, and his brother and sister.

He did so, he said, because he needed help running the store. He was a rarity. Many sutlers, if not most, ran operations not unlike the company stores of mining fame. Blackbeard and Henry Morgan, those princes among pirates, would have blushed at the greed at many forts. Timothy Balliett, however, was honest, despised graft, admired soldiering (having done it), and had been in love with Annette Walls since first he saw her. Six months after Mac Walls' death, they married.

The fort's commander went hunting several times with fourteen-year-old Dobey, or Tom as he was known then. When he was comfortable with young Tom's handling of the Paterson shotgun, he made a gift of it. It was an old Model 1839 sixteen gauge six-shot revolver with a twenty-four-inch barrel. An incident with it soon saved several lives, took several others, and won Tom a four-year trip to West Point.

The incident began when the Indians, over two hundred of them, swarmed over and through Fort Motte at about ten a.m. of a cool spring day. Two of the fort's three mounted rifle companies were on long patrol, as the Indians well knew, leaving about fifty fighters at the post.

Five soldiers and two civilians were caught by the stables and slaughtered immediately. All the horses were taken, but then brisk defensive fire from the barracks and headquarters area staggered the attack. In the sutler's store about seventy yards away were Balliett and his bride Annette, her two sons Tom and Tad, and three soldiers. Annette's daughter Becky, age eight, was in the outhouse.

Balliett passed out an assortment of weapons, and they drove off the first charge. Then things went to pieces.

When Annette realized her daughter was missing, she tried to run to the outhouse. Balliett pulled her back, and armed with a Hall carbine and a Paterson revolver, had tried it himself. One soldier with a Dragoon Colt ran with him, but they were both pierced by arrows and pinned down by the water trough, halfway to the outhouse. Seven Kiowa warriors raced to the corral, dismounted, crawled through the fence, and charged across the open area, determined to finish the two men with tomahawks and clubs.

At that point, Tom advanced on the Kiowa, firing that shotgun. He hit all seven of them. Balliett and the soldier undoubtedly hit some of them too, but there was no question that what dropped them was the six blasts of buckshot from that old Paterson, coming from the side.

Tom had grabbed the pistol from his wounded stepfather to cover their retreat to the store, when his sister decided to make a break for them, running screaming from the far end of the corral. That attracted the attention of three more Kiowa, as well as that of brother Tad, who was reloading carbines for the two soldiers still in the store.

Tad rushed out with a 10 gauge double but took an arrow through his cheek and a musket ball in the knee before he could fire.

Tom picked up the big double gun and accidentally touched off both barrels simultaneously toward the attackers. The recoil dislocated his right thumb and shoulder and blackened his eye, but when the smoke cleared there were no more Kiowa standing near the corral.

Back in the store, they beat off two more half-hearted charges, but the Kiowa had lost enough men and captured enough horses so as to bring hostilities to a sudden end.

☆ ☆ ☆

"That was why I got to go to West Point, more or less," finished Dobey.

"Well, I ain't surprised, after all that. I'm just surprised they's still any hostiles left for us to fool with."

"Nobody likes a smart-ass, Melton. Remember, you're not a real sergeant yet."

Melton grinned. "Where's the family now?"

"Baby sister died of a fever the next year. The rest of 'em are still at Fort Motte."

"You sure? I heard they was closing."

Dobey pulled up, stunned. "Jesus Lord, I feel like I been hit in the chest. I mean, what would happen to...? Where would...? Damn, Jimmy, I haven't seen my mother in over five years as it is, and now..." He nudged his horse back into motion, easing up beside Melton again. "I was hoping to get a furlough, and go see her..."

Melton said, "I'm sorry, Lieutenant. You miss her most, I guess?"

Dobey nodded. "You got to know her to understand. That Kiowa raid? I told you my brother was shot in the knee? Part of the ball stayed in. We put him on a table. My stepfather held his shoulders, me his legs, and ma cut open his knee, dug out that fragment. Well, I fainted. Right on him." Dobey blushed, then shrugged. "Ma got her elbow under my chin, hooked my legs from under me, and dropped me on my butt, on the floor, out cold. Lucky for him, my brother passed out then too, prob'ly from me falling on his legs. Ma was crying the whole time, 'My baby, my baby.' 'Course he wasn't the baby, Becky was, but I guess we were all her babies. God Almighty, I hope she's all right."

Dobey suddenly stiffened and took a deep breath. "Hell, I sound like a little girl. It's just that..." He trailed off again. Melton rode silently, leaving Dobey to his thoughts.

By the fire that night, Melton said, "You was some embarrassed today. Don't be. Hard as it might be to believe, some other of us dog-assed soldiers had mothers too." He poured Dobey some coffee.

Dobey stared at him a moment. "Oh. I guess I was on a pity streak. You said 'had'?"

Melton nodded. "Mine died of the bloody flux when I's fourteen. Felt like I'd been gutted."

That night, Jimmy Melton found Swede Wenstrom by his wagon.

"You find out where they hid the fight money, Swede?"

"No. But I will beat it out of them before we get back to Fort Gibson. Then we don't need them no more. Found the gloves, for sure. In Potter's saddlebags."

"I was thinking. They must have won near two hundred dollars. Hardly nobody bet on Pudgy Potter. They wouldn't of left it at the fort. You searched 'em good?"

"Buck-ass naked, I did."

"Where are them saddlebags?"

Apparently the fat laundress had been busy. There were false bottoms sewed in both men's bags. Potter had over fifty dollars, Reid one hundred twenty-eight. There were also three pocket watches, some rings, silver belt buckles and four gold crosses.

Wenstrom took a five-dollar bill and stuffed it in his shirt. "How much did you bet? We gonna give this to the ones that bet on McDowell?"

"Gimme four. Naw. We don't know McDowell would have won anyhow. Amick kept the betting book. We'll just give back what everybody bet. Keep what's left over. I think them crosses was stolen."

✲ ✲ ✲

Chouteau kept them locked in a storeroom in the rear of his store. Once a day, a squaw brought them each a plate of food and a can of water; once a day they were led, separately, to the outhouse. Chouteau always covered them with that shotgun, and checked their bindings. He'd tied them, ankles and wrists in front, so they could eat and hobble to the outhouse.

Reid had found a loose board at the bottom of the wall. Unfortunately, there was dirt mounded against it outside and they couldn't just kick it out, as Chouteau slept in the store. They'd push it with their legs and as dirt fell inside, they'd scoop that up and hide it behind some barrels. A few more inches, and the skinny Reid would be able to wiggle out. He'd then pull enough dirt away for Potter to follow.

"One more day and they'll be back here. We got to finish this, get out of here 'fore daybreak. Push, dammit."

Potter pushed. Wretched, filthy, hungry, he'd hardly slept in days, but the fear of prison drove him. "I won't do well there," he moaned, for the tenth time.

"Prison? I doubt you need fear that," Reid whispered as he shoveled dirt with his hands.

Noises at the door froze them.

"Damn! They're early. It ain't even light." They pulled the board back into place and Potter pivoted to lay on his side in front of it. As the door started to swing outward, Reid saw the arm of a blue jacket in the light of a lantern.

He lunged against the door, hoping to knock down the soldier, break the lantern, start a fire, grab a gun, something. Anything. It should have worked.

Might have, too, with almost anyone else. Fooled badly by these particular men before, the soldier had opened the door left-handed, and stepped aside as Reid crashed into it, pushing against nothing.

Reid would have tripped anyhow, hobbled as he was, but the soldier instinctively stuck out his foot and clubbed him with his carbine as he went down. Potter struggled to get to his feet, only to hear and then feel his nose and several teeth give way as the carbine butt stroke caught him in the face. It was several seconds before the voices made any sense to him.

"Get up. Get outa here. Move, damn your cheating eyes. Both of you."

"I ain't going nowhere with you, McDowell."

"No, you ain't, for a fact. But you're going. There's two horses waiting outside. Half the damn troop already thinks I was in on that fight deal. I ain't having you two stick around to testify to that lie. I come ahead to cut you loose."

McDowell nodded to Chouteau, who knelt and cut their ankle ropes. McDowell motioned them to the open front door with his carbine.

As they shuffled out into the darkness, the prisoners saw two horses, saddled and ready. Hope, nearly throttled, surged again.

"Oh, thank you God," Potter sobbed.

"Shut up, Potter," Reid wheezed. His throat was constricted too. "Them our saddlebags, by chance?"

"Oh, you're a bold one, Granny Alice, ain't you?" A skinny figure appeared beside the horses, presenting a cocked Dragoon. It bucked and roared.

The round ball flattened as it broke Reid's forehead. Not exiting, it transferred all of its energy to his head and snapped his neck.

"That won't no reasonable expectation now, was it, Priscilla? You see that, Corporal Pudgy? I think it broke his neck, though it ain't like it matters. How you like my gold cross?" He fingered it. "The one my momma gave me, 'fore some asshole corporal stole it?"

The second shot took Potter on the bridge of his nose, if not by surprise. It finally imbedded in the wall behind him. He sat down, then flopped backwards, the back of his head gone.

"Jesus, Jones! Melton said they was supposed to be shot escaping." McDowell punched them both in the groin with the barrel of his Sharps, looking for a flinch. "You just had to shoot 'em in the face?"

"Tell Melton they was running backwards. Damn a bunch of old women, anyways."

CHAPTER NINE

Deep in the fall of 1859, Dobey finally learned where his family was. The telegraph had allowed him to confirm Fort Motte's closing months earlier, but the letter from his mother went to West Point, then Washington, and finally through Fort Smith to Dobey. All it said was that the army was leaving, and that they were going to stay and try trading with the Indians and hunters.

Major Caskey knew the odds of Dobey making it to Colorado and back, alone and in winter, ranged from slim to none. His request for furlough was disapproved.

"I could resign, Major. You know that. It's my mother."

"Yes. And you'd be doing the wrong thing for the right reason. You're good and tough, Walls, but you'd probably die. And for what?" Caskey rubbed his face and stared into space.

"I don't ..."

"Shut up. I ain't through. They probably ain't there, you know, where she said they was. I been there. Ain't nothing there, 'cept snakes, buzzards, buffalo, and Indians. If they are there, after a year, they're dead. But come spring, and you're still of a mind to go, I'll send out a long patrol, to escort wagons or something. You can see for yourself. Fair?"

"I'll think on it, sir."

"Do. You'll take my boy with you. Be good experience for him."

"Who?"

"My youngest. Tom. I'm assigning him to "L" Troop. He's a private. Just got here."

☆ ☆ ☆

The winter of 1859-1860 passed like cold molasses, as Dobey trained his troop, chafed, took short patrols, chafed, and sent fruitless telegraph messages from Fort Smith. Two prospective buffalo hunters promised to deliver several letters, if the Ballietts were still at Fort Motte.

☆ ☆ ☆

The trip to Fort Motte in early April of '60 was relatively quiet, at least compared to Dobey's first long patrol. The major let him take his troop and two wagons this time, one of them covered, with ten spare horses and two mules. Accompanying them was a man named Stineman with a full wagon and several horses. He was reported to be an old carpenter who agreed to open a way station halfway between First Fort and Fort Gibson. Black Bob Morrison picked the site on their last patrol, a hundred miles west and south of Fort Gibson.

Dobey was to protect him while he set up, then leave a half section with him and press on to Colorado, another two hundred miles west. On his way back, he was to swing by the great salt deposit, about halfway between the Santa Fe Trail and First Fort, and bring back as much as he could carry.

Caskey didn't give him any guidance on how long he could visit in Fort Motte. *How long does it take to study bones?* Dobey's throat tightened again.

Bent Roof was scouting for them again. When Melton asked why he seemed so happy, he replied that on the last trip, he'd been able to shoot several Mexicans and Texans, and he was always hopeful.

Dobey asked what they should call the way station. Bent Roof announced that the Seminole locally called it Vamoosa.

"Ain't that what Mexicans say, 'vamoose'? You know, like 'move along'?"

"That's what you Texans say they say. What they say is 'vamonos'."

Dobey, who was itching to move, said, "Let's do just that. Vamonos."

They struck north and west from Vamoosa. After four days, the land began to flatten out. There was little rain, but there were plenty of deer and prairie chickens, and enough water and forage for an army.

Twelve days after leaving the Canadian, they crossed the Santa Fe Trail. Four days later they approached Fort Motte, on the Purgatory River.

Dobey was grinning from ear to ear, and had picked up the pace. Melton rode up beside him.

"You feeling some better now, Lieutenant?"

"Oh, you can bet your ass on that, Jimmy. You know what I was just remembering? 'Course not. Well, Tad, my brother, he bit me once. He was still a baby. Got me right in the small of my back, drew blood. I hit him and Ma whacked me, but when she saw what he'd done, she bit him. On the arm. Not enough to draw blood, mind you, but enough to leave tooth marks." Dobey laughed at the memory. "You talk about one shocked baby. He screamed bloody murder. That was morning. Six or seven hours go by, and he was fine, laughing and playing, and my daddy came in from patrol. Minute he walked in, Tad started wailing again, pointing to his arm. 'Ma bit me! She bit me!' Then Ma started crying too. 'I did Mac, I'm so sorry. I didn't know what else to do.' Ma told me you never saw anybody more confused than my daddy right then."

There were several adobe and wooden buildings, an outhouse, a barn, and two corrals. There were around twenty horses at a water tank near one corral. As they rode closer, the horses raced away to the north.

"Hell, they're wild," said Melton.

Dobey stopped and stared. There was no smoke, no other sign of life, no noise but for an open door creaking as it swung in the wind. He hadn't seen his family in almost six years. Until this moment, he'd had slim hope that that they were alive. It faded.

In the old sutler's store, he found a note nailed to a beam. *Thomas,* he read, *it's no good here. We've gone to Texas. I'll keep sending you letters. Your faithful mother, A.W.B.- P.S. Don't nobody take this down.*

Dobey walked outside. "Get watered up. We're heading back."

✡ ✡ ✡

That had been April and May. Summer ripened into fall, and in late October Major Caskey stopped Dobey as he was leaving his office following an officer's call.

"Walls, you know war is coming. I'm surprised we ain't been sent into Kansas already. Have you thought which way you'll go?"

"A lot, sir. I hope it doesn't happen, but if it does, I don't see how I can go against Texas. Guess I'll have to resign."

"I's afraid of that. I feel the same way about Ohio, though I've spent all my grown days in the South and West. But you ain't had slaves."

"My grand-daddy did, on mama's side. I never saw 'em, but that doesn't seem to matter. It ain't about that, to me. It's about being told what to do, by people who've never been here."

"Yeah. Well, over half my men and officers are from the South. Things are gonna get strange."

"Yessir. You said, a couple of things?"

"Yeah. Melton's time is up next month. With the war coming, do you think he'll ship over, or go to Texas?"

"Damned if I know, sir. I didn't even know his time was coming up. I'll talk with him."

"Do that. Take him, one of your sections and two wagons, head out for Vamoosa Monday. Talk to him, and you do some thinking. Buy us thirty head of horses if you can, and all the buffalo hides you can get in a week. We need 'em for coats and blankets. Take Tom, too."

✧ ✧ ✧

They made good time for four days, with nearly empty wagons. The snowstorm hit them Friday morning. At two p.m. the snow stopped. It was six inches deep, and they were ten miles from Vamoosa. Without the snow they would have never seen the buffalo.

It was a small herd, fewer than fifty. They were sheltering from the wind below a bluff less than a mile away.

"A gift horse," said Dobey.

"No sir, them's buffalo," answered Corporal Jones. McDowell was sick, and Jones was leading the section.

"Thank you," smiled Dobey. "That's even better. I want you to take your section and the wagon with provisions, and kill as many of them as we can skin in three days. Melton and I will take young Caskey and the other wagon on to Vamoosa and see what we can line up for horses and hides there. You better give me two men to help with the horses. We'll be back in a couple of days. Don't spook 'em now."

"Yessir. Just kill 'em. Don't spook 'em." As he wheeled away, Jones muttered, "Look out, girls."

CHAPTER TEN

Vamoosa Station was a log and mud cabin, fair-sized, with a sleeping room off the right rear. As one walked in, on the right there was a crude bar, boards nailed over empty casks, and a Franklin stove back toward the sleeping room. On the left was a wax-papered window, now shuttered, and a large fireplace with a few buffalo hide blankets on the hearth for overnight guests. In the center were two rough tables with wooden crates for chairs.

Around the walls, stacked and on shelves, were trade goods: shovels, picks, saws, harnesses, horseshoes, rope. Behind the bar were tins of food, coffee, sugar, salt, lead, powder, bullet molds, catalogues, newspapers, a couple of Hall carbines, two squirrel guns, three old shotguns, fishing hooks, and the liquor.

Standing behind the bar was the new proprietor: a former carpenter from Savannah, Georgia, forty-two years old, and about to break even on his investment.

He'd just bought twenty horses, saddle-broke, from the three men drinking in front of him. Twelve dollars apiece, and he'd sell them to Fort Smith or Fort Gibson for twenty each. A hundred and sixty profit there; add those seven ponies he'd bought from Seminole boys for five dollars each, he was almost ashamed to think, and he'd have back two hundred sixty-five dollars on his two hundred invested, in less than six months.

Not to mention that these men were now buying liquor with the money he'd paid them. This was definitely better than carpentry.

"What kind of name is that? Stineman?" The big one, the leader, was almost drunk and beginning to get a little surly. He pointed to the new sign behind the bar: "Bill Stineman—Proprietor."

"German. Man of stone, I'm told."

"German. Not a Jew?"

"No sir. I am not a Jew. A simple carpenter, like Jesus, but German. Not a Jew." Stineman smiled at his own little joke.

The big black-haired Irishman smiled too, but it wasn't a sweet smile.

"Well, you robbed us like a damned Jew. You'll probably get sixteen, maybe eighteen dollar a head for them ponies from the army."

The old vaquero nodded and sipped, but the third horse trader, a young tramp, was an instigator. "Tell him, Nigger Jim. Bastard Jew thief."

Stineman began to worry. He had a six-shot pepperbox under his coat, but the little .32 balls might not stop these three. He made a soothing gesture. "Give my money back, and take them to the forts yourselves, then. I'm just offering a convenience. Not trying to cheat you. You want them back?"

The vaquero smiled and said, "We can do that." He looked at his big companion. "Amigo?"

"No, Goddamit, we can't. Me and Toothless here is deserters. We can't go near them forts." He slammed his cup on the bar and shouted, "And this damn Jew knows that, and that's why he's robbing us." He glared, his madness building up to action.

John James Kerrey was a thoroughly oppressed man, and no one knew that better than he, himself. With his thick black hair he could have been called King Kerrey, or at least Prince. But no. The bastards had called him Black Jack as a boy, and now, at thirty-four, he was known as Nigger Jim.

The door opened behind him. The cold blast of air interrupted his thoughts, which really pissed him off. He turned, enraged, to face a sight certain to tip him over the edge: an officer.

There may have been an element of snow blindness that slowed his reaction. Dobey sensed something wrong as he walked in. The hair on his neck stood up, but it just happened too fast.

"Evening, station master, gentlemen." He pulled off his gloves as he spoke, and started to slap snow from his cape and pants, only then noticing that two of the "gentlemen" were wearing army pants. *Deserters?*

The black-haired man exploded. "Bleeding officer," he shouted, and in one motion, drew a short Colt from a shoulder holster, and hit Dobey in the face, backhanded. Nose broken, blood in his eyes, Dobey dropped like a rock. The two deserters began to kick him.

Tom Caskey pushed in at that point, shuddering from the cold and still laughing and looking back at Melton. When he saw Dobey on the floor, he yelled, "Hold it right there." The bigger civilian raised a pistol and shot him in the chest, knocking him back into Melton. Dobey thought, *Oh, Jesus, not Tom.*

Melton shoved young Caskey aside, brought up his Sharps and fired. The big civilian dropped the Colt, and went backwards over a box. The skinny tramp broke left for the window while the man behind the counter stood stupefied. Melton stepped in and butt-stroked the Mexican in the forehead, dropping him cold.

The gunfire, shocking in the enclosed space, startled Dobey back from semi-consciousness. A pistol fell on his head, and he dimly saw one of his attackers step on a box and try to open the window shutters. Dobey picked up the pistol and shot him in the butt. Dust flew from his filthy pants, he screamed, and fell off the box. He began kicking and twisting on the floor, holding himself.

Dobey cocked the Colt again, but almost blacked out before he could fire. Melton drew his Dragoon, stepped over Dobey and shot the tramp twice more. He then swung and pointed it at the counterman. "Friends of yours?"

The voice came to Stineman as in a long tunnel. He was deafened, and stunned by the sudden violence. He nodded stupidly, then shook his head, finally finding his voice. "No. No. Just came in. Horse traders. I just bought horses from them, but I think they meant to rob me. Kept calling me a Jew."

The corporal stared at him, boring into his eyes, then said, "All right," and shot the unconscious Mexican instead. Stineman flinched, but showed no sympathy. The corporal appeared to believe him. "Throw some water on my lieutenant," he ordered, then swung to cover the door as two troopers ran in, carbines ready.

They stared at the carnage, speechless. The big corporal decocked his pistol and said, "Took you long enough, girls. I think Caskey's had it. Check him, and put him in the wagon. The major ain't gonna be happy 'bout this. I'll get Lieutenant Walls on his feet, and see does he want to start back tonight."

CHAPTER ELEVEN

Stineman was an accomplished seamster. He explained that much of his business in Savannah had been furniture building and repair. He expertly stitched Dobey's lip and face, while Melton kept putting packed snow on the broken nose, and pouring whiskey in Dobey's cup.

"Pour some of this on my eyelid, once I get my eye shut tight," muttered Dobey.

"Do what?" Intent on watching the stitching, Melton seemed vexed by the order.

"That whack on the face may have deranged him somewhat," offered Trooper Vinson.

"I don't rule that out," said Dobey, "but the whiskey will kill any germs that might have gotten in those cuts."

Trooper Robertson piped up. "Can you get sickness from a dead man, Lieutenant? From his blood, I mean?"

Everyone stopped and stared at Robertson. "Me and Vinnie got blood all over us, putting young Caskey in the wagon. Maybe we had ought to drink some of that whiskey. Sir."

"Nice try. You and Vinson get all them buffalo hides there loaded on top of Caskey. Count 'em," Melton said. "We got to pay this man for 'em."

"I told you there was twenty-three," Stineman said, looking up from his sewing.

"Count 'em twice."

Dobey decided that there was no rush to get the dead boy back to his father. "This cold will keep him from spoiling. Send Vinson and Robertson back down the trail to bring Jones and his men in tonight. We'll need 'em to help with the wagon and horses." Dobey touched the stitches over his eye, and winced, "First thing in the morning, we'll move camp to the kill site, finish skinning whatever they shot, then head home. Take some meat. It'll keep too."

Melton dispatched the two unhappily sober troopers. "Keep the river on your right side, and stay alert. 'Specially after you cross that second creek."

"For hostiles, Corporal?"

"No, Jesus, Vinnie, ain't no sane hostiles gonna be out on a night like this. Just be careful you don't startle Jones and the others. Might think you're hostiles. Make some noise after that creek." Melton hesitated. "Might be I could convince the Lieutenant to let everybody have a little nip afore we put you girls to bed. If you ain't too slow getting back here."

Melton turned back in time to hear the end of Stineman's plan for dividing the loot.

"... and since these men have no survivors that we know of, the rule of 'habeas corpus' applies. We split their money, and possessions."

"'Habeas corpus'? What money?" Melton perked up.

"'Habeas corpus' means, 'We have their corpses.' French, I think," Stineman said, with some arrogance.

"Not exactly," mumbled Dobey, his head splitting with pain.

"Anyhow, they got some money which I just paid them." Stineman laid out a quick plan for cheating Major Caskey and the army while enriching himself, Dobey, and Melton. Dobey stared at him, dumbfounded. He'd heard of the graft among tradesman dealing with the military, but Major Caskey didn't tolerate it, and so this was his first exposure. He turned to Melton, who was crunching the numbers and waiting for Dobey's reaction.

"It's twenty dollars for saddle-broke horses, sir. Ain't half of them saddle-broke. Maybe none. Them's unshod Indian ponies, probably stolen. We ought not to pay over sixteen for 'em."

"Why, those lying bastards. They assured me that all twenty were broken to the saddle. I paid, uh, fifteen for them." Stineman's confidence seemed to be slipping away.

Melton smiled. "All twenty of 'em? I counted twenty-seven."

"Oh. I mean, uh, ohh!"

The 'dead' Mexican, prostrate beside Stineman, ended the discussion by shouting, "Puta!" He sat up and jammed his knife up between Stineman's legs.

Dobey, sitting at a table and fiddling with the dead deserter's sawed-off Navy Colt, instinctively shot the Mexican, knocking him flat. Really dead this time, he was unable to withdraw his knife.

The trader stumbled back several steps, sat down on the protruding knife, and fainted. Fainting was the only truly fortunate thing to happen to him on that day, which had started so well. He bled out in three minutes, without regaining consciousness. Painlessly, as far as anyone knew.

✼ ✼ ✼

Melton searched the four dead men, and kept their boots and weapons and money, before dragging them outside into the snow.

"Rest of their clothes was too filthy. And bloody." He began dividing the money. "We'll have the boys bury them in the morning, if the ground ain't frozen. If it is, we'll tote 'em off a half mile and leave 'em in a gully. They's all four thieves, anyhow."

Melton poured Dobey some whiskey. "I sent word I'd let the boys have a taste of this when they get in here."

"You giving away a dead man's liquor?"

"Ain't his no more, Lieutenant. Habeas corpus." Melton poured himself some and sat down. "You know my time's up, less than a month?"

"I heard it was soon."

"Here's what I'm thinking. There's almost four hundred dollars here. We'll split that, for starts. Then there's this place, all the stuff in it."

"Inventory."

"Yessir. Inventory, and them twenty-seven ponies, and Stineman's wagon and mules. Somebody's got to run this place. I want to try it."

"You? But ..."

"Yessir. Hear me out. I'll stay here and run it for now. You go tell the major that I want to finish my time here. Tell him I worked out a deal with Stineman."

"Corporal Melton, I won't lie to Major Caskey."

"Sir, I'll go put a silver dollar in that dead sumbitch's pants right now. Just tell the major I bought him out." When Dobey hesitated, Melton pushed on. "If the major says I got to come in, I will, but I really want to try this. Being a storekeeper, I mean."

"Hell, Jimmy, by the time we get back and tell him, and he sends somebody back out here to get you, your time's up anyhow."

Melton smiled. "Yessir. Now, on this other stuff: we're halves on it all. You pay me sixteen dollar a head for half the ponies, with the major's money, and pay yourself for the other half. You take the odd one. Same deal for the buffalo hides."

"You take the odd one." Dobey was starting to feel generous.

"Yessir. Now on the rest of it, I need to buy you out, 'less you're gonna resign and come run it with me. Can you?"

Dobey shook his head. "Don't know as I'd want to, but they wouldn't release me for that, anyhow. And I've got years still to go on my hitch."

"All right. Well, I guess the inventory was about two hundred, so I owe you another hundred for that. That fair?"

Dobey nodded, astounded by his sudden wealth. "I'd like to keep this cut-down Colt and shoulder holster."

"Yessir. You done right well with that. And I'd like to wait a while to pay you that last hundred, see how things go here. Maybe in the spring?"

"Of course, Jimmy. I wouldn't have thought of any of this. Of course. What about your things?"

"You better take all that back with you. Major Caskey will have to account for it. Yessir. Take it. Horse, guns, sword, saddle and harness. Lemme keep my uniform, though. Tell the major to take it from my last month's pay. Say I didn't have nothing fit to wear."

Dobey smiled. "Well, you can afford it now. But you keep your horse. I'll give the major the odd one."

"And we better go search young Caskey's body. You can take whatever he has back to his daddy. We don't do that, my boys'll have it all 'fore daybreak. And you ought to wear his sling and carbine for the trip home. Ain't no good to him. Hang his pistol and gunbelt on your pommel, too."

Tom Caskey's pockets were empty. They removed his weapons, and were starting to place the hides back on top of his body, when he murmured, "Thanks. I'm cold."

✶ ✶ ✶

Kerrey's bullet had hit Tom Caskey's carbine barrel, knocking it into his forehead. Slowed considerably, somewhat flattened, it had then passed through his carbine sling and thumped him soundly in the chest, over the heart. It had barely broken the skin, but gave him an egg-sized bruise. It was now in his pocket, along with his once-missing stash of three dollars and seventy-five cents, pocketknife, and a silver comb.

"The double-whack, head and chest, knocked his little butt out cold," explained Vinson, to the rest of his squad around the fire. "All that blood came from his forehead. I swear he won't breathing when we put him in the wagon."

"God's pure truth," added Robertson. "We'd never of tooken his stuff, had we knowed he won't finished."

"You gave it back fast enough, once you seen him."

"That I did, Shaun Patrick. My own heart stopped for a moment," Robertson shuddered, as the others laughed. "He stood to hug me, but I thought it was his ghost coming after my thieving ass."

"Aye," said Patrick, turning to the others. "Me own brother Brian was there and seen it, so he did. Old Vic here and Vinnie pulled out them treasures so fast, they dropped 'em all. And Vic says, 'We wasn't gonna keep it.'" Patrick paused, choking with laughter. "What was you gonna do, Vic, give it to the poor?"

✶ ✶ ✶

In the morning, they clinked and clattered away. Dobey looked back, and Melton saluted, then waved. The vision would stick with Dobey for some time: the cabin, framed by snow-covered evergreens; Jimmy's horse and cow snorting white vapor in the cold; the mist of light snow falling while

Jimmy stood in the open doorway, the fireplace bright behind him. Dobey waved back, and Melton stepped inside and closed the door. Dobey wondered if he'd ever see him again.

He'd never felt so lonely.

Chapter Twelve

The second of June, 1861, was a typical glorious spring day for the region, which meant unpredictable. It had snowed ten days earlier. It was now raining hard, with gusting winds. And it was still a little cold.

Major Caskey let Dobey keep his pants and boots, and let him buy his gloves and cape and hat. He bought a horse and saddle in Fort Gibson. That little storekeeper's Colt was under his left arm, and a brand new Colt Navy hung on his pommel.

Black Bob Morrison had resigned too, and left the day before for Georgia. A cousin back there, a politician, had promised him a regiment. Dobey was heading for Texas with no such expectations, no prospects whatsoever.

Major Caskey decided to send McDowell's old section with Dobey to Vamoosa. McDowell was troop sergeant now, replacing Melton, and Corporal Jeff Jones was now the section leader. Their mission, supposedly, was to buy as many horses as Melton had, and to try to talk him into re-enlisting.

Of course their real mission was to escort Dobey there, on his way to Texas. Caskey was a little emotional. "Probably get lost, by yourself. Dumb-assed Rebel. Keep your head down. Maybe see you again, when this is over, a year or so.

Tell Melton thanks for saving my boy. Take you further, but you bastards are attacking us already."

Dobey tried to thank him, but couldn't speak.

And now they rode, south and west, miserable. Dobey's replacement, one Lieutenant Pendleton, was nominally in charge.

✫ ✫ ✫

The rain slowed to a drizzle as they rode up to the station. Dobey started to hail, but Melton stepped into the doorway, covering them with a sawed-off ten gauge double. "State your business. And if it's looking for deserters, you can just ride on."

"Jesus, Corporal, you got a beard. You gonna take on twenty men?" Jones kept one hand on his pommel, and lifted his hat.

"Hell, that you, Jones? Losing some hair, ain't you?"

"Look who I brung you." Jones nodded at Dobey.

Melton squinted. Dobey had grown a mustache over the winter. "Lieutenant?"

"Not no more, he ain't." Jones' head bobbed as he grinned. "Tole us just to call him 'Dobey' now. Din't you, Lieutenant?"

Inside, two nervous civilians sat by the fireplace, backs to the wall, carbines over their laps.

Melton started to pour drinks for Dobey, Jones and Pendleton. "Can we do this, sir?" Pendleton addressed Dobey.

Dobey smiled. "You're in charge. If it were me, I'd say yes."

"You listen to him, Lieutenant Pinkleton. Ol' Dobey will steer you right. Yes sir." Jones took a drink, glared back at the civilians, and whispered to Melton, "They's just like two rabbits, ready to bolt. Deserters, you think?"

"If they is, it ain't no business of yours in my store. See, I told them they was safe here. Which means they's safer than you, as I got no agreement with you here, whatsoever."

"Hell, them ladies don't faze me none. I ain't scared of you, Melton, but we ain't got no mission as to deserters. Has we, Lieutenant Pinkelton?"

"It's Pendleton, Corporal Jones. I've told you that over and over again. And I don't know the protocol here." He was more nervous than the civilians.

"You're here to buy horses. Have a friendly drink on a cool day, and buy horses," Dobey said calmly. "And then ride back, soon as you can, before a big Texas volunteer cavalry unit takes you prisoner."

Pendleton nodded, and licked his lips.

"And there ain't no horses for you, Lieutenant. Lieutenant Walls sent me a letter, and I just been waiting for him to get here. We're taking the horses and everything I can pack into that wagon, and we're heading for Texas, with our two new friends over there. Closing the store." Melton poured another round.

✫ ✫ ✫

They crossed the Canadian at dawn, and found Jeff Jones waiting a half-mile south.

"Got ol' Lieutenant Pinky drunk as a skunk. Some of the boys, too. They won't be fit to ride for a half a day, no how. Damn girls." He handed Sharps carbines to Melton and Dobey. "Doubt they'd chase us, even was they sober."

Dobey and Melton stared at the guns.

"I seen y'all was gonna pack them old Hall carbines. These'll be some better. I borrowed them from the heavy sleepers. Nice new Navy Colt from Miss Pinky, too." He patted the addition to his own arsenal. "Bunch of ammo for them Sharps on Pinky's horse, there in them trees."

Melton laughed, and Dobey said, "Thank you. We'll pay you for them. Fifteen dollars apiece?" Melton had paid him the hundred he'd owed for 'inventory' and so Dobey was flush. He handed Jones six five-dollar gold coins. "And how is Pinky, ah, Pendleton to get back to Fort Gibson? Walk?"

"I 'spect he'll ride with his new friend, Private Bishop. I think I heard Bishop teaching Pinky the ways of the West, out in the bushes last night."

☆ ☆ ☆

Melton's 'new friends,' Harvey and McConegly, had deserted from Fort Leavenworth two weeks earlier. They were well mounted and equipped, compliments of the U.S. Army, with Colt revolving carbines, five shooters, .56 caliber, and two Remington revolvers each.

Harvey's family had written that a Colonel Terry was raising a regiment of cavalry back home, to be called the Rangers. In fact, many of the men were former Texas Rangers, the state constabulary that policed the Texas frontier. They had a reputation for being hard, independent fighters.

Melton plied the two men with food and drink to wait and take him and Dobey with them. While he waited, Melton sawed off two shotguns, for himself and Dobey, and put shoulder straps on them. These street sweepers now hung off their pommels.

Colonel Ben Terry would be happy to see them. But it was a long, long ride to Houston. And it would be a long, long time before they passed near Vamoosa again.

CHAPTER THIRTEEN

"Can you believe how we complained about that ride to Houston?" Lieutenant Harvey stared out the window, as the train finally pulled into Bowling Green, Kentucky.

"Let me see. Do you mean that long, safe, uneventful one—the one with no Indians, nice people willing to feed us, no real schedule—is that the one?" First Sergeant McConegly had an innocent, sardonic sense of humor. "Five short delightful months ago?"

"Seems like five years," put in Dobey.

"Could 'a just come straight here from Vamoosa," said Corporal Melton. "Would 'a been a shorter ride. Could 'a spent the summer drinking Kentucky whiskey. It's famous good, I hear."

Lieutenant Harvey was morose. "Vamoosa? Me and Mac had rid three hundred miles from Leavenworth before we got to your damn little store in Vamoosa, then three hundred on to Houston, at least. Then more than three hundred by train and wading to New Orleans, and then what? Another seven hundred miles, eating train smoke, up to here? Ain't we sort of across the river from where we started?"

"Not exactly."

"All right, Mister West Point know-it-all. Don't forget you's just a dumb-ass private here, while I have been voted a officer and a gentleman." Harvey finally grinned.

Dobey smiled back. Harvey and McConegly were from Fort Bend County, where the Eighth Texas Volunteer Cavalry Regiment was formed. As former regular cavalry non-coms, they were given leadership positions as soon as they got to Houston.

Dobey, Melton, and Jones, however, were just outsiders who'd selected a fine unit to join. Their years of service counted for naught, so far. Melton was a corporal only because he beat the hell out of the scoundrel originally put in charge of his section, and that fine fellow deserted.

The beating was justified and, witnessed by the whole section, kept anyone from wanting to testify against Melton. Nor did they want to be in charge of him, so First Sergeant McConegly happily gave him the section. Melton also had a small line of credit, since he'd brought in some extra horses, guns, and ammo.

Dobey's training in "that Yankee school in New York," actually made him suspect in the ranks, and resented among some of the non-regular officers. Harvey and McConegly spent time with him on the trail, though, and heard about him from Melton and Jones; as a result, certain higher-ups were watching him.

In the meantime, he was given a job in 'C' Company, Eighth Texas, that he was perfectly suited for. He was educated, organized, intelligent, brave, fast on his feet, a scarred veteran, tough, disciplined, witty, thoughtful and energetic. He was thoroughly cognizant of cavalry, infantry, and artillery tactics, knew how to employ sappers to design and destroy fortifications, and knew the written thoughts of all the great military leaders of history. He was made company clerk. Hell, he could write.

Private Jeff Jones, who had some of those same attributes, was made the supply clerk. Hell, he was a thief.

✫ ✫ ✫

"I wouldn't have missed New Orleans, though, for all the rice in South Carolina," mused First Sergeant McConegly.

He, Dobey, and Jones were setting up the 'C' Company command post, a rather grandiose title for the open tent, with an order/movement log, a personnel ledger, and a supply ledger. Those were Dobey's ideas. Later, they would all agree that the supply ledger was a great source of toilet paper. No one wanted a written record of Jones' supply transactions, and besides, he couldn't write.

"You still thinking about that girl, Mac, uh, 'scuse me, First Sergeant?" Jones stopped stacking cartridge boxes and wiped his forehead.

"You may call me Topkick. I've always liked that title. 'Your Majesty' don't sound bad, neither. But yes. Yes, I was thinking about her." McConegly stopped smiling. "Think about her all the damn time. I mean to go back there and marry her. Who do you think I was writing on them trains?"

They'd all had varying measures of luck with the ladies of New Orleans, but McConegly was smitten with a raven-haired, sloe-eyed, slow-talking beauty named Diane Duquesne. The eighteen-year-old widow had already lost two husbands in duels.

No one doubted McConegly's ability as a swordsman. He was bigger and better looking than Melton, a great talker, and according to his friend Harvey, something of a legend among married women, around certain army posts. But Lady Diane had taken him off the market, tout de suite.

Corporal Hodges from Melton's section approached with a request for supplies, and heard the last comment.

"Jesus, Mac, you gonna marry that Frenchy? She must 'a been some kind of a seamstress."

Before McConegly could get to him, Jones stood, drew his Colt, reversed it, and said, "Looky here a minute." He then bashed Hodges with the butt. Hodges trembled for a second, then toppled.

"She won't that kind of seamstress, you dumb sumbitch. She sewed ladies dresses, made 'em up, entire. And you don't never talk about a man's intended, even was she a hooker." Hodges got up and wobbled off.

McConegly and Dobey were astounded. That was more than they'd heard Jones say about any one subject, ever, and with more emotion. He apparently approved of Mac's choice.

"Thank you, Jeff. But you can't go around hammering corporals on the forehead."

"Him? Hell, Top, that's just Prissy Hodges. I've knowed him for months. He ain't right."

Chapter Fourteen

They drew horses in Bowling Green, fresh Kentucky mounts, and the regiment was now split up to "show the flag" in company-sized patrolling operations. Not expecting to meet Union forces, they wanted to learn their horses, learn each other, gain confidence, and intimidate any locals who were still on the fence.

"That would be about half the population," surmised First Sergeant McConegly. He, Dobey, and Jones were scouting for a campsite for the night.

"Yeah," answered Jones. "Some of these good ol' boys opened fire on 'D' Company yesterday. What kind of campsite we looking for, anyways?"

"Tell him, Dobey."

Dobey figured he was being tested again. "Well, me, I'd want a little hill, with trees or rocks for cover. Creek at the bottom, so we could refill canteens and water the horses. Road nearby, so we could find ourselves on a map, and let regiment know." He paused.

"Good so far. Go on."

"Lieutenant Harvey said they'd meet us at a church this side of that next little town around four p.m., so I'd want a place not too far from that. Not too close to that village, though, or the boys'll be sneaking away tonight looking for ladies and liquor."

Lieutenant Harvey and the rest of 'C' Company had circled to the north of the crossroads village, and would ride back through it late in the day to impress the townspeople. "See if we can pick up a few recruits," he'd said.

McConegly's group found a good site by two-thirty, and headed for the rendezvous. As they approached, they saw a small gathering by the church. "Well, I guess we get to meet the local churchgoers," said McConegly, after scanning them with his telescope. "Bunch of old men in black suits."

"Ain't Sunday," said Jones.

As they rode close, the civilians turned to stare. McConegly doffed his hat and said, "Hope we're not interrupting a service."

All of the civilians were armed. Alarm bells went off in Dobey's subconscious.

"Well, brother, we are about to conduct a service, of sorts. Sort of doing your job for you." The leader, a tall severe man with scar tissue for his right eye, waved toward an open wagon. The old man and two boys in the back were tied, hands behind them, and were gagged. The hair stood on the back of Dobey's neck.

Realizing that the soldiers still didn't understand, the big man continued. "Slave holding scum. We warned them to leave the county. They didn't, so today we'll hang them." He smiled a fierce, hideous grin. "Already gave their farm to their slaves."

Dobey realized that he, Mac and Jones were all wearing their blue capes against the autumn chill. Mac looked at him, dumbfounded. Dobey said "Abolitionists," and cocked his shotgun. Mac flipped his cape aside to draw a Remington, and shouted, "Don't move!"

The sight of Mac's gray uniform under his cape startled the entire seven-man lynch mob. Their leader pointed his cane and shouted, "Secesh! Get 'em." A cross-eyed man dropped his rifle; another ran.

One man raised a carbine, so Dobey shot him first. Their leader dropped his cane and tried to pull a big horse pistol from his belt, so he went next. Jones shot the driver off the wagon with his Sharps. Mac banged off four shots with his Remington as Jones and Dobey got their pistols out, and then it was quickly over, with the abolitionists only managing a few shots.

Jones galloped after the runner, and rode him down. The man lost his shotgun in the trampling, but jumped up and drew a short sword. Jones reined around and pointed the big Dragoon at him.

"Put that down this minute, Edna."

The man threw down the sword, and Jones shot him, knocking him off his feet. He struggled to get up again, so Jones shot him twice more.

Only the cross-eyed man remained standing, hands raised, terrified.

"We're trying to discourage the taking of property and the hanging of families," said McConegly, as Dobey freed the prisoners. "Perhaps you'll tell others how this works. Now get out of here. Spread the word."

The cross-eyed man's head bobbed as he slobbered, "Yessir. Yes, sir, I will. I din't mean no harm. Din't know they was going to hang no one."

"Liar. Lying, nigger-loving son of a bitch," the man in the wagon sputtered as he ripped off his gag. "Two of the others said to let us go, but he voted to hang us. Over two old niggers we've had for fifteen years. Liar."

"I'll jes' head on out, start spreading the word, Captain, like you told me."

"He ain't no captain, Ruth Anne. And you're just having a bad day." Jones leaned down and shot him between his crossed eyes.

"Damn it, Jones. I wanted him as a messenger."

Jones looked at McConegly, astounded. "Hell, Top, you knew I was gonna kill him, the minute he lied to you. 'Sides, we don't need him. These three we saved can tell everyone. Don't worry so much. Are you all right?"

McConegly gave them a wan smile. "I don't know. May just need to borrow this wagon for a ride back to Bowling Green." He fell from his saddle.

✲ ✲ ✲

The musket ball had broken two ribs on Mac's left side, and a pistol ball had broken his left forearm. Heavily bandaged and sedated with Kentucky whiskey, he lay in a wagon full of straw, waiting for the Corinth train.

"You look like a cigar, or something," said Melton.

"Mummy," offered Dobey. Mac had also cut his head when he fell from his horse.

"'Wrapped in swaddling clothes, laying in a manger,' is what I am."

"My mummy didn't look nothing like that," Jones looked askance at Dobey, then faced Mac. "Now, I still don't know who shot you. I didn't know you was shot 'til you passed out."

"Well, I certainly knew it. Immediately. You hadn't been so busy killing prisoners, you might have noticed, too."

"They wasn't prisoners, Top. Like Dobey explained to the captain, they was murderous particles."

"Partisans. You mean to say partisans."

"Whatever. Whatever they was, they just had to go."

Chapter Fifteen

"How many, son?" Colonel Ben Terry believed that leaders should lead, and on this bitter December day he was riding with his lead company. Which just happened to be 'C' Company.

The scout took a deep breath. "I ain't sure, Colonel. Some of 'em is in the trees. I'd guess a hundred or more, skirmishers, and a whole bunch more a couple or three hundred yards behind 'em. Got to be the ones we was looking for."

The whispered word went back through the regiment like the wind. Yankees, right ahead. The Eighth Texas had been waiting for this word.

"And, Colonel, some is in a hayfield. We go hard at 'em, we can get right amongst 'em 'fore they's sure who we is."

"Captain Ferrell, bring up 'A' and 'D' Companies on line on our left. I'll take 'C' and 'E'. Scouts, you lead us. Soon as we see them, get up close and blister them with shotguns and pistols. Major Harrison, you hold the reserves. Billy, you ride back and tell that General Hindman what's happening. Tell him to hurry. We'll hold 'em for him."

✠ ✠ ✠

Corporal Hans Winkler was having a bad day. As if being on the skirmish line, hundreds of yards in front of the others, wasn't bad enough, he'd missed the sausages and dark bread at noon, and twisted his ankle. And the Herr Hauptman seemed to believe that they would run into Rebels today. "We'll burn their asses today," he'd said. Of course, the Herr Hauptman was back there with the whole damned Thirty-Second Indiana Infantry Regiment, solid German riflemen, all around him. And, suddenly, here was the enemy. He fired, part of a ragged volley, and the enemy charged right at him.

The screaming and yelling startled him, but he wasn't afraid. At a glance, he saw dozens of gray-clad horsemen charging across a wide front through the trees and underbrush. One big officer, lots of braid and waving a pistol, shot the men on either side of him, and bore down on him. He braced his Springfield against a tree and fired again. The rider and horse tumbled out of his own gun-smoke, and almost rolled over him. He thought, *My bullet must have gone through the horse's neck, and hit him in the face.*

"Back to the main line, men. Steady. Fix bayonets and fall back . . ." The rest was lost in the booming of shotguns and the banging of pistols. Winkler fixed his bayonet and began backing up. He turned to run, only to face another horseman. Behind him.

He thought, *this isn't good.* The blast caught him in the shoulder and knocked him down. He thought he heard the man call him "Trudy."

✳ ✳ ✳

Lieutenant Colonel Lubbock, regimental executive officer, stopped for another fit of coughing. He was not a well man. The assembled officers were not smoking as a concession to his condition.

"In case somebody don't know, Colonel Terry was probably the first man killed this afternoon in the charge. I'll take over 'til we can re-vote, but I think we should adopt the name of Terry's Texas Rangers, in his honor." More coughing. "We had three others killed and eight wounded, but the Yankees left thirty-eight dead and wounded. Tell the men to be proud. Major Harrison will sort of run things 'til I get back on my feet."

There was some muttering when Lieutenant Harvey relayed the information to 'C' Company's non-coms. Their captain was one of the wounded, and Harvey was now the acting commander.

"I'm just glad I ain't the supply corporal no more, is what I'm saying." Jones had taken over Melton's section, when Melton replaced McConegly as first sergeant. "That damn Major Harrison is a stickler for paperwork. And they didn't do much over on the left today."

"Didn't do much paperwork?" Dobey winked at Melton.

"No, I mean fighting. That major was in charge on the left, and they didn't do nothing."

Melton poured coffee. "Jones, there was a hell of a fight on the left. I talked to First Sergeant Baines from 'D' Company, and he said they charged just fine, but the Yanks was behind fences and haystacks, and shot 'em up pretty good. And Major Harrison was back with the reserves."

"All's I know is we did all the killing. I think Harrison's a old woman. But I do admire this Colt carbine that Top Sergeant Mac left me. Anybody know how he's doing?"

A month later, they would find out.

✳ ✳ ✳

"What's the name again? McConkle? I don't think he made it."

"It's McConegly, sir. Come in here maybe six weeks ago."
Lieutenant Harvey was beat, dripping wet, bedraggled. So
were Dobey and Jones. The pullback to Corinth, Mississippi,
in the first month of 1862, was through constant rain and
snow. They had left Melton to set up camp, and came straight
here.

"Yeah, I remember him. He's gone, I'm sorry to tell you."
The old major commanding the hospital appeared to be near
the end of his rope, too. "Likeable cuss. But that wound fes-
tered, and we had to take off the limb. He didn't last a week
after that. Shot himself. Told the orderly that he wasn't a man
anymore, and his woman wouldn't have him that way."

They re-mounted in the freezing drizzle, and found
nothing to talk about on the ride back to their base camp.
Miserable sentries steered them to the 'C' Company command
post, a line shack along the rail line that they were guarding.
Melton had a lantern and a fire sizzling inside.

Melton poured coffee all around, and gave Lieutenant
Harvey a quick rundown on their positions. When he fin-
ished, it was quiet. No one wanted to tell Melton. Finally
Melton smiled and said, "You missed him, didn't you?"

Harvey looked pained. "Yeah, Jimmy. He was gone long
before we got there."

"I know. Well, least ways you know where the hospital is,
so your trip won't wasted."

They were shocked by Melton's callousness. Dobey recovered first. "How'd you know?"

"Hell, I'm the one that sent him back out for some liquor.
Had some in his saddlebags, but he'd parked his horse at the
regimental command post, and walked here. You must have
just missed him again in the rain."

✶ ✶ ✶

McConegly took a nip. "His name was McMonigal. Poor lad, hit in the balls and leg with buckshot. They couldn't keep our names apart. Whose horse do you think I'm riding? Damn, it's good to see you all. I have a letter from Lady Diane. Drink up—y'all act like you've seen a ghost."

CHAPTER SIXTEEN

"Where the hell are we, anyhow?"

"Hell, Melton, we's in the woods. Middle of nowheres, like always. You gone blind?" Jones bit off some jerky and laughed at his own joke.

Melton kicked out the fire. "Throw some creek water on that, Corporal Smart-Ass. Maybe our brand new Corporal Walls knows something."

Dobey clattered up to them and dismounted. "Damn. Missed coffee, huh?"

Melton passed Dobey his cup. "Finish mine. You know where we are?"

Dobey gulped the coffee and took a piece of jerky from Jones. "Closest place on the map is a church named Shiloh. Harvey sent me to tell you we're pulling back. General Johnston was killed, which has left some confusion." Dobey remounted. "Anyhow, we're on rear guard again. Major Harrison's got us and another company. We'll be with some Tennessee cavalry, under their Colonel. Name's Forrest. Meet by the edge of that corn field back there."

☆ ☆ ☆

93

"I hope this Colonel Forrest ain't a 'nother old woman, like Major Harrison. That's all we need. Hell, I thought we was winning here. Thankee, Sergeant." Jones accepted the tobacco plug from Melton.

They wore their capes. Early April was still cool, and the sun was barely up.

"We was winning, for a while." Melton spat. They were on a trail, riding at the head of Melton's section and just behind Major Harrison, Lieutenant Harvey, McConegly and Dobey. "Now, tell me something. Do you just hate women? Is that why you call people by women's names?"

"Naw, Sergeant. Hell, I'm married. Got three daughters. They just didn't bring me no consolation, so I joined the cavalry."

"Jesus, Jones, how old are you?"

"Damn near twenty-four."

"Riders on the left," someone shouted. Major Harrison halted the column, and commanded, "Face left."

The three riders were led by a big man in gray on a huge black charger. He wore a saber, and two revolvers.

"I am Forrest. Are you the Eighth Texas?"

"We are, sir. I am Harrison, the major. I have two companies."

"I have but one of mine, so you are a welcome sight. There is a Yankee infantry brigade, not a quarter mile through those trees. If you'll bring your men on line, we'll attack and drive them back." He drew his saber, wheeled away, and shouted, "Prepare to trot."

Major Harrison drew a Tranter revolver, and yelled, "They're in those trees. Follow me."

As the Tennessee cavalry went through their drill of trot, gallop, and charge, Harrison led the Texans on a wild charge around their right flank and straight into the Union infantry. Their skirmishers heard the charge before they saw it, fired a loose volley, and ran back to join their main force.

The Yanks were well drilled. They formed a rough oblong box, bayonets fixed to repel cavalry. As the skirmishers joined them, they knelt and placed their rifle butts on the ground and fixed bayonets too. They became a hedgehog for horses and men to impale themselves upon.

The Rangers rode screaming to within twenty yards, halted, and blasted the formation with buckshot and carbine fire. Emptied, those weapons were slung on their high pommels, and the bloody work was finished with pistols.

The box broke. Joined now by the astounded Colonel Forrest and his Tennessee horsemen, the Rangers chased the tattered remainder back to its supporting force. Forrest fought his way to the head of the charge and was briefly surrounded and wounded, but cut his way out. As he rode by Major Harrison, he said, "Well done, sir. Very well done. Let's us go and re-load, before their cavalry finds us."

Harvey volunteered 'C' Company to cover the withdrawal. As soon as the rest were out of sight, he yelled, "Check the dead. Leave the wounded be. You're looking for money, carbines, pistols, watches, ammunition, boots, socks. Move quick, boys. They might actually have some cavalry."

As they searched, Melton caught up with Jones. "What you think of our Major now, Jonesy?"

"Hell, I'd follow him anywhere. He plumb startled me."

"You don't look so good."

"Swallowed that tobacco, when we charged."

☆ ☆ ☆

The summer of 1862 bled over into 1863. The regiment fought in over forty engagements during this time, but only took thirty casualties. Murfreesboro, Tennessee. Perryville,

Kentucky. Murfreesboro again. They earned a reputation for ferocity and competence.

Drawn up on line with the 1st Georgia Cavalry, they faced a fresh Union cavalry brigade near Stone's River, across fairly open ground. Bugles blared, sabers flashed, and the Yanks began their drill: trot, gallop, charge.

"Steady, boys. Pay attention. The bluecoats are going to show us how to do a charge. Bugles, swords, by the numbers. Damn, that's impressive." McConegly and Harvey rode up and down behind 'C' Company, calming them. When the Union cavalry closed to within thirty yards, the entire line lit up as those shotguns roared once, then again. Hundreds of them, plus the First Georgia's Enfields.

Horses and blue-coated men went down, en masse, and the brave charge floundered. Pistols finished it.

Nathan Bedford Forrest was now a general, and had earned his nickname: The Wizard. Whenever he could get them, he took Terry's Rangers into his brigade.

In January, he took them on a raid into western Tennessee. The spring was spent patrolling the despised General Bragg's line along the Duck River, then screening his next retreat, to Chattanooga in June and July.

Dobey, now a sergeant, rode with Melton on the retreat. "I don't know how much longer we can stand Bragg as a Commander. The whole Army of Tennessee must be demoralized."

"Ever' time we've whupped somebody, Bragg has run from 'em. I wouldn't cross the road to piss on him, if he was laying in the ditch, on fire."

'C' Company was down to forty men, mainly due to sickness. The Eighth Texas, eleven hundred strong one and one half years earlier, was now composed of four hundred and twelve troopers. The armament changed, too. A few Spencers, lots of captured Sharps, a few Colt carbines. Shotguns, however, were still their forte. Every veteran had two or more revolvers.

In September, they routed the Union right wing at Chickamauga, taking twenty casualties, while inflicting over one hundred and thirty. Once again, their latest regimental commander was one of the wounded, shot while leading a charge.

Dobey, McConegly, and Jones had each been wounded twice, Melton three times, Harvey killed. Captain Dave Hunter now commanded 'C' Company and Melton took over as his first sergeant, when McConegly became the regimental sergeant major. Dobey and Jones were section leaders. They were all tired.

In November, they caught a break. Terry's Texas Rangers were detached to participate in the siege of Knoxville. Stuck in that failed effort, they weren't able to rejoin the Army of Tennessee until the spring of '64.

In April, the Wizard asked for the Eighth Texas again, and with two brigades, took them to a small community forty miles north of Memphis, on the Mississippi River. It was called Fort Pillow.

CHAPTER
SEVENTEEN

The eleventh of April 1864 ended in a miserable drizzle for the garrison of Fort Pillow, Tennessee. The weather was not their greatest source of misery, however. Rumors abounded that the Wizard himself, General Nathan Bedford Forrest, had decided to cook their hash. He was especially upset, allegedly, that of the five hundred and thirty-six Union soldiers in the fort, over three hundred were Negro artillerymen, serving the fort's six cannons. To make things worse, the remaining soldiers were "homegrown Yankees," from the 13th Tennessee Cavalry (U.S.A.), who had, allegedly, committed untold numbers of unspeakable depredations on nearby southern sympathizers.

Except for perhaps three men, the Negro artillerymen were all former slaves, who'd run or been freed from Tennessee and Mississippi plantations. Some of the 13th Tennessee were former Confederates, who'd deserted or been captured and changed sides. Forrest, a former successful slave trader, was determined to return the slaves to their owners and punish the 13th Tennessee, for "encouragement of the others."

When the word spread that the depredations were actually by the black artillerymen, and against the local flowers of southern womanhood, Rebel temperatures went off the scale. The fact that the artillerymen were trapped in Fort Pillow without horses, unable to get out to do the evil deeds, didn't emerge until it was much too late.

The morning of the 12th was worse. At 0530 hours the "Missouri Mongols" of Black Bob McCulloch's 2nd Brigade killed several Union pickets and drove the others in. By 0600, it was apparent that another twenty men had deserted from the garrison, leaving 516 men to face the Wizard.

Fort Pillow's gun emplacement, about seventy-five yards square, sat on a high bluff overlooking the juncture of Coal Creek and the Mississippi River. Half-moon shaped, the fort's six gun embrasures faced away from the river, to the south and east. A dry moat encircled its parapet, six to eight feet deep and about fourteen feet wide. Beyond that were some rifle pits for skirmishers, and the trees were cleared for half a mile or so.

Just south of the fort itself were three rows of barracks, perhaps forty yards from the moat. One hundred fifty yards southwest of the gun positions was the camp of the 13th Tennessee Cavalry, on a low bluff. One hundred yards south of that were the boat landing, the 'town,' and a hospital. At the landing were several coal barges, and the Union gunboat *New Era*.

Seven small hills surrounded the fort from one hundred to two hundred yards distant. The Rebels occupied these, and sharpshooters began firing on the gunboat and the gun positions. By eight a.m., most of the Union cavalrymen had joined the black artillerymen inside the parapet. At nine a.m., the fort's commander, Major Lionel Booth, was shot dead standing beside Gun Number Two. His replacement, Major

Bradford of the 13th Tennessee, immediately ordered the last of his cavalry skirmishers out of the rifle pits and into the fort.

The *New Era,* ordered to take refugee non-combatants to safety, began towing the coal barge they'd occupied to a point upstream. At mid-morning, the Wizard himself arrived. Told that the fort could not be taken without heavy cost, Forrest immediately rode out for a personal reconnaissance of the entire perimeter. During this one hour ride, two horses were killed under him, and the third wounded.

He then ordered his 3rd Brigade under Colonel Tyree Bell to close on the fort from the north and east, and sent Black Bob McCulloch's 2nd Brigade up from the south to take the barracks near the parapet. Terry's Rangers were part of McCulloch's Brigade.

"'Nother Black-Hearted Bob, huh, Dobey? Like ol' Captain Morrison?" Jones, Captain Hunter, First Sergeant Melton and Dobey were waiting for the regimental commander behind one of the captured barracks.

"Goddamit, Jones, you call him 'Dobey' one more time and I'll break your jaw. He's been a lieutenant again for over a month." Melton's ferocity surprised them all.

"Jesus, Top, I'm sorry. Sir." Jones nodded contritely to Dobey.

Jones had two of his troopers firing Enfields around each end of the barracks, in slow aimed fire. The rest of his twenty-man section sat around their leaders, in relative safety. The cannon in the fort could not be depressed enough to engage them, and the Wizard's three rifled cannons had arrived at noon and driven off the Yankee gunboat. Now they waited for food, ammunition resupply, and orders.

'C' Company, down to fifty-one men, had eight Spencers, eleven short Enfields, twenty-four Sharps carbines and rifles, and eight men still carrying shotguns. The other nine companies of the Eighth Texas looked about the same. But each company had to leave ten men with their horses.

A runner came dodging around the last row of barracks and jogged up to them. "The colonel wants the officers back there behind the last row. And you can send a couple of men from each section for food and bullets."

The runner waited until Dobey and Captain Hunter left, then turned to whisper to Melton. "Second Missouri found a bunch of liquor and food in them Yankees' camp back there." He nodded toward the former camp of the 13ᵗʰ Tennessee (U.S.A.). "In case you wanna send a runner there, too."

Melton put his finger in the man's face. "Don't say another word about that to no one. No one. You do, I'll hurt you. Clear enough?"

"Clear. But, shit, Sergeant, them niggers up there is already drunk Ain't you heard 'em?"

"I heard 'em. We want them drunk. But I see a man drinking in 'C' Company before we take that fort, I'll kill him." Melton looked around at the nearby Rangers. "Any of you boys been listening to us, you just focus on that last part."

Jones stretched and glared at his men. "These girls know they don't drink afore I do. They know I'll kill 'em."

"He would, too, First Sergeant." Corporal Marcus Skipper giggled. "He'd do it. He's crazy as hell."

☆ ☆ ☆

"We're gonna have a truce. Wizard wants to give 'em a chance to give up, since they ain't got no other chance." Captain Hunter stopped to take a bite of cold chicken. "Long as the truce flag flies, we ain't supposed to move up. 'Less, of course, they start cheating."

"How can they, Captain? We got 'em circled."

"We don't neither, Jones. The river. They can reinforce from boats behind the fort, or start to slip out by boat. You can see smoke down river. Means more boats is coming. Wizard's gonna give 'em one chance, but we got to finish this this afternoon."

"What do we do, if we 'spect they is cheating?"

"We'll move through the smoke of them barracks burning in front of us, get in that ditch, right under 'em. When the general sounds the charge, we'll be on top of 'em 'fore they know it. All right. Check guns and water. And stay clear of them drunk bastards from Missouri on our left."

As more men from the Eighth Texas moved up to join 'C' Company behind the barracks, they saw General Forrest ride into plain view of the negotiators, on their left. He was also seen and recognized inside the little fort. Bluecoats, black and white alike, began taunting him. Butts were exposed, challenges shouted. In no way did those actions please the Wizard, or his men.

Dobey rejoined Jones, Melton, and Captain Hunter.

"What's a chicken-shit rear echelon staff officer doing way up here? Lost again?" Hunter asked, grinning. Dobey, the new Regimental Intelligence Officer, had actually led the regiment on their march here the previous night.

"Colonel says I can go in with you. I told him you were a mess, and needed help. Sir." Dobey grinned back. "He did say to pass the word: General Forrest don't want us to kill any of those contraband that we don't have to. He thinks they'll surrender, but if they don't by four o'clock, we're going in."

Captain Hunter stood. "How much time we got?"

"It's after 3:30 now."

"I'll be happy to have you with us, if we go in. You and Melton take his old section, and I'll go with Jonesy. Right now, I think you and me better split up and pass that word about the contrabands. The other companies probably ought to hear that from an officer."

As they jogged off, Jones stood and yelled "Hey—there's the Wizard hisself again." Forrest galloped up to their left flank, beyond the barracks, to the second meeting at the truce flag. For all to hear, he shouted "That gives you twenty minutes to surrender. I am General Forrest."

At ten minutes to four, the regimental commander joined 'C' Company. "Now, Forrest has changed his mind. He don't think they're gonna quit. They been signaling those boats. They think they're gonna be rescued; either by slipping out to them boats, or having a whole bunch of fresh Yankees come run us off. Ain't neither one gonna happen. We got sharp-shooters covering both sides of the back of their hill. Now listen. We got a deserter, says there's a ditch just under the wall. Maybe six feet deep. Then, there's a ledge right under their wall. When the 'Charge' is sounded, get our boys in that ditch with no yelling or shooting. Forrest will have sharp-shooters sweeping the wall. Half the men squat down, other half steps on 'em, gets up on the ledge, then pulls up the other half. Soon as we're set, we wave off the sharpshooters and go in among 'em. Questions?"

"The general still don't want us to kill the contraband?"

"No, he don't. Nor do I. But when we go over that wall, you blister everything, everybody in sight. They throw down and quit, let 'em. What we want is them cannons, turned around and pointed at them riverboats, before they bring us mischief."

✡ ✡ ✡

At four p.m. the fort's commander refused the surrender offer, and within seconds Forrest signaled the charge. Minutes later six hundred Rebel cavalrymen hunkered unseen below the lip of the parapet, and on a signal two hundred and fifty sharpshooters stopped firing.

The six hundred Rebels in the first wave stood and fired, point-blank, into the shocked defenders; perhaps four hundred and eighty of them were still packed into the small fort. Thirty-five or forty had already been wounded or killed, and been sent down the back of the hill to the river.

When the Rebels emptied their shotguns, carbines, and rifles, they drew their revolvers and blazed away with them. Most of the defenders were hit in those first few minutes. About a hundred were killed; a hundred, wounded, tried to surrender. The others, wounded, began to flee over the back wall. As they did, the second wave of Confederates came over the front walls, fired into the retreating mass, and dove into the melee. In less than ten minutes after the charge was sounded, Fort Pillow was overrun. Dead men were strewn everywhere, and the moaning of the wounded filled the air.

As the Texans consolidated and began rounding up prisoners, two things happened. Someone on the left, maybe in the 5th Mississippi, yelled, "No quarter. General Forrest said kill 'em all." This regiment had lost several officers, including its commander, as they rushed the ditch. They had also been drinking. At the same time, on the other side, Colonel Barteau's 22nd Tennessee found the 6th Colored Artillery's open liquor.

The mixture was now complete. A lack of leadership in some units, with hatred, racism, fear, blood lust, vengeance, vile challenges, rage, and liquor, set the stage. The lie of "no quarter" capped it.

The second slaughter, the indefensible one, began. Every Rebel unit, including the Texans, began robbing the survivors, as was normal. Perhaps one hundred and fifty of the fifteen hundred-man assault force began shooting the prisoners, the wounded, and those trying to surrender.

Several Rebel companies charged over the back wall, chasing those who had fled to the river. Many of the survivors continued fighting and firing at the attackers from the bottom of the hill. Some acted from drunkenness, others in sheer desperation. Whatever their reasons, their actions allowed some of the Rebels to continue firing, long after the fort's flag was lowered.

✲ ✲ ✲

In the center of the fort, a white sergeant from the 6th Colored Artillery knelt and calmly picked his targets. Twice wounded himself, he didn't expect to be treated well by these southerners. No one serving with colored troops ever was.

Captain Dave Hunter, standing on the parapet, took a bullet in his thigh and tumbled into a gun emplacement. The Henry barked again, and Sergeant Jeff Jones was hit in the face. He fell back into the moat.

✲ ✲ ✲

Dobey, scanning the interior of the fort for resistance, saw the flash of the brass Henry as the artillery sergeant levered it again. They fired simultaneously. The sergeant missed, and was knocked over a box of fuses. Dobey jumped off the parapet, retrieved the Henry, and as the second wave came over the wall, went looking for Jimmy Melton.

"Lieutenant Walls. Hey—you all right?" Melton limped up, his left leg bleeding.

Dobey nodded, and pointed at Melton's leg.

"Yeah. Contraband gunner stuck me with a bayonet when I jumped in his pit." Melton grimaced. "You seen Captain Hunter? We got over thirty contraband prisoners, and maybe fifteen whites. The cannons is all secured."

Hunter hobbled up, using a captured Springfield as a crutch. "Put the prisoners in the moat, and put a good guard on 'em. Them drunk bastards from Missouri and Mississippi is shouting 'no quarter' and shooting prisoners left and right. The Wizard ain't here yet." As Melton moved off, Hunter winced and sat on some ammo boxes. "I guess we better try to get some of these guns turned around."

"I'd help, Captain, but the colonel told me to collect whatever information I could, quick, in case we get chased off."

"Information?" Hunter was a fighter, with no formal military training. He didn't care who he was fighting.

"Yessir. What units were here, how many men and horses, size of the guns, like that. I'm looking for documents, maps, and officers to question."

"Oh. Damn, this hurts. Well, you better get on with it. I'll send Melton to help you, soon as he's back. I seen some tents there toward the back." He stood suddenly. "Here comes the general."

Forrest was injured and blood-spattered, but the blood was from two dead horses, and the injuries were from being thrown when they were killed. His blood was always up in a fight, and now he was livid, shouting orders.

"They're shooting contraband, Goddamit. You officers and sergeants put a stop to it. Get those guns turned around.

Goddamn. Do I have to do everything?" He dismounted, and limped to help manhandle one of the guns to face the river.

Two sergeants from 'B' Company, distinguished as Rangers by the Lone Star emblem on their hats, pushed ten more Negro prisoners toward the moat. The Wizard saw them.

"You there. Rangers. That's the way. At least somebody listened to my orders. Take care of 'em, boys. They're valuable property."

Dobey moved off. There was still heavy firing beyond the rear embankment, and sporadic yelling and pistol shots inside the fort. As Dobey moved through the first tent, two things were apparent: it was a hospital tent, and all of the wounded had been executed. There were shots and shouting from the next tent. Dobey had slung the captured Henry; he cocked the Spencer and started into the next tent.

A wounded Negro stumbled out and into him, holding his bleeding neck. Wide-eyed in fear, he fell back from Dobey. Dobey pointed toward the area held by the Texans, and said, "Go there. You'll be helped."

As Dobey started to push open the flap, a drunken Rebel sergeant ran into him, shouting, "Get back in here, nigger. I ain't through with you." He tried to push Dobey aside, and fired his pistol at the Negro soldier, missing him.

"Yes, you are." Dobey butt-stroked the sergeant's jaw, knocking him back into the tent and down. Dobey stepped over his legs inside and yelled, "Hold what you got."

There were four rows of cots full of bluecoats, with other wounded on the plank floors. Five Rebels, searching the dead, looked up stupidly. One, a sergeant, lurched toward Dobey, waving a Starr revolver. "These are ours. You get outta here. We got these, and we'll do what we please with 'em." He stopped suddenly, looked down at a wounded Negro sergeant, and said, "Gonna rise up against your masters, was you?"

He shot the Negro, and Dobey shot him. The big carbine bullet knocked the sergeant over a cot.

Behind Dobey someone yelled, "You killed Shoe, you sumbitch!" Starting to turn, Dobey felt a paralyzing pain in his right side and fell between two cots. There were two quick pistol shots, and the sergeant that Dobey had clubbed fell on top of him, moaning.

"Get off my officer, you back-stabbing little son of a bitch. Rest of you get outta here. I see you hurt another prisoner, I'll kill every damn one of you." Melton swung his Colt, inviting defiance.

The Rebel sergeant pushed himself off of Dobey, and sat up. "Can't breathe," he moaned.

"That's even better," said Melton, and shot him in the eye.

Chapter Eighteen

"I've been hurt worse than this, and never was sent to Atlanta. It's just a stab wound. Melton was stabbed too, and he's not here."

"Melton didn't take an Arkansas Toothpick all the way through his side, Dobey." Captain Hunter grimaced as the ambulance wagon bounced over the railroad tracks. "Bayonet was in his thigh, and it didn't fester. Yours did."

"That's just so much horse droppings, and you know it. I poured whiskey on it, and it cleared up on the train ride here."

Hunter was quiet for a moment. "All right. I ast the colonel to send you with me, to keep 'em from taking my leg. I been dosing it with whiskey too, but I don't trust 'em. All's they know is cut, cut, cut."

Jeff Jones suddenly sat up. The .44 Henry bullet that broke his jaw also took out three lower teeth. The fall into the moat broke a leg. He had been unconscious for most of the last three days, mainly from the two bottles of brandy that Melton put in his musette bag. "Got to loothen thith up." He pulled at his bandages. "Can't talk wuth a damn."

"You couldn't talk worth a damn before you was shot. There's the outside chance that folks will be able to understand you now." Hunter grinned, and Dobey nodded agreement. "Ain't no chance your mouth is infected."

✯ ✯ ✯

The hospital was overflowing. Since Dobey didn't want to be there anyhow, he made a financial arrangement with the chief orderly. Melton had given Dobey two hundred dollars, "donated" by the prisoners at Fort Pillow. Dobey paid the orderly thirty dollars to let him check in every day, but stay elsewhere. For another ten, the orderly was to take special care of Jones and Hunter.

"You notice I didn't try to negotiate you down," Dobey said to the old sergeant. When the orderly nodded, Dobey added, "That's because I want your help to be willing and full. And there's one other small qualifier. If Captain Hunter loses that leg without my prior approval, you will lose one of yours. So will the cutter."

The old sergeant smiled condescendingly, expectantly, waiting for Dobey's 'just joking, of course.' When that wasn't forthcoming, his look turned to one of consternation.

Captain Hunter, pleasantly drunk, said, "He's very serious."

Dobey unwrapped his bedroll, taking out the Henry rifle and slipping on his shoulder holster and short Colt. He pulled his jacket over it, slung the Henry, and said, "See you tomorrow."

✯ ✯ ✯

"Where to stay? I dunno, sir." The young orderly scratched his head. "I heard some officers say to a cabbie they was going to 'Shadow Blank' or something like that. Cabbies'll probably know."

There were no cabs in sight. It was raining, of course, but mid-April wasn't too cold. Dobey slung the Henry upside down, pulled up his collar, and started walking. After a mile, thoroughly soaked, he came to a tavern. Halfway through a rum, honey, and water, he asked the owner if he had a room.

"Ain't no room at the inn, son. Whole town is full."

"What about this Hotel Shadow Blank?"

The tavern owner mulled that for a second, then exploded in laughter. "You mean the Chateau Blanc. You got plenty of money, that would work. Second best whorehouse in Atlanta. The White House."

By the time Dobey finished his drink, it seemed like a positively wonderful idea.

Madame Gloria Constance Marie Laval studied the young transient. An officer, well-spoken, scarred but still handsome, clean, soaking wet, but shaven, and no smell to him. Maybe twenty-five. Hard.

In turn, she could tell that Dobey was appraising her. Red hair, burning green eyes, small waisted but buxom, almost as tall as himself. Maybe thirty-five. Hard.

She decided. "All right. The room is thirty a week, U.S., in advance. The ladies are separate. We have no boys. You can drink all you want here, but if you make trouble, drunk or sober, you're out. And no refunds. Denny—come in please."

A hulking bald man stepped in, stared at Dobey, and asked, "Yes ma'am?"

"This is Lieutenant Walls, Denny. Texas horse soldier. He may be staying a while. May he keep his guns?"

"Don't matter none to me, Miz Laval."

"What if he cuts up?"

"Then I'll take 'em away and make him eat them." He spoke in a dull monotone.

"Thank you, Denny." As the huge man left, Laval raised an eyebrow to Dobey. "Deal?"

Dobey grinned and said, "Here's thirty. I'll take your advice on companionship, unless …"

"What?"

"I suppose everyone asks for you. Is that a possibility?" His eyes bore into hers.

"Not everyone is bold enough. But no. Before I established this house, I worked in one. I've had enough pizzle sticks to last a lifetime. Still, thanks for asking. I'll send you a couple to look over. Will you eat here, too?"

✳ ✳ ✳

Steak. Potatoes. Gravy. Carrots, a hint of sugar. Bordeaux. Dobey looked up from his empty plate, shook his head, and said, "This can't be happening."

Madame Laval smiled, and sat down. Dobey tried to get her chair, but was too slow. "Sorry," he muttered. He was surprised by her blush.

"Some different from campaigning, eh?"

"You don't know." Dobey looked up as Denny appeared from nowhere and placed a demitasse of coffee in front of the madame, then disappeared.

"Where'd you find him?"

"Denny? In the gutter." She sipped her coffee.

"A drunk, was he?"

"No. In the gutter. Right out front. Used to be a cabby. Three provost officers disagreed with his price and beat him senseless with their shillelaghs."

"Their what?"

"Nightsticks. Smarmy bastards near killed him. I saved him. He loves me. End of story."

"Why'd you save him? I mean, you see lots of stray dogs here."

Laval thought about that. "Not sure. Maybe because I hate the damned provosts so much myself. They come in, terrorize anyone who ain't important, take what they want, and never pay. I hate them."

"I understand. Two of them tried to take my rifle on the way here yesterday." He put his hand over hers. She pulled hers away.

He did understand. When he was twelve, two older boys and a drunk soldier had taunted him into a fight that he really wanted to avoid, and then pounded him. His father had pounded the soldier, and both boys' fathers.

She asked, "How'd you handle them?"

"Who?" Could she read his mind?

"The provosts. Who else?"

"I'm sorry. I was eight hundred miles away and fifteen years back in time. Well, I sort of suggested that they eat horse droppings and die."

She laughed, roaring like a man. She put her hand over his. He did not pull away. "No, really." She stared at him.

"Oh. Really. Well, I said, 'Why don't you just take it?' They looked funny for a minute, then left."

"God, I wish I'd seen it." She laughed some more.

"Listen. I can't get my friends out of that hospital. Can you get me two meals like this tomorrow, so I can take them some real food?"

"Maybe eleven in the morning?"

✡ ✡ ✡

Dobey picked up the basket, and paid the cook two dollars. When Hunter and Jones opened it, they found the same meal Dobey had eaten, plus an apple pie, and soft bread. The old orderly heated up the steaks and potatoes in exchange for a slice of pie.

"When you think we'll get out of here, Lieutenant?"

"Soon as y'all are healed. I'm ready to go."

CHAPTER NINETEEN

A doctor checked Dobey's wound at mid afternoon, and pronounced it to be healing well. Dobey splashed some of Jones' rum on it, before letting the old orderly re-dress it, and left for the White House before dark.

Laval was in the kitchen when he returned the basket. Normally composed and in charge, she was nervously biting a nail. When he thanked her, she stared blankly at him, and asked, "For what?"

He held up the basket. "The meals. My friends. Just what planet are you on right now?"

"I'm so sorry. It's those provosts. Colonel Fortson just left, and warned me they're coming tonight. I have to keep Denny away from them or they may go after him again. Or cause me more trouble, for harboring him. It's my problem, though," she smiled suddenly, "and I should not let it bother paying guests."

"I don't plan to let them bother me. Or you, for that matter."

"You are sweet. But best you just lay low. You happy with that Kathy, are you? She wasn't too old?"

"Oh, no—she was as good as you said. And she gave me a powder to stop the itching on this cut."

"Yes. She worked for a drug compounder before she came to me. Which means she has a couple of useful talents here. But she's brought in a young relative, my most beautiful girl, whom I've named Bridget. You may want to try her tonight."

"Bridget?"

"Yes. Very blond, very Swedish-looking, very young. You'd be doing me a favor. I want to keep her away from the rough trade, as much as possible. Kathy said you were strong, but not rough. Stay in with Miss Bridget tonight. Stay out of trouble. She'll bring some food and wine."

"All right. I'll pay for it, of course."

"You most certainly will."

"Can I get a hot bath first?"

"Yes. How nice. I'll have Old Bill and Just Bill bring the tub to your room and fill it."

✼ ✼ ✼

The two slaves had his bath ready twenty minutes later, and left a brush, soap, towel, Bordeaux, and two glasses on a chair by the tub.

Dobey undressed quickly, putting his Colt and money under the mattress and his Henry, knife, and shoulder holster under the bed. He folded his clothes on the other chair, and stepped gingerly into the tub, holding his privates against the scalding water.

A half glass of wine later, he was dozing off when the door opened, and a fair-skinned blond girl of maybe eighteen years stepped in. She was very pretty, and very scared.

"Lock it," he said. "I didn't expect you so soon. Haven't finished my bath. Barely started, in fact. You must be Bridget."

"I am now. I got to get used to that." She smiled nervously. "Can't lock up, just yet. That house darky, Just Bill, is bringing us up some food in a minute. Miz Laval said to lock up when he leaves. You want some help with that bath?"

"Yes. Yes, I do." He smiled. "How'd you know that?"

"Listen. I'm scared, but it ain't of you. Miz Laval said to do whatever you wanted, that you wouldn't hurt me none. But she said some mean men was coming tonight, and I was lucky to be taken up with you. You ain't gonna let them have me, is you?"

"No, Miss Bridget. Not tonight. Why don't you get out of that dress and take this brush to my back, before this water cools off?"

She did. In her undershift and pantaloons, she folded a throw rug by the tub and knelt on it. "What do I call you, sir?"

"Name's Dobey. How long you been at this particular occupation?"

"All week." She scrubbed furiously, trying to avoid his scars and his bandage.

"Well, there's no substitute for experience," he said, dead-pan. It flew over her head. "When that bandage gets soaked, it'll come right off. We'll put a little liquor on my cut, and you'll dress it up again for me. The makings are up there on the dresser."

"Damn Yankee done this to you?"

"Nope. One of our own, drunk as a skunk."

"What happened to him?"

"He didn't make it."

The girl relaxed somewhat, and just as the bath began to get interesting, Just Bill arrived with their food. Noticing their blushing, he averted his eyes and hurried out.

"Good thing he didn't get here three minutes later." She smiled coyly, and began to wash him again.

"Maybe you'd better lock that door first."

She squeezed him, stood, and walked to the door. Before she reached it, it flew open. Three men walked in: a major and a lieutenant, both pudgy, in immaculate gray dress uniforms, and a hawk-faced sergeant in butternut.

"Here she is. Just like we heard, too pretty to believe." The major glanced at Dobey's folded jacket. "And way too nice for a dog-assed cavalry lieutenant." The girl started crying.

"Hold on, there." Dobey tried to stand. His feet slipped in the tub and he flopped back. He made it to his knees before the Provost sergeant clubbed him with his nightstick. He chipped a tooth on the edge of the tub, went under, and came up sputtering and dizzy. Blood and soap were in his eyes.

"Oh. You probably already paid. Well, you can have her when we're through. We'll be right down the hall."

"We might be a while," added the chubby lieutenant, dragging the girl out.

"Might not be interested in what's left," the sergeant leered. "And we'll just borrow this wine, too. Don't do nothing stupid, Lieutenant, sir. You don't want to sleep in my jail. Nossir, you don't." Pointing a Colt at the stupefied Dobey, he backed out.

Hands folded, bleeding from a cut above his eye, the slave Just Bill stood just inside the door. "I'm sorry, Master Dobey. They made me tell. Had to have that little golden girl. Miz Laval gwine to kill me."

Dobey wiped his face and eyes. "Maybe not." He pulled on the shoulder holster, shirtless, stuck the sawed-off Colt in it, and grabbed the Henry. There were eight rounds left in it. "You go, right now, and see if there's any more of them outside. Come straight back and tell me. I'll be in their room. And tell Miz Laval to bring me another pistol." He pulled on his boots.

"She down. They bonked her on the head when she tried to stop 'em."

"Throw water on her then, Goddammit. You bring me a pistol if she can't. Hurry!"

The screaming led him to the right door. He kicked it beside the handle. The frame splintered, and the door swung in. Bridget was face down on the bed, fighting and screaming, as two men held her and the third tried to tear off her shift. They all turned to face the intrusion.

The two officers were outraged, and the sergeant reached for his pistol. Dobey shot him first. He went down like an empty sack. The lieutenant, kneeling beside Bridget, tried to unsnap his holster. Dobey shot him next, and he fell off the bed. The major released Bridget and stood, pointing a finger at Dobey. "You have no idea how much trouble ..."

Dobey thought, *eventually he'll go for his pistol*. Dobey shot him in the chest. The .44 Henry rim-fire was essentially a big pistol bullet. Well placed, it would certainly kill, but it lacked knockdown power. The major staggered, began wheezing, and started pulling at his coat buttons.

Dobey levered in a fourth round and shot him in the head. He fell backwards like an oak as Bridget scrambled off the bed and past Dobey into the hall.

Dobey worked the Henry's action again, and moved to his right until his sights covered the downed lieutenant, sitting in a fetal position on the far side of the bed. Dobey shot him in the side of the head, and he fell over.

He spun back to cover the door as he heard yelling in the hall. Not well lit to begin with, the room was now filled with his gun smoke. His ears rang from the enclosed gunfire and his eyes still smarted from the soap.

"Walk through that door and you'll die," he said, not realizing he was shouting.

"Lieutenant Walls, it's Marie Laval. Don't shoot."

"All right. Come in," he shouted.

She eased in holding a Colt Pocket Model. Behind her, Just Bill stepped in with a shotgun. "Ain't no more of 'em, Boss. I brung you this gun."

"Thank you," Dobey said, too loudly. Just Bill stepped back.

"Nice outfit," Laval said.

"What?" Dobey shouted at her.

"I said, 'Nice outfit.' You look like a pervert." She smiled and shouted back. "Were you and Bridget playing games?"

Dobey realized he was wearing his shoulder holster and boots. And a dumb smile. He brought the rifle to the position of present arms, which covered him. Sort of.

✫ ✫ ✫

"You'll be fine here. Those bodies won't never be found. Old Bill and Just Bill will sell their horses and traps, and ain't no one in Atlanta going to miss those men. Their mothers could not have loved them. You're bleeding."

"Why do you call him Just Bill? He some kind of darky magistrate?"

"No, honey. He used to be named William Rice. He ran from a bad owner, so now he's Just Bill." Laval dressed his wound, pouring equal parts of brandy on it and in him.

"You smell good. Where's Bridget?" He winced. "We didn't finish."

"That's lavender. And I gave Bridget the rest of the night off. You relax here a while, and I'll send some one else up, special for you. She'll have a key. And wear this for her."

"What is that?"

"Called a sheath. Sheep's gut. You'll figure it out."

An hour later, he heard the key in the door. A husky voice whispered, "Blow out that light." He put down the Colt and snuffed the candle.

He made out her dim outline, as she dropped her robe. She slipped under the cover, and snuggled against him. Buxom, he noted. Small-waisted.

"What's your name?"

"Sue," she whispered. "Just Sue."

He caught a whiff of lavender.

☆ ☆ ☆

"Hey, Lieutenant Dobey, cap'n ith doing better, and tho am I. You 'bout ready to get back to the wegiment? Sthit. Sthill can't talk good."

"No rush, Jeff. I just want to make sure y'all are fully recovered. We're still all right on money. I sold that Henry. Y'all take your time. I'll find something to do."

Captain Hunter came back from the privy. "Hey, Dobey. I see you growed that mustache again. I like that. Covers some of your scars. You smell good, too. You wearing foo-foo water?"

Chapter Twenty

They finally ran short of money and excuses. The cash disappeared quickly once Hunter and Jones were able to get passes from the hospital, and began to spend time at Marie Laval's White House.

Before the war, Dave Hunter raised hunting dogs outside of Houston. At Chateau Blanc, he settled in with Linda, who loved most animals. She kept a small dog, Poco Charlie, in her room. For anyone other than Hunter, some of Charlie's licking might have been considered inopportune as to timing and location.

Kathy the compounder and her cousin Bridget adopted the wild man Jones. In the last week, a stream of well-dressed, well-heeled staff officers, bootleggers, and merchants were humiliated as Bridget passed them up for Jeff's energy and humor. Kathy brought experience to the table, as well as painkillers and a salve to help with his facial scar tissue.

The same men, pouting over Jones' good fortune, also deeply resented Dobey.

"What's that lieutenant got that we don't have?" A passed-over lumber broker moaned.

"Let's see. Youth, fearlessness, good looks, and Madame Marie Laval. Not a damn thing that I don't wish I had." The colonel shook his head, and patted the arm of the skinny young whore he settled for.

✷ ✷ ✷

There were invariably women present for train departures from Atlanta. Seldom was the platform so graced with well dressed beauties as it was this morning.

Kathy and Bridget sobbed over Jones, begging him to desert and let them take care of him. Linda cried softly, telling Hunter she'd go to Texas with him if he'd let her. She'd help him with them dogs. Promise. Even though they was trained to hunt other poor animals and birds.

Marie Laval stood regally, holding Dobey's arm and staring fiercely at the women who snubbed her, and smiling inside when men pretended not to know her. Several men were openly polite, realizing that with Dobey's departure, they might once again have a chance.

Old Bill touched her arm. "Miz Laval, that lady there, one in the blue dress, she ast can she come speak wid you." He twisted his hat in his hands. "Say she doan want to bother you. She seem nice."

Marie smiled and nodded to the woman, a slim well-dressed matron. The woman approached and nodded to Dobey. "Lieutenant. Madame Laval. I apologize for the intrusion, and the rudeness of some of our citizens. I felt that I must speak. I believe that it was you who sent the food and clothing and money to the orphanage last Christmas. I recognized your Negro as the delivery man. I had long suspected it." Pale, almost fragile, her smile was refreshing.

Laval and Dobey were taken aback. Recovering somewhat, Laval said "I heard that there was such a gift, and that it was s'posed to be anonymous."

There was a brief impasse, as the matron's head bobbed and tears welled up.

Kathy whispered to Jeff and Bridget, "Miz Laval was a orphan, you know. She ain't really French."

The woman reached out and touched Marie's arm. "Yes. It was. Which makes the gift both gracious and generous. As a trustee, I can assure you it was one of the most generous gifts we've received. Perhaps, if you learn the identity of our benefactress, you could simply assure her that she has a friend in Mrs. Betty Todd. My card, Madame Laval."

As he boarded, Laval kissed him and whispered, "It's Brendan."

"What?"

"Brendan. Sue Brendan. Don't tell, but don't forget," she sniffled. "It's Irish. I ain't really French."

Kathy elbowed Jeff. "You see? Orphan. Told ya so."

"Maybe we can get hit again, and come back." Sergeant Jones was pensive, as the train pulled away. They waved again at the women.

As they steamed north, Dobey opened the basket and passed out fried chicken legs. "It ain't gonna be the same. Even if we do get back here, it won't ever be the same."

CHAPTER TWENTY-ONE

As they slowed for Cassville Station, Jones stood and announced, "I got to get off and go back."

Hunter stared at him. "You deserting?"

"Oh, hell no, Cap'n. I mean, I got to go see my family. Wife and daughters. It's been eight years. Ain't been this close for a while. I'll come back."

"Eight years? Didn't want to spoil 'em, did you? Where are they?"

"Franklin, Georgia. On the Chattahoochee River. I got some stuff I stold and traded in that hospital. They might use some of it."

"Didn't know you was married. I'll write you out a pass."

From May through the end of summer, the Eighth Texas served as part of the rear guard for the Army of Tennessee as it retreated from Chattanooga to Atlanta. The Rangers fought at Resaca, Cassville, New Hope Church, and Big Shanty, trying to slow Sherman's advance.

Sergeant Major McConegly was commissioned a captain after Resaca, as they backed down the Georgia railroad toward Atlanta. He was judged deranged after being hit in the head at Cassville, and was discharged medically.

The Union cavalry forces were always dashing and brave and well-equipped, but were largely untrained and inept during the early years of the war compared to the southern horsemen, who grew up with guns and horses. Things had changed. Yankee cavalrymen were still as dashing and brave as ever, but were well-trained, well-led, and armed almost entirely with repeating carbines. In short, they were more than a match for their Rebel counterparts. And there were way too many of them.

Jeff Jones rejoined them just before the fight at New Hope Church. He had changed, too. "Laurie, my wife, she thought I's dead, so she taken up with a cousin. Had to run him off, but anyhow, boys, I got me a son. Seems she was pregnant again when I left, so I got this eight year old boy named Ben Franklin, after the town, you see. I might 'a worried, 'cept he's a spitting image of me. Not so tall, of course."

"And the girls?"

"Nine, ten, and eleven. Pretty things, and just sweet as you please. Like to have spoilt me rotten. They help Laurie with the moonshine business."

"And your wife, she took you back?"

"Well, not willful, not right off, but I begged and begged and she came around. I mean, damn, boys, y'all should see her. She ain't all fat no more. Pretty as a ten-dollar bill, and put together nice."

"Hellfire, Jones, she must 'a been pregnant the whole time you was with her before. No surprise she's some smaller."

"You know, Melton, you might be on to something there."

✡ ✡ ✡

At Big Shanty, with the Rangers fighting dismounted, a Minie ball hit Jones' carbine as he was re-loading. It took off a finger of his left hand, and the impact knocked him ass-over-teakettle. As he fell backwards, his left foot came up and a second bullet passed through his boot, taking off one and one-half toes.

He hobbled back to the horse-holder, mounted, rode back to the front and yelled, "You know what? To hell with this. I'm going home. Y'all want some free likker, come to Franklin." He spun and galloped south in a hail of bullets.

✡ ✡ ✡

After the fall of Atlanta, the Eighth was part of General Wheeler's Cavalry Corps, harassing Sherman's flanks as he pushed toward Savannah. It was decided that a special unit was needed to deal with the hundreds of Union and southern deserters who were looting and raping throughout the countryside. 'C' Company, now under Captain Alexander Shannon, had the highest concentration of veterans and repeaters. Fleshed out, they were completely equipped with Henrys and Spencers, and captured blue capes and pants. They became Shannon's Raiders, with Jimmy Melton as first sergeant and Dobey, promoted to captain, attached as the regimental special intelligence officer.

CHAPTER
TWENTY-TWO

"Good to have you back riding with 'C' Company, Cap'n Walls. They's just up ahead. Watch your step." Sergeant Skipper led Dobey through heavy underbrush on the edge of a swamp, eighteen miles southwest of Atlanta. It was close to ten p.m. and there was no moon.

"Good to be back, Marcus. Your father said to tell you, 'Do God's work, keep the faith, and the Lord will protect you.' I'm pretty sure those were his words, exact."

"Yessir. Sounds like him, the woolly old fart." Jerry Ray Skipper was the regimental chaplain, known for his white suit, his unruly thick black hair and beard, and his refusal to wear a hat, even in the rain. He was also, unofficially, the regimental commander's personal bodyguard, carrying a three-barreled long gun and four Colts. His other son, Buddy, helped him with services and, as regimental clerk, tried to keep a history of the unit.

They stumbled through a shallow creek. "Does daddy still think he's the Protector of the Crown?"

Dobey laughed. "Oh, yes. Don't nobody want to mess with the Eighth Texas' colonel, not with Reverend Skipper nearby."

"You'd think the fact that about every damn colonel we've had has been shot or died would depress him somewhat. Daddy's always long on faith, short on logic. Here they is, sir."

Captain Shannon and First Sergeant Melton were in an old bootlegger's cabin on the edge of a pond; a lantern fully lit the one room.

"Hey, Dobey. Come on in. Skipper, get Sergeant Cullen, and y'all join us. Captain Walls is gonna tell us what we're up to."

☆ ☆ ☆

What they were up to was a raid into Atlanta. General Wheeler had civilian complaints of widespread looting and shooting by deserters; he didn't think there were any regular units still there. He felt that if the Raiders made a quick sweep, performed a few public executions, that maybe the rest of the scoundrels would flee.

"Any other guidance from on high, Dobey?"

"No, Xander, and I think this is sort of how it's gonna be for us. I don't think they want to know too much about what we do. They'll tell us a problem area, try to keep us from bumping into our own forces or main Yankee units, but we're pretty much an independent command."

"Then we'll do what seems right 'til they tell us to stop. Here's my take on it: we're going after anybody hurting or stealing from civilians. I ain't looking to hang every Confederate deserter I see, if they's just trying to get home, but we better not catch 'em twice. Any Yankee is fair game, specially foragers and deserters. Special crimes, rape or murder, we'll hang 'em, leave a sign on 'em what for." He looked around. "Y'all was here under Captain Hunter. Is this gonna go down all right with the men?"

The sergeants nodded, and Dobey said, "They don't hold with killing prisoners, not regular ones, but that's not what you're talking about here."

"No. I'm the same way. Hell, I was at Pillow. We're talking about taking out criminals. Robbers, thieves, murderers, rapists. We overtake and capture some regular Yankee patrol, we'll send 'em back to regiment, or strip 'em and parole 'em ourselves. Dobey, you was in Atlanta not long back. How you think we ought to do this tomorrow?"

They settled on splitting the company. Dobey and Melton would come in from the west on the Birmingham Road with Sergeant Cullen's section, while Shannon and Sergeant Skipper would come up the Montgomery Road from the south. They'd move fast, taking targets of opportunity in broad daylight, and try to meet at the main train depot by noon. If there was no real resistance, they'd reassess then, and probably sweep on through to the northeast.

In case of real resistance, rally points would be north of Stone Mountain, or back here to the swamp, depending on how they were pushed. If they were really separated, they'd meet in Carrollton in two days.

Captain Shannon stood and stretched. "Let's get some sleep. We'll get up at six, and be rolling by seven."

Dobey's group followed the east bank of the Chattahoochee River til they cut the Birmingham Road, and were in the city's outskirts before nine a.m. As they got closer to the center they put out scouts and flankers to look for activity. Corporal Jack Sterne's squad was the first to score.

A flanker reported yelling from a large house near the Marietta Road, and it was quietly surrounded. Before Sterne's men could dismount, three bluecoat deserters burst out onto the porch laughing and carrying pillowcases, which jangled with silver flatware and candelabra. They shouted another threat back into the home before they saw the blue-caped riders along the front hedge.

"Y'all come on down, boys," shouted Sterne. "No need to haul them heavy bags. Just leave 'em on the porch."

The sound of ten Spencers being brought to full cock caused the robbers' hair to stand on end.

"Hey, listen. We'll share. And there's some women in there, still got plenty of good use left."

"That ain't what this is about."

"Are you provosts, or something?"

"Not exactly."

"You going to arrest us?"

"Not exactly."

✳ ✳ ✳

"First blood," Dobey muttered. The volley, maybe a half-mile north, wasn't irregular enough for a gunfight. Just ahead, an old black woman sat on the ground at an intersection, sobbing, nursing an obviously broken forearm. Speer, the Raider's medico, trotted up and dismounted.

"We're looking for troublemakers, Mammy. I can set this. It'll hurt, then feel better."

"Yassuh. And thank you, suh. Glad all you Yankees ain't bad. Oh, Jesus," she yelled as he reset the bone.

"You seen some bad Yankees, Mammy?"

"Right over there in that house. They hurt me and ever'body in there. They mean and drunk. Sleeping now. Already done their business."

"Any guns?"

Cullen's men dismounted and surrounded the home.

"They boss, he gots a pistol. Other three, they gots bay'net knives."

Five minutes later, the sorry, hung-over lot stood on the roadside. From the porch, the battered family watched sullenly, not expecting much justice from the blue-caped Union cavalrymen.

Melton dismounted, carrying his shotgun in his left hand. He faced the leader, a corporal, and said, "Well, girls, there's good news and bad news. The good news is, we ain't got time to hang you. Bad news is, we ain't Yankees."

He drew the sawed-off Colt and shot the corporal in the head, re-holstered, and shotgunned two of the others. The fourth bolted, but three Spencers knocked him down.

Melton tipped his hat to the people on the porch. "Compliments of the Eighth Texas. Just leave the scum out here. They'll all be dead soon, and maybe it'll discourage such behavior."

Dobey pulled up. "Jimmy, we ain't far from that White House I told you about. No sign of Regulars, yet, so I want to ride by there and check on 'em."

Melton nodded. "I'll go with you. Cullen, keep criss-crossing this main road til you get to the train tracks, then turn left. We'll catch you before you get to the depot."

✲ ✲ ✲

"No suh, Mister Dobey, they gone," said Old Bill. "Miz Laval, Mizzes Kathy and Britches, Mister Denny, Miz Linda, Just Bill. Gone to Savannah. Just Old Bill, that you might know. I'se here wid that trashy whore, Miz Fancy Stine, that Miz Laval sold out to. Her and her whores, that is."

"Savannah. Well, they'll have to run again. Sherman's going there now."

"Yassuh. Mister Dobey, don't you take no chances wid dese whores here. Ain't had no doctor since Miz Laval left. Now, you ain't changed sides, is you?"

"No, Old Bill. These capes are just to fool the Yankees. Any soldiers in there now?"

"Yassuh. Yankees got them some mean-assed provosts too, same as us. Two of 'em up dere wid Miz Fancy all night."

Ordered from their room into the hallway, the two provost sergeants were feisty and threatening until it sank in that these two blue-clad troopers holding guns on them were in fact Confederates. They now wore a distinctly worried look.

"Y'all been out doing your job, we wouldn't even be here. Cap'n, you think we should shoot 'em, or just turn 'em out naked and unarmed, maybe let the locals and looters take care of 'em?" As he spoke, Melton turned to face Dobey.

At that moment, the irate and drunken Madame Fancy suddenly pushed between the provosts and stuck a little .41 Deringer almost in Melton's face. Melton threw up a hand as she fired, and the two provosts bolted back into their room.

The underpowered fat little ball took off the top joint of Melton's left middle finger, and hit him in the forehead. His shotgun went off as he fell backwards, cutting the madame's legs from under her.

Dobey pumped two rounds from his Spencer through the wall into the provosts' room, drawing a yelp and a flurry of pistol shots in return. He slung the Spencer, drew a Colt left-handed, and grabbed Melton's collar with his stronger right. The madame, moaning, sat up in the doorway. She was immediately hit by one of the provosts' pistol shots, and slumped.

The semiconscious Melton still held his shotgun with one hand as he wiped the blood from his eyes. As Dobey dragged him around a corner, one of the provosts stepped into the doorway, firing. Melton fired the second barrel at the noise, driving the man back into his room, dinged by three ricochets and splinters.

Dobey bounced Melton down the steps, missing the last few himself and winding up in a heap on the floor with Melton on top of him. Melton rolled off him, drew a Colt and fired two shots up the stairs to discourage pursuit.

In a stage whisper, Old Bill said, "Mister Dobey. Mister Dobey—over here." They crawled toward him, and out a side door onto the verandah.

"Can you ride, Jimmy?"

"Hell, I can dance. I just can't see." He tumbled backwards down the step into the yard.

Dobey and Old Bill got him to his horse. He mounted, and said, "Where to?"

Dobey grabbed Jimmy's reins, and said, "Just hold on to that pommel and keep your head down." They galloped off, expecting a bullet in the back, but the provosts had had enough. As they swung onto the railroad tracks, Dobey asked, "When did you learn to dance?"

At the depot, Speer wiped the wound clean to find solid bone. "Judas Priest, First Sergeant, it glanced off. I knowed you was hardheaded, but Jesus. It did take the top off your ear, howsomever. Lay still, and I'll sew up your forehead."

CHAPTER
TWENTY-THREE

"Listen, Daddy, it was a good raid. Top Sergeant Melton was the only one hit, and we must of killed twenny deserters from both sides, and captured seven regulars. Now, why in Hell would you . . . owww!"

"Mind your tongue, Marcus Aurelius." Reverend Skipper waved his cane at his oldest son. "Your mother would choke in her grave if she heard that filth pouring from you. And you can tell your heathen comrades that while I ride with you, I'll not tolerate such profanity. I'll smite them heel and toe."

"Ain't that 'head and toe,' Daddy?"

"Buddy, just shut up. I'm talking to your brother." The old man ran his hand through his tangled mop of hair to regain his thoughts. "I am not sent here to correct your conversation, though I may. Your captain expressed concern about the executions. He doesn't want to exceed his authority. So, if there is a life or death question for these pond scum that we wish to exterminate, I will be a sort of moral compass to the Raiders."

"Well, good," said Melton. "Now they'll have a fair chance."

The old zealot's eyes blazed with religious fervor, as he nodded agreement. He was, at such times, the incarnation of John the Baptist, raving in the wilderness. In a white suit, of course, and shaking a fist at the heavens. During the next three months, over four hundred deserters and looters were shot or hanged by Shannon's Raiders; for many of them, their last earthly vision was of that deadly apparition, the right Reverend Jerry Ray Skipper.

✫ ✫ ✫

They camped at a destroyed plantation, west of Savannah. The slaves' quarters had been spared by Sherman's men, but the slaves had followed him to Savannah. Dobey, Captain Shannon, and Reverend Skipper were having coffee when the first patrol came in.

Sergeant Cullen took a swallow of coffee before reporting. "We got one of ours, says he escaped from the Yankees. Got three Yankees, had two little nigger girls in a barn, taking turns with 'em. Is that the same as raping white women? I mean, to us?"

The reverend stood and trembled. "It's worse. Far worse. These men are seen by the Negro as liberators. It is a terrible betrayal of trust, on top of a heinous crime."

"Yessir. They was on top of their hineys, for sure."

The three officers walked out to face the doomed men, shivering in cold and fear.

"Now you shall know the wrath of God."

"Hey, ain't you John Brown? I thought you was hanged. I seen your picture in a newspaper."

"You, sir, will meet John Brown in Hell in a few minutes. Hang all three of them."

"Over by the road, Cullen. Put a sign on 'em. 'These raped the girls they set free.' Buddy will write it up for you."

Captain Shannon turned to the Rebel prisoner. "Where you from, son?"

"Augusta, sir. I ain't no deserter."

"Which way was he heading when you took him, Cullen?"

"West. But he run from us."

"You Goddam right I run. Y'all wearing blue capes, I thought I was captured again. Oowww!"

The reverend had stepped off the porch and caned him.

"Jesus Christ, you old fool, I might take that damn stick and . . . owww!" He went down.

"I was you, I'd stop cussing. Reverend Skipper is against it." Cullen smiled. "I seen him whack his own son."

"All right. All right. But you listen. I ain't no deserter, and this ain't right. Only reason I's captured in the first place, was our Goddamned major surrendered. Hold on there, Reverend, I'm sorry, but I'm hot about this. We run out of bullets, and I wanted to run, but he surrendered. Hell, you give me a gun and some cartridges, I'll ride with you. I'm sorry again, Reverend."

"What's your name, son?"

"Skip Todd, sir. And I was a sergeant. My uniform rotted off me, so I got this old coat with no stripes."

"You take him and watch him, Cullen. He can help hang those three. It's a good thing you wasn't walking toward Augusta, Todd."

Melton returned from checking the guards and joined the officers back inside the cabin. "Reverend, we got some captured Spencers. You still want to carry that cannon?"

"That cannon, James Melton, is a very well-made Pennsylvania drilling. The name comes from the Germanic word for three, 'drei,' as it has three barrels. I chose a fifty caliber rifle, with two twelve gauge smooth bores. But they come in all sorts of combinations. I almost chose one with a

.32 caliber squirrel rifle, a .40 caliber rifle for deer, and a ten gauge for ducks."

"Or Yankees."

"Amen, Brother Melton."

In December '64, they rejoined the regiment, now down to two hundred and fifty men. Melton became the regimental sergeant major, Dobey the operations officer.

With the rest of Wheeler's cavalry, they screened the Confederates retreat north into North Carolina, first ambushing Kilpatrick's Yankee cavalry near Aiken, then fighting them around Columbia. They overran Kilpatrick's camp at a small crossroads near Fayetteville, and would fight their last real battle at Bentonville, North Carolina, from March 19-21, 1865.

Dobey was exhausted as he rode into 'K' Company's lines. Two wounded Rangers looked up from reloading their pistols, stared at him blank-faced for a moment, then pointed to a tobacco curing shed at the edge of some pines.

One of the grimy soldiers stood, wiped blood from his face, and said, "Doc, uh, Captain Matthews is having a meeting with what's left of our sergeants and officers. In that corn crib, or whatever it is." He touched a Colt to his temple in a salute, and sat down again.

The meeting was breaking up as Dobey rode up. Doc Matthews, the youthful company commander, shielded his eyes against the afternoon sun and faced Dobey expectantly. Nervously. Resigned. Hell, a visit from regimental staff couldn't be good.

"Y'all better stick around til I learn what Captain Walls has in store for us. Prob'ly wants us to go on one of his little rides." His subordinates gave strained laughs.

Dobey dismounted, and saluted Matthews. "Captain Matthews, men." He nodded to the others. "Y'all did a fine job today, And no, I don't have any special mission for your company."

"Well, my stars, Dobey, ain't we formal? What's up then?"

"Doc, I don't know if y'all heard yet, but Colonel Cook, Lieutenant Colonel Christian, and Major Jarmon have all been hit bad. You're next senior. There's no time for elections, Doc, so you're the new regimental commander. Better turn things over here, and come on back with me. Tomorrow's gonna be busy, too."

"Hell, Dobey, you should do it. You got a hell of a lot more experience than me."

"You know that's not how it works, Doc. You outrank me by a week or two. Sir." Dobey smiled. Artillery fire behind them caused the smile to disappear. "We better ride."

The regimental command post consisted of a group of messengers huddled around Sergeant Major Melton and three junior officers. As Dobey and Matthews rode up, so did General Wheeler.

"Where's the regimental commander? This is the Eighth Texas, right?"

"I've just learned that would be me, General," Matthews saluted him.

"Well, Captain, that fire you hear is Yankees trying to take our bridge back there. We must not lose it. Our supplies and ammunition must come over it. I've sent some Tennessee infantry toward it, but they'll likely not arrive in time. Mount your men, go as fast as you can and charge whatever you find at that bridge."

As they raced toward the bridge, Sergeant Major Melton shouted, "Welcome to regiment, sir."

Matthews looked askance at him and said, "Jimmy, you know I ain't had any experience at this."

Melton yelled back, "Hell, Cap'n, we ain't much more than a company no how."

They galloped past the Tennessee infantry, Brown's brigade, double-timing along, and were cheered on. Topping a small rise, Matthews, Dobey, and Melton halted to allow the Eighth Texas to close on them. Here also waited General Hardee and his staff, with a great view of the enemy, five hundred yards away across an open field. They were in sparse woods, closing on the bridge.

The Texans saluted, and General Hardee asked who they were.

"We're the Eighth Texas, sir," said Matthews. "And General Wheeler told us to run off anybody 'round that bridge, and hold it."

Hardee looked at the mass of blue infantry at the bridge, shook his head, and said, "Then execute your orders."

Matthews drew a Colt and yelled, "Charge right in front!"

It was to be the last charge of the Eighth Texas, and the last cavalry charge of the Army of Tennessee. It was, in every sense of the word, a smashing success.

Screaming to beat the band, the Texas horsemen plowed into the Union infantry, almost head to head, as the bluecoats ran toward the bridge. The angle of attack precluded all but the skirmishers and front runners of the foot soldiers from firing their single shot rifles, and they had no chance to form a hedgehog.

Dobey trampled an officer waving a sword, then in rapid sequence, shot a sergeant trying to reload, a flag-bearer, and three more riflemen, while his big bay ran over four others.

Deep in the ranks of the enemy, he drew a second Colt and quickly emptied it around him, as his charger kicked and bit anyone on the ground.

At a full run, Melton fired both barrels of his 10 gauge into the packed ranks, slung it and drew his pommel Dragoon before slamming into the mass. He used the pistol to parry a bayonet thrust, then clubbed the rifleman before shooting four more. His horse screamed as she took a bayonet in the neck, then stomped the man that stabbed her.

As the bluecoat scrambled to get away from the slashing hooves. Melton yelled, "You son of a bitch," and shot him in the back. Another bayonet struck in the wooden part of Melton's saddle narrowly missing his left leg. Melton shot the soldier in the face as he tried to withdraw his bayonet. Dropping the empty Dragoon back in the pommel holster, he changed reins to his right hand, and drew a belt pistol left handed.

Doc Matthews shot two skirmishers as he rode toward the blue ranks, then singled out a mounted major. He hit the major in the leg with a pistol shot before ramming into his horse, broadsides. Yankee horse and rider went down in a tumble. As Matthews backed away, a sergeant jumped and grabbed him around the waist, trying to drag him from the saddle.

Melton shot Matthews' assailant in the back; the man arched, screamed, and fell away. Matthews spun his horse to step on the man several times, then began firing at other targets.

Around the three riders, wounded men dropped their weapons and crawled to get away from the horses and pistol fire. Along the line, the scene was repeated a hundred times. And as the Texans emptied their third or fourth revolvers, Brown's Tennesseans piled into the crush, their own blood-curdling yells helping to break the line.

The Union forces abandoned the bridge, leaving two hundred prisoners, and many more dead and wounded. As they pulled away, the Rangers lashed them with carbine fire.

* * *

Melton made a swing through the companies, speaking with each first sergeant. He caught up to Dobey and Doc Matthews as they followed the prisoners to the rear. Dobey could see that something was terribly wrong.

"You all right, Jimmy?"

"No sir. You remember General Hardee's boy, that run away from school last year to join us?"

Matthews said, "Yeah. Sixteen-year-old. General sent him home, but he come back yesterday, I heard."

"That's right," said Dobey. "General told Kyle to swear him into 'D' Company. Why?"

"He was killed. First damn action, and the boy's dead. Who's gonna tell the general?" Melton's voice cracked.

Captain Doc Matthews, only twenty-two years old himself, said, "Shit. Murdering hellfire shit damnation." He yanked his reins to the left and trotted up the little hill to General Hardee's vantage point.

* * *

Around a small fire that night, Dobey poured Doc Matthews a brandy. "You done good, Doc. It was a damn good charge."

Matthews just stared into the fire. After a moment, he looked around and said, "You know what he said when I told him? He said he thought he'd sent us all to our death, and that Jeb Stuart could not have done any better. Said his son was exactly where he wanted to be, and he was damned proud of him, and damned proud of us." He took a sip. "Ain't that something?"

BOOK TWO

April 1865

CHAPTER TWENTY-FOUR

"Wrong answer," said Jimmy. He shot the prisoner, then levered open the breech of the Sharps and loaded another linen cartridge. "Same question," he said to the second man.

They stood under a chinaberry tree in the empty back lot of an almost empty farmhouse. As he cocked the carbine, Jimmy thought, *There ought to be chickens here, and goats, and cows. And children.*

"I ain't no deserter, and I ain't raped no nigger wench. He done it," the man said, knees wobbling, nodding at the dead man.

"Well, that's better than he come up with." Jimmy smiled. The blast, even half-expected, was startling. "Still wrong." He reloaded, and turned to the Skipper brothers. "Dump both of 'em in the well. I'm gonna grab a bite to eat."

As Buddy dragged one of the barefoot dead men to the well, he muttered, "I know our daddy would have approved, but I still think Melton's a hard man."

Marcus grunted as he tilted the first body into the well; there was a thud as it hit bottom. "Listen, Buddy. The scouts caught these two, pants down, buggering that little contraband girl in that barn, right there." He wiped his fore-head; body disposal was warm work, even in April. "Besides of which, they had to be the ones as killed the old couple that lived here. Their bodies was still warm."

The second Yankee was heavier. They struggled to get his upper half over the edge of the well, then each grabbed an ankle and tipped him in.

"Anyways, I guess these two wisht they'd stayed with Sherman." Marcus wiped his bloody hands in the sandy soil. After inspecting the result, he added, "Let's us go to that creek."

What was left of the Eighth Texas Cavalry was bivouacked comfortably somewhere in central North Carolina. The temporary commander, Captain J.F. 'Doc' Matthews of 'K' Company, didn't know exactly where, nor did he worry much about it. The regiment had overrun a Union cavalry camp at Monroe's Crossroads prior to their last battle at Bentonville, and was still eating well.

Matthews was still in command since Bentonville, when Colonel Cooke and several other officers were wounded. Rocking on the porch of a small farmhouse, he was now pondering the awesome responsibility of leading a regiment, albeit a small one, in an army that had been defeated and was getting ready to quit. He was also enjoying his new boots, which a few weeks ago had graced the legs of Union Major General H.J. Kilpatrick; as he considered and waited for Captain Walls and Sergeant Major Melton, he sipped some captured brandy from a battered tin cup.

Captain Walls and Sergeant Major Melton soon appeared from the back yard. Each had a metal plate tucked under his pistol belt and a tin cup hanging from a revolver hammer.

Melton stopped at the bottom of the stairs and leaned on his Sharps carbine, but Walls marched onto the porch, stamped his heels, and with his best impression of a British open palm salute, snapped, "Captain Walls reports to the regimental commander as ordered, sir!"

Leaving Walls in that position for a moment, Matthews nodded to the grinning Sergeant Melton and said, "Jimmy." He then turned back to Walls, gave him a casual salute, and said, "I'm glad somebody is impressed with the task I have. I was just sitting here, studying on it."

Walls dropped his mock salute and produced a sandwich from behind his back. He'd made it by putting some bacon between two thick slices of hard cheese. He now broke it, and handed half to Captain Matthews. "You so busy and important, you probably ain't had time to eat. Make me your deputy commander, and me 'n Jimmy will take good care of you all the time."

"That's you, Dobey. Give, give, never take." He grinned at his own sarcasm, then continued. "Want some brandy? Jimmy?" He poured both men some in their own cups, and studied them while they sipped.

Captain Thomas McDougall Walls, U.S. Military Academy Class of 1858, was the twenty-seven years old deputy commander of the regiment by default, but in Matthews's opinion he should be commanding it. Dobey Walls had more combat experience than any other officer in the Rangers. He'd grown up fighting Indians; his father had been a career cavalry sergeant, killed by Kiowas in '52. After West Point Dobey had served three years in the cavalry out west before the War of Northern Aggression. When it started, he'd resigned his commission and rode south to join Terry's Rangers as a private. A former U.S. Cavalry corporal named Jimmy Melton rode with him.

Sergeant Melton was now thirty-three, nearly six feet tall, and weighed about 200 pounds when well fed. Just now he was about 180. He took a sip and said, "What's up, Cap'n?"

Matthews blew smoke and said, "Little while back, my daddy wrote and said since the Yankees left north Texas, the Kiowas was acting up again. You hear that?"

Dobey replied, "I heard that, Doc, and I worry. My ma and my brother are still out there somewhere, if they're still alive."

Matthews nodded. "I heard something else, too. My daddy said he was in Fort Worth, and some Mexicans was talking about trading with some other Mexes at a little post up in the Panhandle, on the Canadian River."

"So?"

"Said they was a old white woman and a crippled man that owned it. Said some folks called the place Canadian Fort; others said Canadian Ford."

"Doc, you just trying to get my hopes up?" Dobey was pacing the porch and fidgeting now. "How many little stores in Texas is run by some old woman and a crippled man? Fifty? A hundred, maybe?"

"Maybe. But Daddy said the locals called the place Balliett's Post. Now, Dobey, that was months ago, but . . ."

Dobey stared at Doc, stunned. Doc nodded, then continued. "Here's the thing. Within a month, we're gonna be ordered to join the rest of the Army of Tennessee, and go lay down our guns. They may take our horses."

Dobey looked away. "It's over, then? All done? They'll take our guns and horses?"

Matthews said, "It's over."

Jimmy Melton muttered, "Jesus," and drained his brandy.

Matthews sipped again. "Now, if someone was off to the west on a recon patrol, he wouldn't know about that surrender order. Even if he heard about it, he wouldn't know where to go. I expect he'd just keep heading west, trying to avoid blue suits and big towns. Maybe drop down into South Carolina, pass north of Atlanta, and pick up the Tupelo road north of Birmingham. I got a cousin in Tupelo might tell him how to get to the big river, and then get a boat down to the Arkansas River, and up it to the Canadian."

Matthews paused and handed each man a cigar. "Captain Walls, you are ordered to take a patrol consisting of Sergeant Major Melton and yourself, and recon to the west. Take what extra ammo and food you can put on a spare horse. I've written down a suggested route on the back of this map, along with my cousin's name. He's on the Corinth road, just outside Tupelo. Don't report back til you hear from me. Tell Billy Johnson that I've promoted him to captain, and he's to take over your duties. Sergeant Major, who should replace you?"

"Patch Dunphy, from 'B' Company, but wait a minute. Why me?"

"'Cause I said so, Jimmy. You brought him to the Rangers, you take him home. Hell, he needs help finding his own butt with both hands." The men smiled; everyone knew Dobey was the best map-reader in the regiment. Matthews continued, "Y'all leave as soon as you're packed. My cook will give you all the jerky you can carry, with beans and extra canteens. We'll be eating good for at least two more weeks on this captured Yankee stuff. Get moving."

Dobey stood, wiped off crumbs, and shook Matthews' hand. He tried to say thanks, but couldn't speak. Melton stood fidgeting, obviously agitated. Matthews said softly to him, "Listen, Jimmy, you're not gonna miss any fighting. I'm gonna keep us out of contact til they order me to come in and quit. There's only two hundred and fifty of us left out of eleven hundred, and we're all from around Houston. We already whipped our Indians. Go help him with those Kiowas."

Jimmy said, "Yessir," and turned to leave.

Matthews said, "Jimmy?" Melton turned back. "I heard the shots. What did you do with the bodies?"

"Medicos tried to save the girl, but they'd beat her too bad. I had the Yankees bury her and the old white couple. Put the Yankees in the well."

"Jesus, Jimmy. The well?"

Melton flared, then took a deep breath and spoke slowly. "It's dry, Doc. And if Yankee cavalry finds them two bodies, they won't care was they deserters, murderers, or what. They'd hang some civilians or Rebel prisoners as pay-back. You know that," he added as if speaking to a child. "Do you know the first one said they didn't kill the old couple, and that the girl was 'only a nigger'? Whose side they supposed to be on?"

Two hours later, Dobey and Melton rode southwest.

CHAPTER
TWENTY-FIVE

They were relieved to be heading home after four years, but they were not at all relaxed. The war was not over, and they needed to get through about 1,200 miles of Union patrols, Regulators and Home Guard looking for deserters, deserters looking for anything they could rob or steal, and farmers—angry old men tired of being robbed by both sides. As they got closer to home, there would be the added excitement of hostile Indians, bold after years of the white army's absence.

Though a small force, they were a force to be reckoned with. Under Dobey's leg was snugged a Spencer carbine, and on his pommel was holstered a Navy Colt revolver. On his hips were two more of the .36 caliber Colts. In a shoulder holster hung a fourth Navy. The loading lever was removed, and the barrel had been shortened to four inches. It was a gunfighter's pistol, his face had been scarred by it, and he was never, ever, without it.

Jimmy Melton also carried a sawed-off Colt, but his was a bigger 1860 Army model, and he wore it butt forward on his left hip. He had another .44 caliber Army on his right hip, and in his pommel holster was a Dragoon Colt, an old four-pounder. The newer Colts were lighter and easier to handle, but it was a good spare, and God only knew how many times the Confederate cavalry had turned the tide in fights because of their extra six-shooters.

In addition to his revolvers, Jimmy Melton had his Sharps carbine in a saddle scabbard. Like the Dragoon Colt, Jimmy had carried it and fought with it for ten years. His new main gun though, was a Colt revolving shotgun, and he wore it slung over his back, barrel up. It was a 10 gauge, five shot model 1855 Sporter, that until recently had been a hunting weapon for a Union brigade commander. After liberating it on their last raid, Jimmy had the Ranger armorer cut the barrel down to 22 inches; each chamber was loaded with "Buck-and-Ball"—one ¾-inch round ball, and six .31 caliber buckshot, on top of a huge charge of powder. At thirty-five yards or less it was a devastating weapon. The armorer had named it, "The Avenging Angel."

Both men wore gray jackets, and brimmed hats with the "Lone Star" emblem of the Rangers; their pants were light blue with a yellow stripe, acquired at Monroe's Crossroads, along with their new plaid shirts.

Draped across their bodies were leather slings, which could be quickly attached to sling-rings on the left side of their carbines. They carried large knives on their pistol belts; there were bedrolls, ponchos, canteens, tin cups, forage bags, and saddlebags on their individual horses. In the saddle bags were jerky, extra cartridges, tins of primer caps, powder flasks, razors, soap, curry brushes, hammers, horseshoes, nails, rags, socks, spare shirts, and matches. On the spare horse were a bucket, axe, shovel, two shelter halves, stakes, rope, more forage, sugar, hard cheese, bacon, a ham, jerky, coffee, a pot, a pan, apples, tobacco, rice, some potatoes, canned tomatoes, and more canteens, brandy, and ammunition. And a nice break-down fishing pole, with all the trimmings, another gift from a Union colonel.

They were as well set-up as they could be, much better than for most of the last four years. Wounded several times, each had healed; they were hard and sound. Dobey Walls learned basic hygiene at West Point, and insisted on it for his troopers. Jimmy Melton long ago noticed that Dobey was hardly ever sick, and that his men suffered less sickness than those in other units, so he became a believer too.

They could cover twenty-five to thirty-five miles per day without pushing. Sometimes they did better, but mountains and rivers and Union patrols slowed them down. Both men had captured some U.S. currency and coins on the last raid, and started with almost sixty dollars between them. By occasionally buying some eggs or corn dodgers from poor locals, they stretched their supplies and usually received excellent intelligence on that area.

They had ridden and fought together for over seven years. They seldom had long conversations but when they did talk, they used an abbreviated patois, common in the South and West. Words considered unnecessary were simply dropped.

"If he wants to talk to me, then he will have to come here," became, "He wants to talk, he better come here."

And "Are you finished?" became, "Through?"

"I'm not certain that he's completely sane" became, "He ain't right." Or "This isn't working so we'd better try something different," might become, "Ain't no good like it is."

CHAPTER TWENTY-SIX

Eleven days into their journey found them in northern Georgia, near the Alabama line. April was still cool in the mountains, and the smell of smoke late in the day brought them to a farmhouse.

From sixty yards out, Jimmy yelled, "Halloooo, the cabin." Ten seconds later, an old man sidled onto the porch with a long double barreled shotgun, and said warily, "We ain't got nothing left to take."

Jimmy stood in the stirrups and yelled back, "We ain't gonna try to take nothing. We're pretty well set, but our horses could stand some grain. And if you got somebody can cook real food, we'll pay for it." Dobey saw movement behind the house.

"War's about over, and Rebel paper ain't never been worth a damn no how. Y'all jes' ride on back to Tennessee. My grandson's in the barn by now, with a rifle, an' my boys will be here in five minutes, if shots are fired. Jes' ride on. Better for all of us."

"We are not Tennessee raiders," Dobey shouted. "I'm Captain Walls, and this is Sergeant Major Melton. We're the advanced element of our regiment, heading home to Louisiana.

We have captured Yankee dollars. You don't want 'em, we'll buy food at the next farm."

There was some debate with someone inside the house, and Jimmy muttered, "Damn, you talk good. So, we still saying we from Louisiana?"

"Yup," said Dobey. "Nobody needs to know where we're heading, less they're trying to capture us. The boy is behind that shed, with a squirrel rifle. You make him?"

Jimmy nodded, and yelled again. "You listen—That boy does hit me with that pea-shooter, it'll only make me mad. I'll kill him, you-all, your dogs, and burn your house. Tell him to point it away while we yell at each other."

The old man made a decision, nodding his head to the person inside and leaning his gun against the wall. "All right, y'all come on in. Billy, come back round here and don't aim at 'em no more. You hear me?" A barefoot boy, maybe twelve years old, came trotting to join the old man, who put his hand on the boy's head and said, "You done good, Billy."

"Durn, Pap, lookit all them guns." Billy was wide-eyed.

The old man patted him again, shushed him, and said, "I'm sorry for being unneighborly, but them raiders has 'bout wiped us out three times. Smokehouse emptied, taters, corn, my pigs—hell, they butchered my milk cow. I don't know whose side they's on, though they wear the gray."

Billy piped up, "Yeah, we had to get another cow, and keep her hid," then yelped as his Pap pinched him.

Dobey smiled. "No worry—we don't kill or take milk cows. I might eat some buttermilk biscuits, though." He dismounted and handed the reins to the boy. "Would you feed these horses for ten Yankee cents?"

The boy looked to his grandpa, who nodded, so the boy said, "Yessir. Yessir." He took the reins for Dobey's horse and the spare, then looked up at Jimmy, who had not dismounted.

Jimmy took one more long look around, fixed the old man with a stare, and asked, "No surprises here tonight, old man?"

The farmer stared back, eye to eye, and said, "No, sir. Y'all will be fine. You can stay in the barn if'n you want."

Dobey believed him, but Jimmy pushed, "What about your boys who listen out for you?"

The old man looked down for a second or two. "They's both dead. One died of fever in camp, and this boy's daddy was kilt riding with General Forrest in Tennessee, a year ago."

Jimmy softened, dismounted, and handed his reins to the boy too. Billy's head bobbed, and he said, "Yessir. He were a hero." A confused look came over his face, and he added, "But he were kilt by some niggers in a pillow fight."

Jimmy and Dobey both turned to stare at him. "Do what?" said Jimmy.

Dobey just murmured, "Pillow. Last April."

The old man shushed Billy again, and told him to get on with the horses. Turning back to the Texans, he said, "He don't understand. It were Fort Pillow, and they was a bunch of niggers in the fort, and my boy got kilt there. My sister's boy was there too, and he came by an' tole us."

He thought a moment, then continued. "Said he 'uz wounded, but I seen no sign of it. I think he jus' run. Said my Bill was kilt goin' over the wall, so he couldn't help with killing all the niggers when it was over." Swallowing hard, he said, "Though I doubt my Bill would've helped kill prisoners no how."

Jimmy Melton stiffened again. "Even as they was only niggers?"

The old man didn't notice that Jimmy's hackles were up. He shrugged, "Don't know how y'all feel 'bout 'em. They ain't never bothered me. I wisht I had one or two to help here, with my boys dead. But we din't kill prisoners when I was in

Texas, in the Messican War. Damn Messicans, they did, but we din't. And I don't think Bill would've, either."

"So—you fought in Texas. Against the Mexicans," Dobey said. "You remember where?"

"Saint Jack-Ass, or somethin' like 'at. Whupped 'em, too. Took a passel of prisoners, and their general. Din't kill 'em, though."

Dobey smiled. "San Jacinto. Y'all whipped them good. Caught 'em taking siesta, didn't you?"

"Tha's right, by damn. Nobody 'round here knows 'bout it. They's all sure I'm lying, or crazy. How come you know?" The old man was beaming.

The excitement in his voice finally brought his wife, a skinny shy woman, onto the porch. Nervously picking at her apron, she whispered, "Is ever'thing all right, William?"

Bobbing up and down, old William said, "Yes, Lottie Mae, it's all right. These men know 'bout that big battle I was in, one where I got shot an kilt some Messicans." Turning back, he asked again, "How do you know?"

Dobey started to answer, but Jimmy interrupted, saying, "The captain here was trained at West Point. He knows all the famous battles. Talk your head off about 'em, if you let him. But we're both from Texas, and everybody there over six years old knows about San Jacinto."

Dobey nodded, looking at the old woman. "That was almost thirty years ago, and it was the beginning of the state of Texas. The general your husband help beat and capture was Santa Ana, and he was also president of Mexico. It's a famous fight, all right."

The old woman just clucked and whispered, "Well, I never...".

William pulled up his pants leg to show a scar on his left calf. "Seventy-five caliber ball, from a damn old Brown Bess musket. I kilt the one who did that, though. Pistol ball in the chest. Famous, huh? Y'all are true?"

* * *

After a meal of ham, beans, corn mush, honey, and buttermilk biscuits, old William said, "So which is it—Louisiana, or Texas?" He was grinning.

Dobey pushed back and smiled. "It's hard to live a lie. You caught us. Louisiana, if anybody asks."

"Home guard is all right, around here. But I'll still tell 'em y'all went due south. Wisht y'all could stay a few days and tell some o' my friends about San Jack-sento, but the main thing was for Billy and Lottie Mae to hear it. You don't know how much that means. An' you ain't paying for the meal."

"Are, too," said Jimmy. "You're too old and small to argue with me about it. I said we'd pay and that's that. They wouldn't likely even be no Texas, if y'all hadn't come and beat Santa Ana back then. This here is a Yankee silver dollar. Let's go outside and smoke a fine Yankee cigar."

He held out the coin, and when old William didn't take it, he handed it to Billy, who lit up like fire, and said, "Thankee, sir. Thankee. Ain't never seen one of these, no sir."

William stood, trembling, and said loudly, "No. Give it back, boy. Now!" He turned to Dobey and said, "I know I held out on you to start with, and poor-mouthed myself. But you see we've a cow and some pigs hid over the ridge, and we can be as hospitable as the next. The boy don't know better. He was clubbed by them raiders when he tried to save a pig I'd give him. In the head. Purty bad."

Jimmy took the coin back, and said "No offense meant. The meal was sure worth it. Now will you smoke?"

"None taken. And yes, I will. Cap'n, you too?"

Dobey smiled. "Y'all go on. I'll be out after one more biscuit and honey."

When they left, he turned to the woman said, "Poor but proud, huh?"

"Oh, yes. But y'all have sure done him right today."

"And Billy's mom? Where's she?"

"Left with one of them Tennessee raiders, next time after they whacked Billy on to the head. Husband dead, an' said she couldn't handle a boy that acted like he was touched in the head."

"Billy seems just fine to me. He's sure better off with you-all, than with a mother like that."

She shook all over, and nodded, "No kind of mother at-all, she weren't. And he is sweet, and fine, and gets better and smarter all the time. William dotes on him and tries to teach him, but ain't neither of us smart anyways."

"Well, Mrs. Clark—I think y'all have done real good with Billy. Can you read?"

"Yessir I do. Read the scripture all the time. Make Billy read, too, and listen."

"Yes, ma'am. Well, I've got a couple of books on my horse that I want to give Billy. Took 'em from a Yankee, like most of my things. I've read 'em. And I'm going to give you two Yankee dollars. Hold it," he put up his hand to stop her protest. "What you do now is, you take these, hide 'em til we're gone, and say, 'Thank you.'"

She did.

✳ ✳ ✳

They slept well that night, the first time in weeks, aided by a nip of brandy shared with William Clark. The older Clarks slept well too, though Billy was too excited. At dawn, he tiptoed out to the barn to find the Rangers were up already, shirts off, bathing and shaving in a pan of water they took from a rain barrel. Shirts off, but armed.

The captain was wearing a shoulder holster, and the big man had on his pistol belt, with two revolvers. Billy said, "Morning," and stared at the muscles and scars. The captain had an obvious broken nose, and a scar up from the edge of his right eye, that made it seem he was always smiling. He wore a thick brown mustache, but when he did smile you could see another scar on his left upper lip. Then there was one on his left forearm, a bad one, and another two on his right side, front and back. The black-haired sergeant was missing a one-inch portion of his right ear as well as the tip of his left middle finger—the whole joint. He had scars on his forehead and jaw, one going into the hair over his right ear, and two long stitch scars—one on his back near the right shoulder, and another around his left rib cage. Billy wondered about their legs.

"It ain't Friday," he said.

"Ever'day is Friday with the captain," Jimmy laughed.

Dobey laughed too, and said, "We try to wash and shave every day, Billy. We don't always get to. But we smell better, and feel better, and don't seem to get sick so much."

"I'm gonna do it, too, then. I'm gonna be a sojer, like you and my Daddy. Yessir. Y'all want some tea? Granny will make some directly. It he'ps us wake up."

Jimmy wiped dry, pulled on his shirt, and said, "You stay and talk to the captain about soldiering, and I'll make us some coffee instead."

Billy said, "We ain't had coffee in a right good while, I'm sorry to tell you."

"We have some today."

"Yessir." Billy turned back to the captain. "You think I can be a sojer too, when I'm older?"

Dobey looked straight at him. "You'll make a fine soldier, if you choose. I could see that yesterday, when you went out to the shed to cover your grandpa."

"Cover him?"

"It means to help him, to protect him. You did that, and you didn't show fear. Weren't you afraid?"

"Some. But Pap don't never tell me to do nothing wrong. Mostly, I just do what he says."

"That's a good thing, Billy. You'll be fine. And you read every book you can. I did. We were poor, and my daddy was killed too. I did read a lot, though, and got to go to a good school."

"Did niggers kill your daddy too?"

"No, Billy. Kiowa Indians killed my daddy. They were fighting each other. Like the black soldiers your daddy was fighting with, he was trying to kill them, but someone killed him first. Probably not a black man that killed your daddy, though. I was there. Most of the men in the 22nd Tennessee that died were killed by white soldiers, snipers, good rifle shots."

Billy frowned, but seemed to take it in.

"Anyhow, we won that day, and most of the men inside that Fort Pillow were killed. More'n likely, the man who shot your daddy was killed too."

"You think so? I hope so. I miss my daddy. I was nine years old when he left, but I remember him good, and Pap tells me about him."

"Your Pap is a good man. You ask him about the soldier life. It ain't all bad, but it mostly is."

"Why do you do it, then?"

"It's all I know, Billy. I don't know anything else."

✡ ✡ ✡

In the cabin, William Clark was having his first real coffee in two years. He nodded to Dobey as he got a cup and said, "Your sargint tole me y'all was at Fort Pillow."

"We were. I was just telling Billy about it."

"He tole me more'n that. Said a lot of them niggers was drunk, and wouldn't quit fighting you boys."

"True. And some of our boys were drunk too. But a lot of Yankees, white and black, that did quit, surrendered, hands up, wounded, laying on the ground, they were killed too."

"The sargint here says not ever' body was killing the prisoners. That you and him and others, mostly Texans, was trying to stop it. Even ol' Forrest hisself."

"Yes. Probably less than 200 men out of 3,000 that were doing the killing, but they killed over 200 men who had quit."

Jimmy added, "The captain shot one drunken mean son of a bitch who shot two wounded contraband in the hospital. I'm sorry, Miz Clark. But that son of a bitch had a friend who come at the captain's back with a knife, and I killed him. I'm sorry again."

Mrs. Clark nodded as if she heard that language every day, but she blushed blood red.

"It wasn't like a whole bunch of good men just went bad," said Dobey. "They were less than a tenth of us. They were mean or drunk or both, but there are always men like that. Not just soldiers. You must have seen some in Texas."

William nodded. "Yep. I said we din't shoot no Messican prisoners, but they was some men shooting Messicans in the lake. They couldn't swim, and they couldn't come out. Ol' Sam had to slap some of our'n with his sword to stop 'em. I hit one Tennessee man with the flat of my hatchet to stop him. That's why they made me a corporal."

✣ ✣ ✣

Mr. Clark begged them to stay. When they passed on the invitation, his wife gave them a sack of cornbread, fatback, and sliced ham. Both men slipped Billy a few coins, pulled on their ponchos, and rode west in a drizzling rain.

CHAPTER TWENTY-SEVEN

There were other encounters over the next ten days, some as friendly as the Clarks, some cautious, some not so friendly. On a glorious spring morning, they came out of a thick oak forest to find mist rising over a millpond, the mirror image of the millhouse captured on the surface.

"This could be Paradise," Dobey said.

"Yup. Fish just waiting for us. Fried bream for breakfast?"

Crossing a dam at the foot of the pond, they saw men moving from the mill house to cut them off: four men with long guns in civilian clothes on foot, and a fat man in a gray uniform on a mule.

Jimmy asked, "Make a run for it?"

Dobey knew he didn't want to. "No, let's just beat them to the far end of this dike, and lemme talk to 'em. I hate to backtrack."

Jimmy grunted approval, unslung the shotgun, and followed his captain at a trot. At the far end, Dobey reined in and faced the struggling rag-tag band, while Jimmy cocked the shotgun and tied the pack horse to a branch.

The fat rider, who wore a red sash with a pistol and sword, shouted, "Halt, there. Halt, I say."

He brought his mule up sharply to wait for his four men: two scrawny older men and two boys, one of them fat. They closed up, gasping from their seventy-five yard run. They carried three muskets and one shotgun.

"I'm Captain Jones, Alabama Home Guard, and we're checking you over as possible deserters. They's five of us, well-armed, an' we mean business. Throw down your guns and git down. Now, or we'll shoot." He stared at Melton's shotgun, and at the two calm men facing him. He twitched. Just a little.

"I'm Captain Walls of the Texas Rangers. This is my sergeant major. We've written orders, and we don't want to fight with Home Guard just doing their job..."

"But if one of you starts to point a gun at us, I'll kill him," Jimmy Melton interrupted. He glared at the fat man, and added, "I won't stand for no lard-ass make-believe officer yelling at my captain, neither."

The fat man's face betrayed his greed and fear. He thought, *they seem unafraid, but Jesus—that pack horse, with its unknown treasures, those boots, saddles, guns.* In a smaller voice, he said, "We're five against two, and I have more men coming. This is my district—you're under my orders here . . ."

Dobey read his face, and said, "Why don't you move your, uh, steed off to your right, away from your men, Captain Jones, and I'll let you read my orders, and we can all get on with our business. Your men should be careful about what my sergeant said. He's serious." Dobey nudged his horse left, away from Melton.

Jones kicked his mule nearer to Dobey, who leaned out to hand over his orders, left-handed. His right elbow rested on the high pommel, hand inside his jacket.

The old man with the shotgun muttered, "We oughtn't to put up with this shit."

The fat boy piped up, addressing the pompous officer, "Yeah, Daddy, we can take them."

At that point, Jones shouted, "You're under arrest." He tried to grab Dobey's left wrist, and draw his pistol at the same time. Dobey drew the short Colt and shot him quickly in the stomach, and then carefully in the face. The mule bucked away, but Jones stayed in the saddle, screaming. Dobey immediately swung to fire at the men on foot. Jimmy killed the man with the shotgun the moment of Dobey's first shot. As Dobey swung over, Jimmy blasted the other old man and two buckshot hit the skinny boy beside him, who yelled and dropped his musket.

Dobey fired at the fat boy three times fast, hitting him twice in the stomach, then shot the skinny one as he tried to pick up his musket. Empty, Dobey drew another Colt left handed, and fired again at each of the young men.

The fat boy, holding his stomach and moaning, "No, no, no," stumbled to the lake and fell face down in the shallows. The other one, an arm smashed and streaming blood, dragging one leg and his musket, tried to shuffle back to the millhouse.

Jimmy dismounted after his second shot and assured himself that the two older men were finished, then jogged after the fleeing boy and yelled, "Hey!" When the boy turned, Jimmy shot him, and the blast knocked him off his feet and into a crumpled bloody ball.

When that one stopped jerking, Jimmy walked to the water's edge and faced the fat boy, now sitting up, somewhat recovered by the cold water, but still keening, "No, no." Jimmy cocked the shotgun again.

"Gonna rob us, and kill us, wasn't you," said Jimmy, and shot him in the chest point-blank. Despite the boy's size, the

10-gauge buck and ball load knocked him flat on his back in the water. One spasm and he was still.

☆ ☆ ☆

Captain Jones' mule ran about fifty yards before calming and finding a patch of grass. The fat man finally slid from the saddle and sat against the mule's leg, holding the reins with one hand, and his stomach with the other. Dobey's second shot had entered his right cheek under the eye and exited behind his right ear.

As Dobey rode over to him, the fat man could only stare from his left eye. Jones couldn't talk; for some reason his tongue was thick and was sticking out. He seemed to have dropped his pistol. He was deafened, his head and stomach hurt like hell, and he couldn't feel his legs. He felt deeply stupid. *Damn*, he thought, *this regular army asshole is probably going to arrest me and take me to the courthouse. Damnation. I hope my boy doesn't witness this. He'll not let me live it down.*

Dobey leaned down close, and shot him in the forehead. The mule bucked again, and the self-appointed Captain Jones rolled onto his side, stone dead.

☆ ☆ ☆

Dobey rode back, dismounted, picked up the orders he'd dropped, and stuffed them back in his saddle bag. A low cloud of gunsmoke drifted over the pond. Jimmy was reloading the Colt shotgun. He was still breathing hard.

"I won't bury these sorry bastards. Do you wanna hide the bodies, Cap'n? Take the mule, drag 'em in those trees?"

"I don't think so, Jimmy. Let's just leave 'em. They're so shot up, folks might think twenty men shot 'em down. Maybe won't chase us; at least make 'em real cautious." Dobey fought to calm himself too.

"They better be, if they anything like this bunch."

"You don't think we better put some distance on us, 'fore we reload?"

"No, Cap'n. I think we likely to run into some 'nother group, after all this noise. We better be ready."

"Yeah, makes sense. You're right proud of that new shotgun now, aren't you?" As they talked and reloaded, they kept scanning in all directions. Dobey pulled the loaded Navy Colt from his pommel holster and exchanged the loaded and primed cylinder with the empty one in his hide-away pistol; putting it back in his shoulder holster, he then reloaded the pommel gun and his other belt pistol with paper cartridges from his saddle bag.

"Gun's jus' fine," said Jimmy. "Kicks like a mule, and the side-spray is bad, like mos' revolvers, but I like it. Wisht I'd had it that time we caught those Yankees in the box. We had Colt revolving carbines in the ol' 2nd Dragoons before this war, an' I learned to handle them then. They ain't bad."

"Hell, 'A' Company, 3d Regiment, has fought with 'em through most of this war. I'm surprised you didn't find you one sooner."

"They fine in a short fight, such as we jus' had, but if you got to dismount and fight all afternoon—an' how many times we done that?—you better off with a Sharps. I can get off twenny, twenty-five shots with a Sharps 'fore I can do ten with a revolver. Jus' too slow to reload, as you can see." Finished first, Jimmy nodded at Dobey's second pistol, still not reloaded, and said, "I'll water the horses while you finish."

Eight minutes later, they rode on. Jimmy looked back. "Sure wanted to fish that millpond. Some damn paradise."

CHAPTER TWENTY-EIGHT

They rode carefully and steadily, if not hard, for the rest of that day and half of the next. For most of that time, it rained—steadily, if not hard. They camped under a large rock overhang, deep enough for the horses too, and had a fire. With the rain, they were not too worried about being pursued or seen, so they ate hot food and, considering that they were wet, tired, and nervous, they slept well.

But about noon of the second day after the "gunfight in paradise," as Dobey called it later, the rain stopped, the clouds broke, and a hot sun soon had them steaming. The main road veered north, and a small lane continued westerly, through some untended farmland into a patch of pines on a hill.

"What do you think, Cap'n?"

"I know we're s'posed to stay on the main road, but we're also s'posed to be heading west. Let's see what we can see from that hill, other side of those trees. You smell smoke?"

"Mebbe. Yeah, I think mebbe so. This little road's been used by a cart or wagon, since the rain. Turned north, onto that main road." Melton stood in the saddle and looked around.

Dobey kicked his horse into a walk. "We'll spread out." They rode into the pines, staying on opposite sides of the cart path. On the far side of the pines, the path dropped into a small valley, crossed a creek and led up to a substantial farm house, two stories, with a porch and multiple chimneys. Smoke was coming from a fire in the back yard, where a woman stirred a large kettle.

There were stables, a barn, other outbuildings, an honest-to-God pump and a small pond.

"Looks peaceful enough, don't it?" asked Dobey. Jimmy was scanning the valley with his telescope.

"Just don't say one damn word 'bout no 'paradise.' Don't need another one of those, any time soon. Let's stay spread and go in slow."

As they approached it became apparent that the main house, while not grand, was large and probably not more than forty years old. The barn appeared to be much older. At any rate, there had been a home, or homes, here for a very long time; the house was bracketed by three massive oak trees, and they had obviously been planted there, perhaps one hundred and fifty years earlier. As they rode closer they saw the stump of a fourth oak in the back yard. It had been sawed flat, to become a large table.

A dog began barking, and a woman came into the door-way. "You young fellers lost? Or do we know you, maybe?"

Dobey replied, "We're on a scout. Heading for Tupelo. May have taken a wrong turn back over that hill. Don't mean no trouble."

Jimmy stared at her, nodding agreement.

She eased onto the porch but her right hand remained in-side the door. She wasn't pretty, nor was she ugly. Taller than average, full-bodied but not fat. Maybe forty-five, maybe even fifty years old. Clean. Wrinkled, but clean, with a nice smile. Maybe strained.

Another woman came from behind the house, first wiping her hands on her apron, then shielding her eyes to stare at men with some obvious apprehension. "Thought I heard talkin'," she smiled nervously.

"Why'nt you come up on the porch, Bobby Sue?"

Bobby Sue eased up the side steps onto the porch, into the shade. As she dropped her hands back to her apron, the men briefly studied her. Small, five foot—two, maybe forty years old. Tanned, wrinkled some too, but pretty.

The older woman pulled a double-barreled cap-and-ball pistol from her apron, and handed it to Bobby Sue, then brought out an old single barrel ten-gauge fowler from inside the door.

"Easy, now. Easy." This from Jimmy.

"We don't mean to be rude, but we don't have much left to share. Both sides been through here, taking whatever they wanted."

Dobey gave them his best smile, hands raised as if in surrender. "We'd appreciate not being shot at any more. War's over, at least for us, and we're just trying to get home. My momma needs help back there, with her store. Look, if you can't share food, we can. Maybe y'all could cook it, and maybe we could clean up and let these clothes dry some."

Jimmy had hardly taken his eyes off the older woman, and she stared back. Now she made up her mind, and said, "Well, then. Welcome to Four Oaks. I'm Janey Green, and this here's my sister-in-law, Roberta Susan Peterson."

Once the introductions were completed, Janey told them to unsaddle and rest the horses in the stable, out of the sun. Bobby Sue got them some grain, all the while cutting glances at Dobey. "What y'all got to share?" she quizzed him.

"Well, how many we need to feed? Your men coming back for noon meal, or they already eaten?"

"We got no men," she said, her smile gone. "Mine was a colonel, in the artillery. Said it was safer. One of his guns blew up, over near Atlanta. Got him, and two cousins."

"Judas Priest. Him and two of his cousins, same blast?" Jimmy was truly sympathetic; one of his scars was from a burst twelve-pounder cannon, which he had just captured.

"Not his cousins. They's mine." Still downcast, she continued in a monotone, "Anyhow, they brought him here, and he lived a week. He's behind the barn there, in Janey's plot. Our place was burned two years ago, and I moved here."

Gently, Jimmy asked, "An' Janey's husband?"

"He was, or is, a colonel too. Cavalry. I don't think he's coming back either. We ain't heard a thing in over six months, and he would'a sent word. He's my only brother left." She sobbed, "I hope."

"Sorry," said Dobey. He paused a moment, then said, "Look, if you'll take some of this in, y'all can start cooking while we finish with these horses and clean up some."

☆ ☆ ☆

In the kitchen, Bobby Sue dropped her armful on the table. "My God, Janey, lookit this. Part of a ham, deer loin already cooked, taters, bacon, red peppers. There's enough for two meals. I'll get out some onions and corn."

Janey studied the offering, and turned back to the window. "Grown-up men, cleaning up and not told to. Wonders may never cease. An' they weren't as ripe as you might think, when they rode up."

"You think they'd stay a while?"

"Not for long. Not them. But maybe for a while. I know they're young but they're grown up and hard, too. And I don't feel afraid of 'em. Kids won't be back from Huntsville for three-four days. You go up and try to find some shirts and pants that might fit 'em, in Byron's trunk." She grinned warmly now. "I'll have a talk with 'em, over dinner, and maybe they'll stay for supper. And breakfast."

The men hung their wet shirts and jackets on the clothes-line, then pulled two rags, soap, and two old damp shirts from the pack horse. Using the rain barrel, they quickly washed faces, necks, chests and underarms with the rags, hung them up, and donned the damp shirts. Dobey slipped his shoulder holster back on, and they knocked at the kitchen door.

Janey called them in, asking if they felt better.

Jimmy said, "Some better. But we're still pretty rank. Maybe we should eat on that stump out there."

Janey shushed him. "Y'all are fine for the kitchen table. And all these vittles you brought will be ready in a few minutes. How 'bout coffee now? It's thrice brewed, but it's ready."

As she poured the thin stuff, she went on. "Here's my thoughts. Y'all look tired, and a bit scruffy." Bobby Sue walked in with some clothes. "We can put our bathtub on the back porch. Rig a blanket screen around it, heat up some water in that laundry kettle, an' y'all can get a real bath. Shave, if you like. These old clothes will do you for a few hours, and me and Bobby Sue, we'll wash your clothes proper in exchange for the food, which is enough for dinner, and supper too." She glanced at the younger woman, who nodded approval.

Janey looked squarely at Jimmy, and continued, "And to be truthful it would be nice to have the company of two nice men for supper."

"Yes," blushed Bobby Sue. "Two nice clean handsome young men." She smiled at Dobey.

"I can't speak for the sergeant major, but I'd be honored. Jimmy, we in some hurry I don't know about?"

"Nossir, Cap'n." Then, to Janey, "I can speak for both of us, that we ain't had so nice an offer in years. I'll help cook for tonight. Might surprise you-all what I have learned in the cavalry."

Janey winked. "Might not. Let's eat, then get you out of them wet clothes."

None of them seemed too hungry. Plates were soon cleared, and the huge galvanized tub and two kitchen chairs were put near the left end of the back porch. Two blankets were tacked up, blocking the view of the rest of the porch and the backyard. The end looking up the valley road was left open.

Jimmy walked to the stables and returned with his revolving shotgun, Dobey's carbine, soap and the two rags. He leaned the guns on the wall near the open end, and tossed the soap and rags in the tub. Bobby Sue stoked up the fire under the kettle and began filling it with buckets of pump water.

Janey brought out a large pan of soapy water and two stiff brushes. "You do your feet in that pan first. One of you help with the water, other one get started."

"You first, Cap'n. And hurry. These clothes got to dry."

Dobey stepped behind the curtain, and quickly handed out everything but his suspenders, gun belts and boots. "By God, I needed this," he shouted, as he scrubbed his feet. Jimmy soon had the tub half full, and Dobey stepped in.

Turning to Jimmy, Janey said, "Set them next two buckets of hot water on the porch for your bath, and start getting out of them clothes. As you said, we got to wash 'em and get 'em dry."

"You think that will happen by sundown?"

"Maybe. Maybe not." She smiled. "I'll bring y'all some towels."

She waited for his clothes, carried them to Bobby Sue for the kettle, and went inside to have a better look at the now naked men through the kitchen window. She called Bobby Sue to the kitchen door. "Hand them these towels, then come in here for a minute."

After an unhurried examination from behind the window curtain, Bobby Sue smiled and said, "My, my."

Janey said, "Yes, ma'am. I think we better have us a bath, too, after we do their clothes and 'fore we take down those blankets. See if they's smart enough to peek too."

They were.

✫ ✫ ✫

The uniforms were not dry by sunset, to no one's surprise. They were brought in and put on folding racks, near the Franklin stove.

Janey insisted on having supper in the dining room. "Kitchen's too hot, that stove going an' all the cooking, and besides we're all cleaned up. Get out the good stuff."

"What's left of it," giggled Bobby Sue.

Dinner was a great success. They all learned a lot more about each other; they laughed a lot, and there was a fair amount of contact under the table. Sap and hope had been rising in both men all afternoon, especially since they had gone into the kitchen to get the ladies some towels, at Janey's suggestion. "On the counter, by the dish pan," she had said, from behind the blankets.

They had looked, of course. When they did, Janey was sitting in a chair washing her feet; her ample breasts and hips overflowed it. Bobby Sue had been standing in the tub, back to them, washing under an upraised arm. Her small firm snow-white bottom was in stark contrast to her tanned face and neck. Then Janey stood, helped Bobby Sue step out, and stepped in herself.

Great God almighty, thought Jimmy.

Sweet Jesus, I cannot believe my eyes, thought Dobey.

Now, three agonizing hours later, they fumbled to clear dishes.

✫ ✫ ✫

Finally, darkness was upon them. Jimmy went to the barn, and returned with brandy and some sugar. Stirred with water, it was the very last thing that any of them needed.

Janey took Jimmy's hand. "Bring your drink, and let's have some cool air."

As they left, Dobey looked at Bobby Sue, his eyebrow up in question. "No, I think they'd like to be alone." She smiled, "Maybe you'd help me restore that trunk upstairs, being as I wrecked it to find those clothes?"

Leaving a lantern on the kitchen table, they lit a second one and went upstairs to Janey's bedroom in the front of the house, where the trunk was kept. Dobey's West Point training allowed them to repack the wreckage within fifteen minutes.

"What now?" asked Dobey, hopefully.

"Leave the light, and let's go look out my windows and see can we see what they're up to." She giggled again, and led him to her room.

Janey and Jimmy Melton were about 30 yards away, by the large stump. They didn't seem to think that they were being watched.

"What are they doing?" Bobby Sue snuggled against Dobey's left side.

He grinned down at her. "I think that's something he learned from some Indian girls. Or maybe it's something she learned out here on the farm?" He let his left hand slide down her back to rest on her firm butt, and was pleased to note that she wore nothing under her shift. He squeezed her and she turned her face up for a hungry kiss, then pushed him back onto her bed, and began unbuttoning his pants.

"Indian girls ain't the only ones that know how to please a man without getting pregnant." They never did hear the other couple come in, or come upstairs. But when they went by Janey's closed door an hour later to get another drink, it was obvious that the others had gotten tired of the hard surface of the stump table.

It was a long, pleasant, occasionally noisy night.

Dobey struggled out of bed long after daybreak, splashed water in his face, strapped on his shoulder holster and went downstairs. He found a pot of coffee on, real coffee, and took a mug of it out back. He found Jimmy leaning against the stump table having coffee and a cigar.

Jimmy nodded toward the right side of the barn. "Privy is back there. Two-seater, if that don't beat all."

When Dobey returned, he said, "Nice table. Good place for a bite to eat, on a cool evening." He patted the smooth top.

Jimmy looked at him sharply, then decided that there was no hidden jest there. "I ast Janey 'bout that last night. It was one of the 'Four Oaks' that this place was named for, but after lightning killed it, her husband's daddy had the darkies cut it off flat, and rub it smooth. Used it as a serving table, when they'd spit-cook a pig or such." He chuckled, "Said she used to call the place 'Three Oaks, One Stump and an Ol' Holler Log', but the log was used up for firewood over twenny year ago."

Sipping coffee, Dobey said innocently, "I 'spect Janey still enjoys the table."

"Damn it, Cap'n, you did look," Jimmy exploded. "Why din't you just mind your own business? I believe y'all had some fun your own selves, right loud I'd say, an' we din't come peek."

"Thank you, but what happened was, Bobby Sue asked me what y'all were doing, and when I first looked, you were laid back, relaxing on the table. But then, fifteen minutes later, it seemed Janey was on the table, staring up at the stars. I told Bobby Sue I thought you were teaching Janey some Indian tricks."

Jimmy blushed furiously, but finally grinned. "She knew her part just fine, but said ain't nobody ever returned the favor before."

"'Turned the table', so to speak."

"Yeah. Anyhow, how did you do? Janey's too old, but she said Bobby Sue worries about getting pregnant—she's only thirty-nine."

"Well, she had some ideas on that, and that was nice, but I also introduced her to the sheath." The sheath was a sheep's gut condom. Dobey kept the present from an Atlanta madam washed and ready, but almost never got to use it. "Didn't you use the one I gave you?"

"I showed it, but Janey said it was no need."

"Well, I ain't sure I used mine, every time."

Breakfast was late and full of forced cheerfulness. No one wanted the men to leave, but all knew that they must. An hour before noon, they were repacked, saddled and ready.

Dobey reached down to squeeze Bobby Sue's hand. "I haven't had so much fun since before the war, maybe ever."

She teared up. "You didn't have to leave the money. I mean, we need it, but I didn't expect it. You can't think you was paying for our favors."

Janey squinted up at Jimmy and patted his leg. "All that goes double for me. Thought I was too old to have so much fun. You're a generous young man, Jimmy Melton. Glad to have met you. Be safe."

Equipped with directions to put them back on the road to Tupelo, they rode on. Dobey looked over his shoulder, and said, "Whooee, I'm 'bout worn out. What'd you think, old man?"

Jimmy thought a moment. "They was more lonely than loose. I'm gonna miss 'em."

CHAPTER TWENTY-NINE

They experienced no trouble finding Captain Matthews' cousin outside of Tupelo. He told them the war was over, but he was still nervous about them being there. He sketched them a route to a landing on the Mississippi and didn't encourage them to linger. Dobey gave him a dollar, and they slept in the woods that night.

"How come you give that uncivil son of a bitch that money?" Jimmy finally asked.

"Well, he's Matthews' cousin. He did help us, and I wouldn't want Doc to pass here later and think we was uncivil. That man just didn't want his house burned by vengeful Yankees."

"Matthews does come by here and gets treated that rude, or hears that we was, damn house is still likely to get burned."

Three days later, after skirting a large camp of Union cavalry, they met a farmer who had been selling corn whiskey to the Yankees. They overtook his wagon, heading away from the camp. He confirmed that the war had ended.

"They's stopped patrolling and all that," he said. "Jes' waiting to git paid, and hoping to be sent home."

"Good to hear. Guess nobody wants to be the last ones kilt," said Jimmy, "specially when it's s'posed to be over."

"Naw, sir. These boys ain't thinking about killing, I can tell you that. Kinda hate to see 'em leave, now they's halfway friendly. An' they pay good for likker, since they's expecting pay any time. Said most of their officers had rid up to Corinth, so's to see what's to do, uh, do next." He stammered the last bit, and began to shake, realizing he might just have signed his own death warrant.

Sergeant Major Jimmy Melton saw the fear in him, looked at Dobey and said, "Cap'n, he's heading our way. Whyn't we ride a ways with him, see he don't get bushwhacked?"

Dobey nodded. "You've given us good information, sir. 'Fore you make this run again you might bring some friends with guns. And don't tell strangers you're carrying cash."

"Yessir. Yessir. I din't think y'all looked like no robbers nor raiders. But I weren't smart, still, that's fer sure. Mebbe I could give y'all a jug, once I'm safe home?"

Delivering the old bootlegger back to his farm was done with much conversation, mostly one-sided, but without incident, and was not more than two hours out of their way. His wife fed them some ham, beans and cornbread, and he presented them with a half-gallon of his "best stuff."

Mounted again, horses fed, watered, and rested, Dobey leaned down to shake his hand. "Thanks for the grub and information."

"No sir. Thank you for the advice, and for not robbing me. Now, I know y'all have your own plan, but was I you, an' trying to git to a river boat, I'd cut cross that field yonder. They's a road in them trees. Go left on it, maybe twenny miles, you at Weather's ferry. Ol' man's got a store there, too. 'Nuther twenny-five miles, you at the river landing. I sell likker to ol' man Weathers store, and to the people at the landing, for the boat crews. You won't meet no Yankees on that road. Well, mebbe deserters, but why be a deserter, now the war's over?"

Two miles later, in the trees, Jimmy kept turning in the saddle and looking back.

"Specting company, Sergeant Major?"

Jimmy grinned. "Nope. Just afraid he'd follow us to talk some more."

☆ ☆ ☆

An hour later with darkness approaching, a rain squall surprised them. When they kicked the horses into a run and loped into the barn of a burned out farm, they in turn surprised a group of around ten Negroes.

Startled themselves, both Texans pulled revolvers to cover the Negroes before realizing that they were only women and children.

"Sweet Jesus!" blurted Dobey.

"Damn contraband!" said Jimmy, struggling to get his heart back down out of his throat.

"Don' shoot. Pleeeze, don' shoot us."

"Lawdy, mercy, doan kill my babies."

"Wait now, Massa, us ain't armed."

All were begging at once, until a fat woman stepped forward and said, "No need fo' this. Us ain't stealing nuthin, an' us ain't contraband no mo'. War's over, and us is free."

"Where are your menfolk?"

"They gone to try and find us some food."

Dobey took a deep breath, then de-cocked and holstered his pistol. Slowly, Jimmy followed suit. Dobey dismounted, and faced the defiant fat woman.

"No trouble from us. We're just getting out of the storm. The war is over, and we're on our way home—to, uh, Louisiana." He was interrupted by a nearby blast of lightning and thunder. "Let's just mind our own business, and we'll be riding on when this quits."

Mollified, the fat woman said, "Dat's all right, den."

One hour after full dark, screams from the Negroes brought both men up, guns out and cocked.

"Snake. Oh, Jesus—big damn snake!" The Negroes crowded around the armed men and pointed toward the back stall.

Jimmy eased back there, shotgun at the ready, and heard the rattler before he saw it in a flash of lightning. It was enormous: a blond canebrake rattler, coiled and shaking its tail furiously. Jimmy shot it. It twisted, uncoiled, and recoiled for a full minute before going limp. He grabbed the tail, and stretched it. Over eight feet long.

"Cap'n, this thing is eighty pounds if it's an ounce."

"You kilt that devil?" asked the fat woman, her eyes bulging like eggs.

"Yes'm," said Jimmy. "An' he's a big ol' good one, or a good ol' big one. Cut off his head, skin him, an we'll fry him up. Plenty of good meat there."

"White folks eat snake meat?" She was incredulous, but hungry.

"We damn sure do in Texas, ah, Louisiana. Skin it like you would a catfish. Go 'head. We'll start a fire." He tossed Dobey the rattles; fifteen fat ones, three smaller, and the button.

The storm continued through the night. The Texans, having dozed in shifts through the long night, were saddling up after coffee when the fat woman waddled over. "Y'all heading to the big river, catch you a boat?"

When Dobey nodded, she continued, "Yassuh. Den you-all gonna come to the Weather's sto', at the little river first. Dey good folks."

"They? Who's 'they'?"

"Yassuh. Ol' man Weathers and his fambly. Good folks. Dey hepped us wif some food."

Jimmy gave the former slaves some corn bread and fat back, and the two men rode on. As they left, Dobey looked the fat woman in the eye and said, "Y'all might want to try Texas. I believe you'd do better there, though there are a lot of rattlers."

As they rode away, Melton jerked a thumb over his shoulder. "Ol' Mammy had some grit, didn't she?"

"For a fact, she did." Dobey smiled.

"Kind of took me aback, though, coming at us like we was equals."

Dobey thought for a few seconds before answering. "Yeah, how could she come to that? Us being so rich and well-dressed, and successful in our profession, and all."

"I take your point, Cap'n. But if you're trying to make me feel better, it ain't working."

CHAPTER THIRTY

Squatting in the road, Jimmy pointed to several hoofprints. "Looks like three of 'em, heading west too." He stood, stretched, and remounted.

"Probably some more like us, heading home. Too few for a patrol. Still, we get to that store, we'll go up slow."

The tension that they had lived with for most of the last four years had begun to ebb that morning—war over, nearing the Mississippi, heading home finally, a sense of survival started to ease in. All that was now erased again—they were on full alert.

The road bumped against a river and turned left to follow it west through bottomland. A mile later, some fencing told them that they were nearing the store and ferry. A noisy creek crossed under a bridge, and raced into the river, a hundred yards to their right.

The road itself continued west, disappearing across a meadow into trees a mile away. But just forty yards on the other side of the bridge was the store. Three horses were tied to a rail in front.

They broke out their scopes. Dobey said, "There's a house and outbuildings behind the store, over by the river."

Jimmy grunted. "Yeah. Well, those are McClellan saddles, some swords and a Spencer in scabbards, nice and neat. That's By-God Yankee cavalry." He unslung the shotgun, and checked the caps on all five cylinders.

Dobey unsheathed his Spencer, half-cocked it, and levered a cartridge into the chamber.

"Back off, and hide a while?"

"Yeah. These ain't Home Guard." Jimmy reined his horse around.

Unintelligible shouting broke out behind the store, freezing the Rangers.

The storekeeper, a tanned girl in her teens, realized these men meant real trouble for her. She kept smiling, but eased toward the back door.

"And just where do you think you'll be going?" The sergeant moved to block her escape. "Heads up back there, Bailey."

Private Bailey, posted in back on watch, shouted back, "Man coming, Sarge. From the house, wif' a shotgun."

The leader, a big man in cavalry pants and a buckskin jacket, grabbed the girl's wrist. "Quiet now, missy," he menaced.

The girl picked up the cup of whiskey that he had set on the counter, threw it in his face, scratched free and bolted past the distracted sergeant.

The captain shouted, "Stop 'er, Riley." He picked up his Henry rifle and moved into the yard, behind his sergeant.

Private Bailey had tripped the girl and held her down with a boot in the small of her back. She tried to scream a warning to the old man to run.

The old man, white-bearded, maybe sixty years old, fired one barrel of his shotgun into the air and shouted, "Hey there. Stop that, damn you. Get off my daughter."

Sergeant Riley turned and looked at his leader. "Captain Kennedy?"

Kennedy cocked the rifle as he brought it up, and shot the old man in the chest, staggering him. Bailey fired his Spencer, hitting the old man in the stomach. He dropped the shotgun and fell on his back. The girl wriggled free and scrambled to get to him, screaming. Riley grabbed her.

There was a stump table about three feet high, behind the store. "Bend her over that table, Riley. Help him, Bailey." Bailey leaned his Spencer against the back of the store, and grabbed her arm. The big captain grabbed her hair. Shouting at her to shut up, they dragged her to the table.

Kennedy laid the Henry in the grass and dropped his belt and holstered pistol beside it. He began unbuttoning his pants. "Pull them skirts up, laddies. You'll have reason to squeal now, missy."

Dropping his pants to his ankles, he untied her pantaloons, pushed her legs together and yanked the underpants down. Pushing in between her legs, he grabbed her hips as she screamed and twisted.

The redheaded sergeant grinned and said, "Tightly, now, Bailey. And will you save us a wee bit, Captain?" He twisted her right arm.

Private Bailey gripped her other arm more tightly, but could not take his eyes off her twisting buttocks as his captain tried to penetrate her. It would be his last mistake.

✶ ✶ ✶

The shotgun blast, followed quickly by the crack of two rifle shots and screaming, turned the Rangers back toward the store.

"That's a girl, Cap'n—I'm going in. You coming? I think they're behind that store."

"Yeah, Jimmy, but let's do it right. There may still be three of 'em. You go up the creek til you can cross the road, shielded by the store—I'll go this way, and come up on 'em this side. Have 'em in a cross fire." Jimmy nodded and plunged down the bank to the left of the bridge, just as Dobey went down to the right.

The embankment was such that Dobey could just see over it as he trotted downstream. In less than thirty yards, the drama in the back yard unfolded before him—haze of gunsmoke, a man down, a Yankee trooper, a sergeant, and a big civilian in buckskin dragging a screaming girl to a stump table, much like the one in Four Oaks but lower.

As he watched, horrified, the men pulled up the girl's skirts, and the big man dropped his guns and his pants. Dobey yanked the horse to a halt, flipped the reins over a branch, full cocked the Spencer, dismounted and went over the bank. *Where the hell is Jimmy?*, he thought, then, *I can't wait.*

The three men were thirty yards away with their backs to him, and were all focused on the flashing white of the girl's bottom. Dobey jogged twenty yards at high port before the soldier on the left noticed the movement. The soldier let go of the girl's arm with one hand and stammered, "Captain—look—hey!" He held up his hand and said, "Stop, there."

Dobey brought the carbine to his shoulder and fired. The 385-grain bullet went through the soldier's hand, then his chest, and left an inch-wide hole in his back. He made a whuffing sound and fell on his back. Dobey re-cocked, and levered in another round, thinking, *Where the hell is Jimmy?*

Buckskin pushed off the girl and tried to face the threat behind him, but his trousers tripped him. As he turned, Dobey shot him in the left arm. The bullet broke the upper arm, and shattered the shoulder blade. The impact knocked him sideways onto the girl again, then to the ground beside the table. There was a crunch as his right wrist took the full weight of his fall.

Startled, maybe drunk, the Yankee sergeant was slow to release the girl's wrist. At first he tried to hold her with one hand, and unflap his Remington revolver with the other. As Dobey blasted Buckskin, the girl pulled free and scrambled away. Free from the girl, the sergeant stepped away from his fallen captain, yanked the Remington clear and cocked it as he brought it up at the still advancing Dobey. "Damn you, Rebel," he yelled, "I've got you beat."

Dobey started to chamber another cartridge, but it was clear that the Yankee sergeant would get off his shot first. Maybe he'll misfire, Dobey prayed, as he closed the breech and brought up the carbine's barrel. Everything seemed to be happening in slow motion.

The blast came from Dobey's left, and the sergeant's shoulder and jaw dissolved in a red mist. Shoved violently forward, the sergeant fired his revolver into the ground a half second before Dobey shot him in the left breast. He spun, and went down on his face. Dobey chambered another round and stood over him, but he was finished.

"Took your sweet time, Jimmy Melton. He had me beat. Thought I was dead, for sure," Dobey gulped in air. He turned his attention to Buckskin, who was on his side, groaning.

Jimmy said, "They's a wagon coming 'cross the field. Had to make sure they wasn't hostiles 'fore I could come in." He studied Bailey, who was coughing up blood and who had dug a small trench with his heel, his right leg jackknifing spastically. "This one ain't got five minutes left. Eyes already glazing over."

Dobey said, "I think he called Buckskin here a captain, though he might have been addressing me." He noticed that Buckskin was feebly trying to reach something under his jacket. Dobey pushed the jacket aside and saw the butt of a pistol. He pushed the man over on his back with the barrel of his carbine, and retrieved a Smith and Wesson Number 2 Army revolver from the man's shoulder holster. He tossed it to Jimmy, then picked up the girl's cloth pantaloons and carried them to her.

"Thirty-two caliber rim-fire six shooter," said Jimmy. "Barrel cut to three inches. Nice gun. Big Jack Talbert had one. Hell, this one's serial number 555. Ain't that bad luck, sign of the Devil, sump'n like that?" Jimmy was still breathing hard, starting to calm down.

The girl had been studying them, crouched against the back wall of the store. She spoke up, "You think of the number 666. And that big bastard is a Yankee captain. They were in the store before they attack me. And Papa—mon Dieu, I forget Papa." She ran to the old man, then wailed again when she realized he was dead. "Bastard. That bastard, he kill Papa too." She had some accent, maybe French.

Jimmy leaned over the Yankee officer and his eyes went hard. He nudged the man's shattered wrist with his own pistol, and said "So, Cap'n. You like to have young girls, do you?"

The man yelped, swallowed hard, and rasped out, "No, Sergeant—I'm Captain Kennedy, 15th Massachusetts Cavalry. I'm entitled to proper treatment as a prisoner. Where's your officer?" He groaned, and tried to sit up.

"Was my officer that shot you, you baby-raping son of a bitch." To the girl, he shouted, "Girl—come here."

"She's no baby, now—faith, she begged for it. That was all play-acting—and the old man, he tried to kill us. An', uh, I can ransom myself, if you give me passage." He turned to Dobey to plead his case. "Officer prisoners is ransomed, you know."

Jimmy shouted to the girl again. "Your daddy's dead, girl. Come here and finish this."

She walked to Jimmy as if in a trance and stared at him, not understanding. Jimmy handed her the Yankee's pistol, and said, "Finish it. Finish him, or I will. But you should— you'll feel cleaner."

Dobey could see the comprehension override her shock. She nodded, cocked the .32, and shot the man in the groin. He screamed and bent over. Holding it in both hands, she cocked the little pistol again, muttered, "Bastard," and shot him in the top of his head. He flopped backwards, convulsed, and was still.

She looked to Jimmy for approval. He nodded, and she shot the dead man again, then again. She sobbed, handed the pistol to Jimmy, and walked back to her dead father.

Jimmy said, "You'll be all right, now. You did good." Turning to Dobey, he spoke. "Might've never told you. Two soldiers from my own company beat and raped my baby sister, an' her younger than this girl. I do hate a rapist."

Dobey looked at the dead captain, and murmured, "I'd have never guessed it."

The girl picked up her cloth underpants and started for the back door of the store, but the clatter of a wagon coming close at full speed stopped her. They all moved to the far side of the store to face it. Jimmy and Dobey instinctively spread out, and re-cocked their weapons.

The driver, a young black man, bucketed off the road into the driveway to the home, then veered toward them when he saw them. The girl turned to the Rangers and said, "Do not shoot—is my mama and brother." A woman jumped clear and ran to the girl, before the wagon fully stopped. She appeared to be a quadroon; light brown skin, mid thirties.

The driver stomped on the brake, reached behind him and produced a shotgun, which he cocked and pointed slightly over Jimmy's head.

Dobey put the Spencer on half-cock, pointed it down, and walked to Jimmy's side. "Easy, son. We came to help her." He nodded at the man's sister.

The girl, hugging her mother, spoke rapidly. "Oh yes, Robert, is all right. But Mama, the Yankees have kill Papa, and try to take me, but these men have kill them, well, they kill two, but I kill their capitaine. Well, the big one there, he let me kill the bastard, an' it was he who kill Papa."

"Shh, Honey-Marie. We are here now. All is all right, non?" Then in a sharp voice, glaring at the Rangers, the woman asked, "Why are you have your pants in your hand? Eh?"

"Mama, I am try to tell you, the Yankee capitaine, he try to take me, from behind, the bugger, as the other two hold me, but I fight, I twist, and he don't get in." She spoke with ferocity, then added softly, "An' then these men come and shoot them, but is too late for Papa."

The woman, turned to the Rangers, tears in her eyes, and said, "Merci. Merci beaucoup." Rubbing her daughter's face and hair, she said, "And now, go in and put those on. Shh—don't cry. Go."

As Honey ran into the store, the woman and her son walked to the body of the old man. She sobbed; the boy knelt and put his hat over the dead man's face.

Looking around, Dobey took a cue from the young black man, and walked over to put the dead captain's hat over his naked bloody groin. As he did so, he noticed a belt under the man's shirt. "What's this?" he muttered, and pushed the shirt up with barrel of his carbine. It was a money belt. There was a second one, above it. *Good thing I didn't shoot him in the stomach,* thought Dobey.

He undid both belts, and pulled them free. Turning his back to the mourning civilians, he opened several pouches on each belt. They were stuffed with United States paper money.

He walked to the corner of the store nearest his horse and said formally, "Sergeant Major, come here a minute, please."

Jimmy, who'd been searching the dead sergeant, picked up on the urgency in Dobey's voice, and said, "Yes Sir." He walked hurriedly to join his captain.

As he turned the corner to where Dobey waited, shielded from the view of the others, Jimmy said, "Jesus, Cap'n, you ain't gonna believe what I just found."

Dobey just stared at him with a dumfounded expression, so Jimmy continued. "That Yankee sergeant had over three hunnert dollars in his shirt. You think they just robbed these folks? I mean,..."

Dobey tossed Jimmy one of the belts. "Put this on, under your shirt. Quick. Then let's get the horses and be ready to ride. You bring the pack horse, too."

Jimmy opened a pouch, saw the money, and looked even more confused. "What in the hell have we stumbled on, Dobey?" He started to pull out his shirt.

Dobey already had his belt on, and was tucking his shirt back into his pants. He picked up his gun belt and put that back on, too.

"There's thousands of dollars in each of these belts, Jimmy. The captain was wearing them. Must have been the payroll for that cavalry unit we skirted two days ago. I think these men were deserting with it. Let's get ready to ride, and then we'll finish the search. Somebody's gonna be looking for these people."

They brought their horses back to the rear of the store, as Honey re-joined the group. The boy was putting the old man's body into the wagon.

The mother faced them, and said, "We will bury my man, then we will take you over on the ferry, and go with you."

Jimmy blurted, "No, hold on...," but Dobey raised a hand to silence him.

"Why?" he asked the woman, who was obviously agitated.

"We cannot stay. The Yankees will come, they will find these men are killed, they burn us down or kill us too. We must go to the river, and take the boat to New Orleans."

CHAPTER THIRTY-ONE

Marie-Louise Boisseau was no stranger to New Orleans. Born there in 1833, she was the daughter of her owner, Henri Boisseau, and one of his favorite slaves, the mulatto Annie Smith. Boisseau was a townsman, the owner of a large warehouse. Marie-Louise became a house slave, a favorite herself. At ten, she began helping her father in the office, soaking up knowledge like a sponge. She became pregnant at fourteen by Henri's carriage driver, a huge slave named only Billy.

When Billy asked if she could be his woman, Henri had him beaten senseless and sold to a plantation in Alabama. Marie-Louise, five months pregnant, was sold to a riverboat captain, who traded her three months later to Bob Weathers for whiskey. When her boy was born in 1848, Weathers gave him his name. Two years later, Marie was born to them and by that time forty-two year old Bob Weathers was hopelessly in love with seventeen-year-old Marie-Louise. His previous wives, both whining, thankless wretches, and all three of their children died many years before, victims of various fevers or water moccasins.

Three years after Marie's birth Weathers gave Marie-Louise a paper attesting to her freedom, as well as Robert's and Marie's. That won her undying loyalty, if not her love. She helped him build and develop his store and ferry business, and raised the children to be frugal, careful, appreciative, hard working, and respectful, and to never take their freedom for granted. "That freedom, it can go faster than it come, I guarantee," she'd say, and often.

She pronounced Robert's name "Ro-Bair," and as he was a husky boy, Pop Weathers naturally began calling him "Bear," and the older he got, the more it became him. Now at seventeen, he was almost six feet tall, and weighed over 200 pounds, all muscle. Marie, with her tawny complexion and sweet disposition, was, of course, "Honey."

But Marie-Louise, now thirty-two years old and still strikingly handsome, had been the undisputed boss of this family for at least ten years, and she was not asking to go to New Orleans. She and her family were going. Perhaps these men would help; that was the only question.

Dobey, not knowing any of this yet, sensed it in her attitude and voice, and saw it in her eyes. She wasn't debating, and her logic cut to the quick.

"What about your things here, your inventory?"

"We will load what we can in the wagon. That wagon, she have more space than you see. She have the "faux"-bottom, for smuggling. And we have a horse, and a mule, and these bastards, they have give us three horses more."

Dobey and Jimmy noticed how quickly she joined them in ownership of the dead Yankees' horses. "We share. We help each other," she finished, with some finality.

Unconvinced, Jimmy asked, "Can that boy shoot and ride?" He nodded toward Robert, now digging a grave for his stepfather. "We might have to fight our way to the river."

Marie-Louise nodded, and Honey spoke up. "Bear the bes' tracker an' hunter round here. One time, that ferry mule, he bite the horse. That horse, he bolt, jump that fence to the swamp. Bear, he track him all day, bring him back."

"Ain't no cows round here now 'cept our milk cow. Soldiers take them all. My boy, he bring us all the venison we can sell or eat. An' wild pig, too. Ain't never had to eat squirrels." Marie-Louise seemed to sense the tide was changing in her favor. "He strong, though he still growing. An' he smart. I school bof' of my children. Numbers, for the store, but read an' write, too."

"Give us a minute," said Dobey, and he and Jimmy walked away for a quick conference.

"Thing is, Jimmy, I think she knows the river and the boat people. They're gonna go anyhow. We might need the extra eyes and firepower, til we get on a boat. Maybe while we're on it too, now we got this money."

Jimmy shrugged agreement, and added, "I'm starting to think like a storekeeper again myself. There's a lot of stuff here, horses, guns, boots and like. They'd help stock us up when we get to your mama's store, even if we split some with these folks."

"All right. You finish searching the bodies and their saddlebags. Collect their guns. We'll redistribute them and the ammunition. I'll lay down some rules for these folks, and get 'em moving. I want to leave inside an hour."

Dobey found Marie-Louise and Honey inside the store, and heard the last of her instructions to Honey. "And before you get those things from the house, you tell Robert, he don't just put your Papa in the ground. He gets him that big coffin off the back porch. An' put his bible in with him. Then bring that other coffin, the one Papa made for me, bring that here."

"Why, Mama?" Honey asked, with a worried look.

"We hide more things in it, cher. Fool people some. Now move—these men will leave us, we don't move real fast, our own selves. Don't forget Papa's clothes." Turning to Dobey, she put her hands on her hips, and smiled. "You decide, no?"

"We decide. Yes. But you do things our way, until we split up. You don't listen to us, do exactly what we say, and when, then we ride away so fast you'll be amazed. Deal?"

"These dead men: we share their things?"

"Listen, Lady. We killed them. Their stuff is ours, by rights. How 'bout this? We don't charge you anything for helping you get to the river." He flared a little. "Maybe we don't charge you extra for slowing us down. Or maybe we don't take half your stuff, for saving your daughter. Don't mistake me, Lady, they'd have killed her when they were all through with her, and killed you and your boy when you rode up."

Shocked at his sudden rage, it also occurred to her that this seemingly nice young man had just helped slaughter three dangerous men. She cowered a little as he now jabbed a finger at her and shouted, "They'd have taken every damn thing of yours they wanted, and then burned this whole place down, to cover it."

He stopped suddenly, and she saw a smile replace the anger. "That's it," he said softly, looking out at the bodies behind the store.

"What's what?" asked Jimmy, who came in to listen to the tirade. He loved it when his captain got mad.

"Yankees will be looking for four people here, dead or alive. You have some coal oil in here, Lady?"

She nodded, afraid again. She had thought he was over his anger. "Oui, there, in the corner."

"Hurry and get what you want out of here. We're gonna strip those men, drag 'em in here and soak 'em in coal oil, and burn this place down on 'em."

Like most successful merchants and smugglers, she was, mentally, quite agile. The light dawned for her even before Jimmy caught on.

"The Yankee's they come, they find these men, burnt to a crisp, they think they have found poor Marie-Louise, Robert, an' Honey—an' then they see that new grave for old Pop and they keep looking for these bastards."

Jimmy smiled. "You do good work, Cap'n." He nodded toward the door. "Got a minute?"

Outside, Jimmy gave him a rundown on the booty. "The cap'n had another four hundred twenty Yankee dollars in his pants, and the private had over forty." He shook his head, amazed, and split with Dobey. "Got you a Henry rifle, with two hundred plus rounds, two more new Spencers with eighty rounds each, two Army Remingtons, and the cap'n had another Navy Colt. And three damn sabers, which I will throw in that river. Tobacco, coffee, more matches, real socks, stuff like that. More jerky. Beans and bacon."

Dobey listened and took it in, as he handled the Henry. "This is sweet. Sixteen shooter. Had one in '64, but traded it in Atlanta when I couldn't get cartridges. Thanks."

The Henry held fifteen rounds in a tube under the barrel, and like the Spencer, was a lever-action. Unlike the Spencer, the action also cocked the weapon. Starting with a round in the chamber, it could be fired sixteen times without removing it from the shoulder. Like the Spencer, it fired a self-contained copper cartridge. Smaller bullet, but faster velocity, flatter trajectory, greater range. *And plenty of ammo for it,* Dobey thought, *now that the damn war is over. Though I expect I'll still have use for it.* He quickly came back to Earth.

Bear and Honey pulled up, a coffin, clothing, food and household items in the wagon. "I got it dug," Bear said. "Took a board, writ his name on it, and the date. Need some help, dropping his coffin in the hole."

Once they finished, Bear asked, "That other coffin, Mama, what we put in him?"

"Make a scarecrow, cher. Use those Yankee's clothes. Stuff him full of their things, belts, boots, blankets, like that, and then wrap him like a dead man in the big sheet. Put a board under him, hide some more things under that. Yankees stop us, we say we taking our dead Papa home to New Orleans. Nail him shut, when you through. Honey-Marie, help me load these store things."

Dobey broke in. "Bear, let's you and me and Jimmy see if any of those boots fits us first. And you strap on these two Remington pistols, and a cap pouch. We'll each take one of these fresh Yankee mounts and trail ours behind the wagon. And we're gonna unload most or all of that stuff on the pack horse, put that in the wagon too. Give him a rest."

Bear, speechless about the guns and horse, looked to his mother, who nodded. Now Jimmy handed him a Spencer and a box with seven speed loading tubes of cartridges for it. "You and me will each take one of these, too. It don't hurt these bullets to get wet. I'll show you how it works, then we'll put my Sharps and Cap'n Walls' old Spencer in the wagon."

"The shotguns?"

"Put yourn and your daddy's in the wagon, hind of the seat. Women can get to 'em there. I'll wear mine." He turned to the women. "Ma'am, you wear this Navy Colt. Just cut and notch the belt to your likings. You know how it works?"

✵ ✵ ✵

Marie-Louise stared at him a full three seconds, then decided she didn't have much choice about him telling her what to do. She pulled a canvas valise from the wagon seat, and opened it to show him her husband's '51 Navy. She also had a powder flask and small sack of loose balls for it, as well as caps.

"Good," Jimmy said, with obvious approval. "Leave it there. Always nice to have a hidden spare. Wear this 'un, though, so folks can see it. And you, girl, you keep this." He handed Honey the sawed-off Smith and Wesson. "You can wear his holster, or put it in a coat pocket. Here's your bullets. Watch while I reload it now." He tilted back the barrel of the little pistol, and removed the cylinder.

Bear opened the false bottom of the wagon, which opened on each side between the wheels, and began hiding things. Jimmy and Dobey wound up with new boots, and Bear got Jimmy's old ones, which were far better than his hobnail shoes. He also took a pair of Yankee pants. The extra shoes and boots and horse harness and pants went in, along with Jimmy's Sharps and the extra Spencer and ammo. The spare saddles went up in the wagon, under the shelter halves. A silver service and several jugs of whiskey were wrapped in blankets and put underneath.

Marie-Louise said, "Put all the women's clothes and the Yankee bedrolls under, too. Don't close it yet. Honey, you come with me." Taking some folded clothing, she and Honey went back in the store. "You men, you don't come in now."

✷ ✷ ✷

During the next ten minutes, Bear levered in and out seven rounds with his new Spencer, and under Jimmy's tutelage, reloaded the magazine. "Always cock first, then lever it. You do it the other way, and when the breech closes, the hammer being down will mash the firing pin slightly into the cartridge. See it there?" Bear nodded. "Often causes a misfire. Do it right, and when you close up, the cartridge pushes out that rebounding firing pin, sets it up to be struck by the hammer. Cap'n Walls taught me that." Bear's open-faced understanding and excitement were a delight to witness.

"Yessir."

"For the same reason, if you de-cock it with a round in the chamber, just lower it to half-cock."

"For to not push in the pin, no?"

"'Zactly right. Now here's how the sling and ring works."

✲ ✲ ✲

The women came out wearing the old man's pants, shirts, and jackets, and placed their own clothing, neatly folded, underneath. "You close him now, Bear. And you, M'sieur Jimmy, you can burn those men and my store." Their hair was pinned up and tucked into felt hats, and the baggy clothes made their gender apparent only to a serious investigator. "Maybe less trouble this way, no?" She strapped on the dead captain's Colt, and used his own knife to refit the belt.

The men dragged the dead Yankees inside, then Bear and Jimmy began soaking them and the store in coal oil. When Bear came out, Dobey asked, "That road y'all came from—what's down there? Anything 'tween us and the Mississippi?"

"Yessir. Little town maybe twenty-five miles, a few more farms. But we don' go that way, not today."

Marie-Louise heard and chimed in. "Non, mon Capitaine. We take the ferry, there behind the house. And once across our petite river, we take the ropes and mule with us, ferry she no good no more. We take the back road to the river, smuggler's road, only eighteen mile to the landing. Yankees want to chase us, they got to go twenty-five miles for the next crossing." She beamed, and so did Dobey.

"Then come fifteen mile north." Bear added.

As the store erupted in flame and black oily smoke, the small army moved past the house and onto the ferry, a hundred yards behind it.

"How does this work?" asked Jimmy, as Marie-Louise and Honey drove the wagon onto the ferry.

"I put all you on, then me and that mule, we pull you across." Bear pointed at a device on a tree. "They's a pulley over there, like this one, so's once you're over, you can send the ferry back for me."

Bear dismounted, and tied off his horse. "Once we across, we take loose these ropes, pull 'em all to us. Mebbe we push her loose, no ropes, an' she go on them rocks. You hear them rocks?"

Now straining, Jimmy and Dobey could just make out the sounds of rapids above the roaring and popping of the blazing store. "What is that, a quarter mile down?"

"More like the half mile, and 'round the bend. Can't see him from here."

"But could cavalry cross at those rapids?" Dobey pressed him, as they started to load the horses.

"Nosir. They try, they will wash away."

Jimmy broke in. "That's all good, Cap'n, but do those Yankees have a tracker with 'em, he'll trail these Yankee horses right to this landing, and know where we're heading."

"Mebbe not," spoke Bear. He explained that the ferry path, which Dobey and Jimmy had originally thought was a driveway to the main house, was a road which forked across the small river, going left to the Mississippi, and right to Corinth, though only if one knew what he was doing.

The *whump* of an explosion stopped all talk. Jimmy and Bear looked at each other, grinning.

"Gunpowder? You left gunpowder in the store?" Dobey was incredulous, and mad.

"Naw, Cap'n, you know me better'n that. It was some coal oil is all."

"Coal oil?" Marie-Louise came running up, and heard the last. "Robert, why you don't bring it, if you don't put it on those men? Coal oil, we can sell. You know that. I taught you that."

"Mama, I put a can in the wagon, I put a can on the men. That was just a piece of a can, most empty. And it was, uh . . ."

"Contaminated." Jimmy finished for him.

"All right, then. I thought you gone crazy. Mon Dieu, crazy like me—I forget the cow. How I do that? Honey-Marie, come—we got to get that cow." She looked at Dobey. "We pull her behind the wagon, but what of my pigs?"

"No pigs. And we ain't got time to butcher 'em."

Anne Marie frowned, but then she and Honey raced to the barn.

"Cap'n, I still think we need to do one more thing. I think the three of us ought to ride these Yankee horses right back by that store and up that road cross the meadow, like they was heading." Jimmy pointed as he spoke.

"Go on," Dobey was interested.

Jimmy turned to Bear. "Can't we peel off somewhere's over in them trees, pick up that creek, and follow it back here to the house?"

"Yessir. That'll work good. Anybody tracking will think three men went the other way, up creek, to hide their tracks. No reason for 'em to come back here."

"Shouldn't take us fifteen minutes, Cap'n. We'll throw down their swords in them woods where they can be found. Make 'em look like deserters, for sure."

"Let's do it."

Before they rode off, Dobey told Marie-Louise what they were up to. "I don't think Yankees are tracking these men yet, but if a patrol shows up, don't surrender to'em. They'll hang you anyways, since those bodies ain't burned yet. Get behind the wagon, and fight 'em. We'll be back fast and drive 'em off or kill 'em."

✫ ✫ ✫

As the men left, Honey said, "They would do it, too, Mama."

"I know, cher. I could maybe feel safe with these men, but they are killers. We must take care. Maybe they want us for our things."

"Mama, for shame. They have save me."

"Shush you-self, cher. Maybe they jus' want us for our selves. We will use them to help us get away, but if they mess with you, I will kill them. If Robert don't kill them first, I guarantee."

✫ ✫ ✫

As they worked their way back down the creek, Dobey spoke. "You gonna tell me what all that was about with that coal oil?"

"What you mean, Cap'n?" Jimmy asked innocently, grinning back at Bear.

"You know damn well what I mean. Y'all grinning like you'd just found a dollar."

"Oh—that. Well, Bear, here, he reckons that if those men don't burn good, it might be noticed that they was three men. 'Stead of two women and a boy. Whips out that filet knife, cuts the privates off the private and the sergeant, neat as you please. Put 'em in that half empty can of oil, and screwed the cap back on it. Won't nobody find 'em now, for sure."

Bear slapped his leg. "'Cut the privates off the private'— that's a good one, Boss." He had a deep belly laugh.

CHAPTER THIRTY-TWO

Bear's plan for getting everyone across worked fine. Before he boarded with his new horse and old mule, he loosened both heavy ropes, which were snugged to trees on the near bank. A smaller rope ran through two high pulleys on the ferry to trees on either side, to help guide it. Once across he chopped that one loose, too, and pushed the ferry away.

Marie-Louise did not want to leave the two heavy hawsers. "Those, I can sell to the landing or to the boat peoples. Good money there, I guarantee."

They were simply too heavy, wet, and muddy, even to load on the mule. Jimmy finally convinced her to sell them at a discount if necessary, sight unseen, to anyone willing to come get them; they were then dragged into a canebrake.

Finally, they rode west. Slowly.

✵ ✵ ✵

Jimmy dropped back, beside the wagon.

"Looks like bad weather behind us."

Marie-Louise looked back, then smiled. "Oui. Yes. Maybe that rain will help cover our tracks, eh?"

Melton shrugged. "Maybe. Just hope it don't put out that fire." He wiped his forehead. "People at this landing—you know 'em?"

"Oui—yes, for sure. And Bear, he does too."

"Can we trust 'em?"

"At the landing, yes. We trade with them. The boat people? One never knows. Better we have more guns than them." She smiled brightly, patting her holstered Colt and nodding toward Jimmy's arsenal. "For now, they will be very trustworthy, I guarantee."

After some thought, she continued. "But I think today, we stop maybe four or three miles from them. Dark by then, for sure. We camp, maybe you and Bear, you, how you say, 'reconnoiter'?"

"Yeah. Recon. I'll see does the cap'n agree."

✳ ✳ ✳

He did. Other than that earth-shattering decision, and the constant if subconscious alert for sounds and movement, there was little to occupy Dobey's mind. Except, of course, those twisting, flashing, almost white buttocks. *Jesus,* he thought, *Am I sweating?* Round, firm, almost muscular. *Glad Jimmy didn't see that,* the selfish thought came to him; *might have been better off if I hadn't. God, she looked good,* as he stopped to scan all around, and of course, briefly stare at her. *Still does look good. Those clothes wouldn't fool me. What am I doing? She's ten, maybe twelve years younger'n me.* "Oh, God," he groaned.

"Say what, Cap'n?"

Dobey looked up sharply from his woolgathering. "Didn't say anything."

"Beg pardon. Thought sure you was praying."

"Oh. Didn't mean to speak out. Just thinking that I'm saddle sore, and hungry."

214

Jimmy smiled, and looked back at Marie-Louise. "Me, too."

☼ ☼ ☼

There were no surprises at the landing. The scurrilous family of smugglers that ran it were at first apprehensive at the sight of the hard men. Even Bear, whom they'd traded with for years, watched him grow up, had changed somehow. Older, overnight. Dangerous, like those gray-clad men. Never seen him with no repeater before, neither, let alone two revolvers.

"We'll get you folks out o' here, no time ay-tall," the filthy old patriarch assured them. "Send my boys out in canoes, flag you down the next good boat. Yessir." *And none too soon,* he thought.

☼ ☼ ☼

The old pirate paid Marie-Louise four gold dollars for the ten dollars worth of hawsers they'd hidden back at the crossing, earning a spate of French language from Marie-Louise that Dobey was fairly sure was profane beyond belief.

"I picked up 'pig,' 'whore,' 'mother,' and 'shit-eater,' I think," he whispered to Jimmy. "The rest evaded me."

"Yep," responded Jimmy. "She's one hell of a merchant. You reckon they'd go with us to Texas?"

"Ain't no way."

At that point, her use of the word 'pig' reminded Marie-Louise of those she had left. "I also have five or four pigs there. You give me one dollar each?" She explained that they had left four, but that one was expecting, that they had left too quickly to butcher them, and that there might be a problem getting the pigs to cross that little river.

"Hell of a merchant," whispered Jimmy.

* * *

The second boat going north was empty, a small sternwheeler heading back to Memphis. The old smuggler sold the captain some bootleg and cotton bales to resell in New Orleans, and Marie-Louise negotiated their passage south. "You pay him, cher," she addressed Jimmy. He paid. She knew that he would, though she still knew nothing of his wealth.

The animals were led on and hobbled, and the wagon was manhandled and winched aboard, but only after it had been half-unloaded. By mid-afternoon, they were steaming south on the Big Muddy.

* * *

There were two cabins for them. Honey and her mother took one, of course, and Bear insisted that Jimmy and Dobey take the other. "Me, I sleep on that wagon. Don't trust these boat people too much, my ownself."

After thinking about that, Dobey decided that the men would take turns: one in the cabin, door locked from the inside, two in the wagon, with one always awake. He and Bear took the first night in the wagon. Dobey was on from seven til ten p.m., and from one until four a.m., and Bear was awake the other six hours, using Dobey's pocketwatch. The second night, it would be Dobey and Jimmy. Then Bear and Jimmy. And so on.

Occasionally crew members would wander by, snooping and trying to engage in conversation, but since one of the Rangers' group was always resting, the visitors were always invited to be quiet and move on. And the team members were too well armed and too touchy to argue with.

In theory, each man would get a good night's sleep at least every third night. And the first night, it was Jimmy's turn.

Unused to the boat's motion, sweating, and full of thoughts of the strong-willed handsome Marie-Louise, he went on deck about 10 p.m. Shirtless, barefoot, but armed. Hearing his door open and close, Marie-Louise soon joined him.

"Is too hot in my room for to sleep." She stared at his muscles and scars.

"Yes'm. You want to try something else?"

She flared. "What are you suggest? Me, did I not just lose my husband two day ago? Are you some Texas goat?"

"No ma'am. Jesus, no. I meant, maybe if we was to go forward, up under the wheelhouse, maybe we'd catch a breeze and get out'a this soot. Maybe. I don't know. I didn't mean nothing bad. Hell, I'm sorry I asked."

Mollified, she said, "Well if that's all you mean, maybe that's all right. Just don't you think I am one who goes crazy over a man in uniform. No sir."

Melton looked down at his bare chest and feet and said, "No ma'am. I wouldn't think that. Uhm, lemme just lock my door."

☆ ☆ ☆

About 2 a.m., Honey awoke, missed her mama, and putting her pistol in her pocket, went down to the wagon to look for her.

There, she found Dobey on guard, who shushed her, and with whom she whispered and giggled for the next three hours, well into Bear's shift. And, after waking Bear an hour late, Dobey slept not at all.

It started when they moved away from the wagon, so as not to waken Bear. Dobey had stretched, and rubbed an aching shoulder. She whispered that her mama had taught her the fine old French art of massage; if he would just sit on that coiled rope, she would show him. He found it to be an incredible experience. He knew that Jimmy would not believe it. How could he explain the punching, the rubbing, the kneading with her elbows, the touch of her firm breasts against his arm? Jimmy's on his own, on this, he decided.

All that, and those visions again, soon had Dobey suffering from an entirely different ache. At that point, Honey experienced a chill. He got his blanket from the wagon, wrapped her and held her close as they whispered to each other.

When they finally kissed, electricity shattered through them like lightning, ensuring that neither would ever recover from that first warm embrace.

She knew about mating; she had grown up on a farm, with an older brother happy to show off his superior knowledge. So she knew. She hadn't tried it. Two local boys had approached her on it once at the store, but Bear had come in and asked them if they'd ever seen what buckshot would do to pigs. The boys quit coming around. Still, she knew enough to realize that now she was on shaky ground, and so she bid Dobey a firm goodnight.

As she climbed back up the deck stairs, she was sure she heard someone groaning. He must be waking up Bear, she thought. Silly Bear, he sounds like a dog in heat.

As she gained the cabin deck, a nearly full moon erupted from the clouds, and she saw some movement forward. Her mother? With a man? She eased closer until she could hear a little above the engine noises. Mon Dieu—it is Mama, and with that man Boss. And she's laughing, like a girl.

Honey turned and crept back into the cabin. Her thoughts swirled. She knew that her Papa's death had built a fence around her heart. She started to cry again thinking of him. But tonight Dobey had removed the top couple of rails. And then she smiled and thought, *Mama, too?*

✵ ✵ ✵

Melton stretched and strolled down to the wagon deck, where he found Dobey leaning against the gunwale.

"Talked to that woman awhile. Still got kind of a wall around her. Seems nice, though. She did allow that the old man had been more of a pappy than a husband to her since the girl was borned."

Dobey smiled. "Yeah, the girl sort of said the same thing. You plan to help with that?"

Melton shrugged. "If she'll let me. I think I like her."

CHAPTER
THIRTY-THREE

On the morning of the second day, a Negro from the engine room named Big William warned Bear that the ship's captain, Figg, would try to extort more money from them before disembarkation. Perhaps for "special handling" of the coffin or wagon, or for mucking up after the animals.

Jimmy Melton had taken a shine to Bear, and continued his education on firearms whenever Marie-Louise was resting. One hour after Bear heard the whispered warning about the ship's captain, Jimmy found the young black man leaning on the deck rail.

"You know why you have to have your own bullet mold for them Remingtons?"

Bear thought a minute, and answered, "They ain't as good as Colts?" He looked suspicious. "That why y'all give 'em to me?"

"Naw, Bear, it ain't like that. They's fine revolvers. Some folks think they's more accurate than Colts. It's just this: a Army Colt uses a ball that's about .45 caliber. Point four-five-one inches across. Remington Army model uses one that's almost .46 caliber. So if I put a Colt ball in your pistols, it'll likely be loose. An your'n are a tad too big for my Colt.

Nothing wrong with your Remingtons, though. Fine pistols. Do you have extra cylinders, they's a lot faster to reload than a Colt, too."

"So why they both called 'forty-fours'? Ain't neither one point forty-four across."

Jimmy smiled. "You figger that one out, you come explain it to me. Just how it is, I guess. Now, when y'all get to New Orleans, get rid of these Yankee holsters an' get some easier for you to use." Because Yankee cavalry regulations called for pistols to be worn butt forward on the right hip, Bear wore one that way, and the other butt-backward on his left hip.

Bear smiled. "I ain't no gunfighter. These work just fine. I'm wrong-handed anyhows, and I can get to both of 'em with my left hand this away. How come the cap'n has all Navy Colts?"

"His hands are smaller'n our'n. And I tell you what—the cap'n is fast with that small one."

"Yeah. You got one of those cut down guns, too. Like the one you gave Honey. You fast with it?"

"Well, I'm faster with it than with the long 'uns. Cap'n says they's called 'Storekeepers,' up East."

"Yassuh. For under the counter, or inside a frock coat, I guess. S'pose I'll has to look for one of them, too, less'n Honey gives me hers. By the way, Boss, that darky there, Big William, he tole me to tell you sump'n.'"

☆ ☆ ☆

There are not many secrets on boats of any size. On one as small as the *Memphis Belle,* there were almost none.

When Bear approached Big William on the third morning to thank him for the warning and offer him a dollar from Jimmy, the big man said, "Din't do it for money, though I'll take it and be glad. Nossir. That woman, the quadroon, she been kind to all the niggers on this boat. Don't treat us like no field hands."

"Woman?" Bear thought his mama's disguise was pretty good.

"Hell, boy, you din't think that woman was gonna fool Big William, did you? All the niggers know, what with her carrying on with that big Rebel. Don' you worry, though, ain't nobody gone tell the mates or the cap'n. An' they ain't guessed a thing. They thinks the two Rebels is poofs, both of 'em carryin' on with the breed and the boy. 'Course, the mates and the cap'n, they poofs them own selves."

"Poofs?"

"Girly-mens. Mean bastids, though. I believe I might earn this here coin. They plan's to try sump'n tonight. I'm s'posed to git you drunk, and they figger the Rebs is 'bout worn out. You jes' ack dumb, but be ready 'bout midnight."

"Damn. For sure, we will be. I'm beholding to you. That's my mama and baby sister. I got to watch for them, since some Yankees kilt my mama's man."

Big William blurted, "For sure?" He had almost blurted, "Your sister?"

"Yassuh. White man. He be the one that freed us. We got papers. An' the Yankees, three of 'em, tried to force 'emselves on my sister too, and these Rebels, they kilt 'em."

"Kilt three of 'em?"

"Shot 'em all to pieces, jus 'fore me an' Mama got there. Where you think these pistols come from? Re-peater carbine, too. Say I could keep 'em, too."

"Sweet as he is on your mama, he likely to say most anything. Wait til y'all gets to N'Orleans."

"You listen to me, old man. I don't think my mama is doing nothing, but he ain't grinding no coffee with Mama, less'n she sweet on him too. We maybe ain't going to no New Orleans. Anyway, I think he's true. Both of em. Boss Jimmy, and Cap'n Dobey, too. And I knows my sister ain't grinding no coffee."

He turned to fix Big William with a cold stare. "I owes you. I owes them more. I will do my dog-assed best to kill anyone tries to come at 'em. I knows that you din't know that was my mama and sister, so I don't hold nuthin' you said aginst you. But you know now. Be careful what you say, from now on."

"Easy, boy. Din't mean no disrespeck. I'm on your side. And I'll tell the other niggers too. Oh, law—we gone to have a laugh. They all thought the little Reb was a poof, with that good-looking white boy. Lawdy, Mercy." He laughed, and some of the tension left Bear.

Satterwhite, one of the two scruffy white mates, came on deck and looked toward them. Big William tipped his hat, suitably obsequious, and whispered, "Just you ack drunk, so's they don't suspeck me for nothin'. And they has keys for your rooms."

✳ ✳ ✳

There were only four white crew members. In addition to the captain, there were the two mates and the quartermaster. In the war council, Bear wasn't sure if the fat quartermaster and the captain were part of the planned shenanigans.

Dobey decided. "The captain will probably stay in the wheelhouse. Him or the quartermaster. Problem is, we don't know whether they'll move against the wagon first, or the cabins, or both at the same time. About 11:30 tonight, Marie-Louise, you and Honey move into our cabin with Jimmy. Don't leave anything important in your room. Jimmy, they'll probably come with knives. Douse the lantern 'fore the women come in, then lock the door. If they come through a locked door, you can kill 'em. Bear and I will act drunk by the wagon, and put down our pistol belts. Honey, give Bear that little .32, to go under his jacket. If y'all start shooting, one of us will come, and the other will watch the wagon. If we start it, y'all stay here, til we call you or comes daylight. Jimmy, you keep that Henry in the cabin."

Marie-Louise asked, "And if these men, they come with guns, they come fast? To your room, I mean?"

"You got that Navy Colt. Take the other one out of your valise and give it to Honey. Mostly, though, you got Sergeant Melton. Just do what he says. Me and Bear will put ourselves where they can't get close 'fore we see 'em."

"Cap'n, you find you forgot somethin' tonight, it wouldn't be no good if you came slipping into the room."

"I ain't even gonna take a key, Jimmy. Bear doesn't have one. Anybody unlocks that door, you can kill 'em. Better if you could take 'em down, but don't take any chances."

In the darkened room, Jimmy told the women to stay behind him, pistols drawn but uncocked, to the left of the door. He sat them in wooden chairs.

"One comes alone, I'm a try to knock him out with this wooden stob. If they's two of 'em, I'm a just shoot 'em. If I go down, y'all stand up and open up and keep shooting til they quit moving. Clear?"

On deck, Dobey and Bear passed the whiskey bottle, which Big William had emptied and filled with cold coffee. By midnight they were stumbling, slurring their conversation in stage whispers. Dobey stood, having seen movement in the shadows, and mumbled, "Can't sleep with these damn pistols on." He fumbled to take off both belts, then dropped them clumsily under the wagon.

Bear giggled loudly, said, "Me too, Cap'n," and followed suit. Both men sat on coiled ropes, backs to the wall, hats over their eyes, and feigned light snoring. Their arms were folded over their chests; each man had one hand on a revolver, under his jacket.

✵ ✵ ✵

After ten minutes of irregular snoring, the first mate, Satterwhite, padded barefoot to Captain Walls and, holding his knife behind his back, bent down to lift the hat brim.

He was shocked to find the captain's eyes open and alert. He registered the distinctive three clicks of a Colt being cocked, before he realized that it was pressed up under his chin. There was a double click. The big Negro stuck something cold in his ear and reached to take the knife. He wet himself. "No, please," he sobbed, dropping to his knees.

"Who's with you?" Dobey whispered fiercely. "Is Figg in on this?"

The man shook his head, trying to control his sobbing.

Bear took a quick pass around the deck nearby, then whispered loudly, "He ain't gonna talk, Cap'n. Lemme cut his throat so's he can't yell, gut him, and throw him off the boat."

"Clinton's gonna try your room," Satterwhite found his voice. "I can call him and stop him. I'll do it if'n y'all won't kill me. Din't mean y'all no harm, I swear. I swear. Jus' looking for easy pickings. Please."

✵ ✵ ✵

Jimmy never heard the footfalls because of the boat's engine and paddles. He did hear the click of the tumblers in the lock.

Clinton pushed the door open with his left hand, and started to step in holding his knife in his right. Jimmy smashed him in the forehead with the wooden pin, and he dropped like an empty sack.

Jimmy cocked the Colt in his left hand as Clinton fell, dropped the pin and drew his short Colt right handed, cocked it, and said loudly, "Y'all come on in." There was dead silence—no running, no whispers. Jimmy waited.

In a normal voice, he said to Marie-Louise and Honey, "Y'all point your pistols at the door. Any movement, anybody comes in, just shoot 'em. Don't tell 'em to stop or nothin'."

He decocked his Colts, holstered them, and dragged the unconscious Clinton inside, then closed and re-locked the door. Taking off the rope that the mate used for a belt, he tied the man's hands behind his back, then cut a sash from the window and tied his feet.

Ten minutes later, he heard loud footsteps, and braced again.

"Boss man?" Big William spoke from outside. "Y'all is awright in there? Your cap'n, he done captured Mistuh Satterwhite trying to rob him, sent me to see is y'all awright."

Jimmy cocked both pistols, opened the door and stepped out quickly, swinging to look both ways. Big William stepped back, both hands up, saying, "It's awright, Boss. Don't shoot."

Jimmy stared at him. "Yeah. It's awright. I need to thank you agin. Now go down there and tell the cap'n we got this 'un. You think anybody else is coming at us?"

When Big William shook his head, Jimmy went on. "Tell him that, too. Say to leave Bear there, and y'all bring the other'n back here with rope. Knock him on the head so's he don't yell."

Big William smiled, nodded and disappeared.

✳ ✳ ✳

Fifteen minutes later with both mates bound and gagged, they began moaning. "Can I hit 'em agin, Boss?" Big William smiled.

Dobey nodded, then turned to the others.

"We're gonna lock 'em in here, for now. We'll take turns sleeping in the other cabin. They act up, I'll take Bear's advice and throw 'em off the boat. Matter of fact, Big William, you go tell that Captain Figg that they tried to rob us, and that we told you that we already threw them off. That way he won't be looking for 'em."

"What if they wake up and untie themselves?"

"Go ahead and smash their hands. I think they meant to cut us, and I want 'em to remember us, anyhow. See how good they handle knots and knives with broken fingers."

They were not totally surprised the next morning when, off the mouth of the Arkansas River, they ran gently aground. A deeply embarrassed Captain Figg explained that they were stuck fast; they'd all be much better off if his mates hadn't been thrown overboard; might be days to get her off; he thought the paddle was damaged. To make up for his blunder, he would ferry the passengers ashore, and would buy their cargo and livestock at what he thought was a very fair price, remembering of course that he was near destitution. They could then purchase more horses ashore, or charter another boat to proceed up the Arkansas or on to New Orleans.

"Destitution," Jimmy repeated. "Is that the name of that town on the bank there? That why I should believe you're near it?" He invited the captain into the wheelhouse for negotiations.

Ten minutes later, Captain Figg had steam up, gently backed the *Memphis Belle* off the bar, and took her expertly to dock. He explained that his black eye came from a collision with the wheel during the grounding. His black steward told Big William that the collision was with the butt end of Jimmy's big knife. Big William looked pleased.

Other than Captain Figg and his quartermaster, no one on the boat seemed surprised when Bear, Marie-Louise and Honey disembarked with the Rangers. The women had decided that male disguises were not so important west of the Mississippi. Driving the wagon was Big William.

✳ ✳ ✳

"This corps has got to get on the move, Colonel. I want us out of Corinth and heading for that Mississippi landing tomorrow morning. And, no, I don't know if we're heading upriver to go home, or south to fight in the west."

The corps headquarters was near chaos, with tents coming down, wagons being packed, and both orders and curses flying freely.

The general lit a cigar and said, "Let's wrap this up. You don't know if that payroll was taken by this Captain Kennedy and his two men, or if they were murdered, mutilated and robbed, and if so, was it by some rebels seen nearby, or by some missing civilians. This is beyond us. Bring in the Pinkertons. This is their bailiwick. Go ahead and pay the Fifteenth Massachusetts, but let their commander sweat whether we're going to charge it off to him or not."

CHAPTER THIRTY-FOUR

The town, if it could be called that, was overly modest. On a point, north of the Arkansas and west of the Mississippi, its one road went up a bank away from the dock, through some Spanish Moss-draped trees, then turned north to parallel the Big Muddy. Backed against the big river were Kate's Brothel, a dentist/barber shop, a two-story hotel, and the livery stable, with a corral behind.

The convoy moved slowly up the street, Dobey leading, Bear trailing, with the wagon, Big William, the women, and livestock in between. On their left they saw Mason's saloon, Sally-Sue's Brothel, Mason's Emporium, and the marshal's office and jail.

Jimmy Melton, his Colt shotgun loose across his left elbow, still stood at the dock, watching the *Memphis Belle* back away. As he started to mount, Bear called back in a low voice, "Trouble ahead, Boss."

Jimmy tied his horse to a bush and jogged upstream to the corral, then cut through it to the far side of the livery.

✲ ✲ ✲

Up front, as Dobey and the wagon approached the livery, a huge bearded man came out of the marshal's office and shouted, "You there, soldier. Hold up."

Dobey stopped and said politely, "You mean me?" The wagon rolled slowly past him.

Two more men came out of the jail, and stood on the porch. One let his right hand rest on the butt of an old Paterson revolver in his belt, as the other leaned on a shotgun, chewing a straw. The big man stepped off the porch, passed Dobey and moved in front of the wagon, grabbing a mule's harness.

"I'm talking to all of you. I'm Marshal Fetterman. We need to search your wagon, and collect taxes on you."

"Taxes," Dobey repeated. "Sort of like a toll, just for passing through?"

"You got that right, little feller." The marshal was well over six feet tall, and close to three hundred pounds. He grinned, "Dollar a head for whites, quarter for niggers, mebbe two dollars for the wagon, depending on what's in it. 'Course if you ain't got coin, we could barter." He leered at the women. "Ain't that right, deputies?"

The one with the pistol laughed and spat. "I 'spect we'll have to take them women as prisoners, least ways for a while."

Grinning at the women, the deputies didn't notice Jimmy move onto the street behind the marshal.

Dobey did notice. He turned back toward Bear, stood in the saddle and yelled, "Sergeant Melton. The marshal here is compelled to search us and collect a tax. We're going to barter."

The deputies stared at Dobey and Bear, dumbfounded, and the marshal stood on his tiptoes, trying to see past the wagon. "Who in hell is Sergeant Melton?"

Behind him, Jimmy cocked the shotgun and said, "That's me."

As Dobey swung out of the saddle the marshal, still holding the harness in his left hand, turned to face the ominous voice behind him. The deputies appeared stunned to see that the Reb who'd just dismounted had spun, produced a short Colt from under his jacket, and was pointing it at them. The quicker one tried to drag the Paterson from his belt.

☆ ☆ ☆

Bear, on horseback behind the wagon, clearly saw everything develop, as if it had been deliberately slowed for him. Better yet, he understood. The captain's shout to him, calling him Sergeant Melton, was really a message to the sergeant; it also confused the lawmen for a moment. And in that moment, the captain's dismount had put his back to the lawmen, allowing him to draw his hidden pistol, wink at Bear, and go into action.

The moment he saw the captain's pistol coming out from under his jacket, Bear drew one of his Remingtons and yelled to Big William and the women, "Get your guns out! Be ready, Mama, watch behind you. Honey, look that way." He pointed back toward Kate's Brothel, while he scanned to their rear, then turned back to the fight. It was over, before he could join in. He was pleased to see Big William standing in the wagon, a cocked shotgun pointed at Sally-Sue's.

Dobey had thumbed off two shots at the deputies, then ducked under his horse's neck to point the Colt at the marshal's stomach. The deputies staggered back a step, both hit.

The marshal glanced from Dobey's Colt to his injured deputies, then jumped as Jimmy fired the shotgun twice at them. Both deputies bounced off the jail's wall and went down; one off the porch into the street, the other onto his knees, vomiting blood. Almost in unison, Big William and the marshal said, "Sweet Jesus!"

Dobey said, "Look at me, marshal. Answer me quick. You got any more men?"

Fetterman shook his head, speechless, still holding the mule and staring at his dying deputies.

"Let go of that damn mule and answer me, Goddammit," Dobey shouted. "Any more men?"

Fetterman raised both hands now and sputtered, "Nossir. A nigger cleans up for me, but he ain't got a gun. Nossir. Damn—my deputies ain't fared too well." He gulped, and licked his lips.

Jimmy called from the porch, "These two are about done. Finish 'em, Cap'n?"

Dobey nodded, and Jimmy drew a long Colt left-handed and shot each man in the head. The marshal jumped at each report.

Dobey had Fetterman put his hands on his head, took the marshal's big Dragoon, and said, "Let's look at your jail."

✵ ✵ ✵

As they moved past the wagon to the jail, Dobey was happy to see that Big William, the women, and Bear all had weapons out, and were watching the few citizens brave enough to venture out.

Dobey asked, "Anybody hurt?"

Big William responded, "None of them got off a shot, Cap'n."

"Yeah. Kind of hard to win a fight that way. Y'all see any more trouble brewing?"

Bear came back this time. "Nossir. These other people, I think they happy to leave us alone."

Inside the jail, an older Negro stood in a corner, wide-eyed, holding a broom. There was a back room and two cells, both occupied. The first held an old man and two teen-aged boys, all badly battered, sullen, still wondering what had happened outside.

The second cell held a middle-aged woman and a young girl, shabby and fearful. Dobey faced the Negro. "You tell me what's happening here."

The old man shook his head, terrified. It seemed to him that, no matter what he said, he would be in deep trouble with someone.

Understanding this, Dobey said, "You don't work for this pig any more. He ain't the Marshal now, and he won't harm you. What happened to these people?"

The old man lowered his head, knowing the fat Fetterman would kill him, or worse, once these men left. "They come to here yesterday on the ferry. Couldn't pay the tax. Marshal was gone, and his men, they beat 'em. Took the mother in back and used her. Took they wagon, too."

Jimmy had walked in, and heard the last. "Unlock them doors."

"Yassah. I ain't harmed 'em none, I swear."

"Keep your damn mouth shut, Rastus. This ain't over," the marshal rasped.

Jimmy took the Marshal's Dragoon Colt from Dobey and swung, hitting the Marshal in the teeth. "It will be soon," he said, as the Marshal sat down.

The family crept out of the cells, not sure that their nightmare was over, still afraid. Jimmy said, "We'll get you your wagon and whatever else you had. Where you heading?"

The father nodded. "Santa Fe."

Jimmy turned back to Fetterman. "Get in that cell. Lock him in, old man. Give me all the keys. Your name really Rastus?"

"Nossuh. I'se Old Ben. Yassuh, here's the keys."

Melton handed the marshal's pistol to Big William, then said to Old Ben, "You're the marshal now. You get these folks back whatever was took from 'em. Tell me if anybody wants to argue about that. And tell whoever you want that I said I want them deputies buried or gone by morning. I don't care if they're fed to the hogs or thrown in the river. You got a doctor here?"

"Yassuh. A tooth doctor, but he drunk all the time."

The rescued family was named Watson. After bathing, they wanted to stay close to the Texans, so camp was established a half mile up the Arkansas; a guard roster was set up, guns were cleaned and reloaded, and horses fed. Bear and Big William brought food from the town. "Din't charge us nuthin, Cap'n. Seemed happy to feed us fo' free." Big William wore a wide grin.

Over brandy, Dobey turned to Melton. "Whatever happened with your sister?"

Jimmy nodded, and was quiet, deep in thought for a while. Finally he spoke. "I tole you she was beat and raped. I was on patrol. When I came in, my daddy said he'd found out who done it and wanted me to help. He was a scout and horse breaker for my regiment. Ol' Second Dragoons."

Jimmy lit a cigar, and sipped. Dobey waited.

"Was two Corporals from my own company, took her into the livery in town. Snatched her, down by the river, late. Liveryman watched, din't take part, but watched and liked it. She tole Daddy, once she could talk. We caught 'em one night coming out the Cantina, drunk again. Took 'em to the same barn, beat hell out of them and the liveryman, tied 'em up. Then Daddy left and brought back my sister. Handed her his ol' Colt, and just said, 'Shoot 'em, now, Little Bit. It'll set you free.' I won't forget that. Set you free, he said." He sipped some more.

Dobey finally said, "And?"

Jimmy snapped out of his reverie, and nodded, saying, "She did. Shot each one of 'em. Didn't kill 'em, though. The fire did that. I hate a rapist."

Dobey took a deep breath. "I figured it was something like that. What happened after?"

"Daddy took the family and headed south. I deserted, re-enlisted in that regiment where you found me. Heard later that we probably could have stayed. It was thought to be an accident, that fire. Couldn't tell they was tied and shot."

"Just like we did with Marie-Louise's store. I be damned."

"Nosir. It won't nothing like that. Weren't trying to hide it. Weren't even quiet. We was just trying to rub it all out, wipe it clean. The place, the people. For Little Bit."

"Your sister? How'd she come out?"

"It didn't set her free. She's a drunk, in Fort Worth. She ain't a well person, if'n she's still alive."

As they finished their brandy, Marie-Louise and Honey came and sat by the fire. Dobey had noticed them in heated, if muted, discussion with Bear and Big William, behind the wagon. Bear and Big William talked for a minute more, then Big William joined the group at the fire.

"Bear says the Watson men is on guard now, and he gone to check 'em. He give 'em two of y'all's shotguns, and one of they own, which we got back from the jail. Say they know how to use 'em."

"The women?"

"They's sleepin' in they wagon, right over there."

"They all right now, you think?"

Big William shrugged, and Marie-Louise answered testily, "No, they not all right now. They scared. The mama, she feels ruint. But they alive, thanks to you and Jimmy. You have done good work today. Again."

She paused, then focused on what would come next. "Bear have searched the dead men and the jail. There was money and jewelry and extra guns. We have give the Watson family their things, and ten dollars. There is now seventy-six dollar for to split." She took a deep breath. "Honey and me, we will keep the jewelry. And there is whiskey, maybe five bottles."

Dobey thought for a moment, then said, "We'll talk." He motioned to Jimmy, and the two Rangers moved off a few yards for a conference.

When the Rangers returned minutes later, Dobey said, "I want you to give another twenty dollars to the Watsons for their troubles, and you, Honey, and Bear split the other cash. We didn't even think to search for it, and so we would not have had it, anyways."

Jimmy asked, "That whiskey. Is it good stuff we should keep?"

"Non, cher. Is rotgut. Maybe William, he can sell it in those drinking places?"

"I was thinking that, too. Big William, you keep what you get for it, but don't you be getting into it yourself, 'less you come up blind, you hear?" He gave Big William a rare grin.

"Yassuh. Yas-*suh*! And mighty kind of you, Boss. Nossuh. Big William ain't no fool. Be gettin' right to that, right now." His grin was infectious. He punched Bear on the shoulder, and left.

Marie-Louise watched him bounce away, then turned to eye Jimmy, then Dobey in turn. "Him, you give a gun already. An' we must feed him. You think is good to give that darky money?"

Dobey looked to Jimmy, who shrugged. "I got a feel for men. Usually I'm right, Cap'n, and you know it. I think this one is all right. He ain't dumb as he lets on. Anyways, he's part of our little army, and he's got to be paid. Least til he messes up."

Dobey nodded agreement, then said, "Wouldn't hurt if you sent Bear along with him, though. That village ain't half empty of villains, yet. And we got to decide what do about that marshal. You want to just run him out of town? Think he's scared enough?"

Jimmy thought for a moment. "Probably is, right now. Let me handle it, Cap'n. I'll feel him out. But you know, if I was him, I'd say anything to keep me from just killing him. They was lawmen we killed. Sooner or later, that marshal's gonna get righteous about that, or about us running him off from this sweet deal he's had here. He'll come, or put out paper on us."

"He doesn't know where we're heading," said Dobey.

"Knows these folks was going to Santa Fe. They knows where we's heading. Let me just handle it."

"All right Jimmy. But if you want him dead, let's have a little military court, try him for armed robbery, helping to rape or something, and hang him front of the town. Make it official."

"Yeah. Like we didn't know the war was over."

An hour later, Bear was back. "Marshal's gone, Boss. Had a key hid somewheres, he did. Took off, had that ferryman put him across the Arkansas River. Him? He gone south."

Melton looked at Dobey. "You see? I should of never locked him up. My gut said, 'Just shoot him.' Ever' damn time I try to do something good, it goes wrong."

Dobey smiled. "No good deed goes unpunished."

✳ ✳ ✳

Over coffee at dawn, the Watsons thanked them solemnly, then asked if they could tag along to Texas with them, as they now could afford a boat trip.

Marie-Louise had no objection, and Jimmy just said, "Free country. Long as they don't slow us down. Hell, I don't know how we could go no slower, no how."

The little army grew.

Five miles below them, Marshal Fetterman stumbled along the banks of the Mississippi, watching for a southbound boat. "Sons a bitches," he muttered, "I'll get 'em." He spat out another dangling tooth. "Last thing I ever do, I'll get 'em."

CHAPTER THIRTY-FIVE

After the noon meal, Bear squatted beside Dobey. "That fambly, they hasn't nothing to eat 'cept beans. Not even corn bread, Cap'n."

"And you were thinking what?"

"Oldest boy, he fifteen. Name Jimmy, but they calls him Buck. He say he can hunt. They's wild pigs in that brush. Seen 'em beyond the edge of town. Might take that boy, see can we kill one or two. Big William, he a cook. Mama says we could share."

"All right. But you hear two or more shots fired from here, y'all come running. It means either trouble or a boat has come."

✼ ✼ ✼

As no westbound boat appeared, the loose camp settled in for a second night. Dobey sent Honey to ask the Watsons to help them eat the one pig that Bear had killed. Big William had it on a spit, sizzling.

The Watsons shuffled over to the cook fire, nervous except for Buck, who had spent an afternoon in the brush, tracking pigs with Bear. The older black boy, much bigger and better armed, was intimidating. Both boys had been on edge, watching for, even expecting a slight. Now at supper, they chattered on about hunting, two old friends.

Dobey stood, indicated some boxes and invited them to sit, but Mrs. Watson hesitated, wringing her hands. "Oh, my. I ain't never sat and et supper with no niggers before."

Dobey rolled his eyes. "Now that's an ice breaker."

Marie-Louise sprang to her feet, pushing Jimmy down as he tried to stand, too. "Non. And I doubt you have been beat and raped before, neither. The times, they change."

Jimmy pushed her hand off his shoulder and scrambled to his feet, choking on cornbread, unable to speak, but scary nevertheless. The Watsons' eyes bulged, collectively about three inches.

Dobey pointed to Marie-Louise. "It was her boy that killed this pig, and Big William there that cooked it. And her that said to invite you." He took a deep breath. "I know you've been through a lot here, and the world is upside down. But I won't tolerate rudeness. Y'all can apologize, set and eat, or go back to your wagon and rejoice in being white."

"Or go straight to hell," added Jimmy, finally gaining his voice. Marie-Louise patted his arm. Mrs. Watson bit her hand and sobbed.

Anger, tension, fear, and hunger overlaid the cook fire in roughly equal parts. Buck broke the spell. "Damn, Momma, they is good people. Prob'ly saved our lives."

Watson snapped at him, "Don't never cuss your mama." Turning to Marie-Louise, he folded his hands as if praying. "Hazel don't mean nuthin bad. She ain't mean. She just says whatever pops into her head. It's her truth. It just ain't always nice. And we don't know whether we's coming or going right now. I guess we should be going. We are sorry, and we know we owe you more than we can even say."

"Fair enough," said Jimmy as he squatted again. Marie-Louise kicked him in the knee. "Or you can stay." he grumbled.

Dobey pointed to the boxes again. "Please. Sit. Everybody is strung out. We need to eat and get guards out. Now where y'all from?"

Slowly, in halting fits and starts, the meal moved from its ragged humble beginning to a surprisingly pleasant conclusion. Big William's food helped. It was better than anything any of them had experienced lately. Or maybe ever.

It turned out that the Watsons - Henry, Hazel, Buck, Amanda, and Abel (called Button) - were on a roll of bad luck, shocking in its length and depth, even in these hard times. They crossed from Mississippi to Mason's Landing to find their latest misfortune. They left behind three dead children, stolen pigs, cows, chickens, and mules, a poisoned well, and a burned farm. Watson had fought for the South briefly in Tennessee before being sent home with head and leg wounds, which left him unsteady on his feet. A runaway slave had knocked Hazel Watson on the head with a board when she caught him in their smoke house, leaving her somewhat addled, two years ago.

"At least, more so than she was before," her husband concluded.

"Which was gracious plenty, afore she was hit," murmured Buck.

"Good food," Hazel said suddenly, smiling at Big William. "Maybe best I ever et. You put onions and apples in these beans, din't you?"

"Yas'm. And some bacon, grapes, and a pepper. Little sugar, too. And tomato sauce."

"Oh, my stars in Heaven. Mandy, 'member all that for me. See, this is just too much at once. Oh, my." She frowned, then brightened again. "Could use honey, hadn't you no sugar, I guess."

"Yas'm. Sure could. Prob'ly better. Now, just you have a lil more here." He spooned the last of the beans to her, Jimmy, Bear and Buck. "Raisins is good as grapes, if'n you has 'em."

She nodded, her eyes wet with wonder and gratitude. "The captain was right. Upside down." Watson hugged her and thanked everyone again.

Honey touched Mandy's arm and whispered, "I got to pee. C'mon."

Bear stretched. "Getting dark." He faced the twelve-year-old Button and said, "You and me will be guards first, then Buck and Big William." He glanced at Jimmy, who nodded and spoke.

"Cap'n and I will go third, then start over. Take the cap'n's watch, and stay awake and on your feet. One of us will be checking on you."

✶ ✶ ✶

As Honey crept into the wagon later, she confided to Marie-Louise that Mandy feared that her mother would be pregnant from the rape. "She bleeding down there, Mama, but she don't know is it the monthlies, or is it torn."

"Morning, we take her to that doctor."

"Mama, he a tooth doctor."

"You know another doctor here? We take her there. Someone takes care of all those whores."

✶ ✶ ✶

The next morning, four women, accompanied by Buck and Bear, prepared to go visit the dentist. They waited for the

Rangers to return from their daily ablutions, but once informed, Jimmy sent the two young men alone.

"Drunk or sober, bring him here. Bring all his stuff, and any helper he might have. I'll have coffee and cold water for him, and hot water for her. Don't let nobody slow you down. Boat might show any minute."

Bear brought him back fifteen minutes later, slung across his horse, protesting mildly. A skinny, scantily clad, barefoot and buck-toothed girl rode behind Buck.

Dumped without ceremony, Doctor John Thomason, a balding forty year old, dusted himself off and adjusted his spectacles. "I fear I've lost all that I ate and drank last night, and your nigra cuffed me. Twice, I believe."

"Puked on my boot," Bear explained, shaking his head in disgust.

"He ain't my 'nigra' nor anyone elses," said Jimmy. "Only reason he din't shoot you is we might need you here. You ain't 'zackly out of danger yet." He poured a bucket of cold water over the stupefied dentist's head.

Jimmy grabbed his ear and took him, gasping and sputtering, to the morning fire. "Set. Drink this coffee, and there's biscuits, do you want one. Don't talk til you're sober, less'n you want dental work yourself." He faced the girl. "You his help?"

"Sort of," she said. She dismounted with help from Buck, and took a leather bag from him. "Thank you," she said sweetly, and squeezed his arm. "I'm the only whore has had any school, so he lets me help when I ain't working. He ain't bad, by the way, when he's sober." She accepted a mug of coffee and a biscuit. "That's generally from about noon til three p.m."

Marie-Louise had guessed right about him, though. Since there was little dental work to be done in Mason's Landing, his side-line of tending the whores in exchange for their favors had become his primary business.

An hour later, relatively sober, he diagnosed Hazel's bleeding as menstrual, and to everyone's relief announced that because of the blood flow, she was probably not pregnant. He dosed her for the possible pox, but assured her that he had dosed all the lawmen too, not long before they died. "And they still perished as a direct result of their fornication," he added, pleased with his little joke, so early in the day.

"Tole you he won't half-bad," giggled the young whore, rubbing his head. "Now that you've seen what a morning looks like, what do you think, Doc?"

"Why, Junebug, my lass, I find it just marvelous. Invigorating. I vaguely remember enjoying them in Saint Louis. Or maybe Cincinnati."

"'Junebug'?" asked Buck, awestruck by the girl and the well-traveled dentist.

"Her name's June, but she has flashes of brilliance." He slapped her bottom. "For me now, all this early motion excites an uneasiness, which would be helped by some whiskey added to this coffee."

"Brandy all right?"

"Far better, Sir. As that looks like good brandy, I may just have it neat."

As Melton poured, Junebug winked at Buck and with a nod, got him to move away from the fire. "Where y'all heading?" She plucked a wildflower and sniffed it as they walked.

Buck's tongue was stiff. "Uh, Santa Fe. Us, I mean. Them, uh, they is heading for north Texas. Some fort, they said."

She stopped and pushed the stem of the flower through one of Buck's buttonholes. "There. That's cute. Like you," she grinned. "Wish I was going somewheres. Hey, you are blood-red in the face."

"Well, you made me," he blushed. "Anyways, why's that old drunk call you Junebug? They's fat and green. Ain't he thinking of lightning bugs? They's the flashy ones."

"Maybe he is. As you might notice, Doc don't have many sober thoughts. He did say, howsomever, that my eyes are big and bright green. Like a Junebug, Mister Smarty-pants." She stopped and stared at him. "What do you think of 'em?"

Buck stared back for a moment, then dropped his head and stammered, "I think, I mean, I know they is the prettiest things I ever seen."

"Well, Mister Buck Watson, what a nice thing to say. And I barely had to drag it out of you." She sauntered on again.

He caught up and gave her back the little flower. "I can't wear this. You know?" His eyes pleaded for understanding.

She grinned and stuck it in her hair. "Oh yeah. Too manly."

"So, where is it you want to go?"

"Anywheres but here or home. Old Butch will come back and be worse than ever. And he ain't gonna forgive y'all beating him up, neither."

"Who?"

"Butch Fetterman. The marshal. He was a butcher up to Cincinnati, is where he got the name. Come here on a boat with Doc, years ago. Meaner than my daddy, and used me just as bad. Never paid, neither."

Buck was thunderstruck. "Your own daddy? Not a step-daddy?"

"My very own." She pulled the flower from her hair and hurled it away. "Gin-drinking, preachy, smooth-talking, fancy-dressing... I still hate him. I'm glad... nothing. Never mind."

"Where was your mama?"

"At the store. But she knew. Had to know, even before I told her. I mean, he was careful, didn't want me pregnant, but that still meant a lot of poking, if you take my meaning."

Buck had no idea what she meant. "But, when you told your ma, what...?"

"Hit me. Said I was a tramp, a thirteen-year-old tramp. Like my sister before me, she said." She sniffled and wiped her nose on her sleeve. "Just didn't want to lose him, I guess."

"Jesus Christ." Buck shook his head.

"Don't say that," she flared and punched his chest with a finger. "It ain't that uncommon, Mister Know-it-all. Half the girls in these here whorehouses was used by family. Daddies, uncles, brothers, step-daddies, half-brothers, you name it. Why you think we run?"

Buck's mind was a black fog. "Well, I ain't no 'know-it-all.' I didn't know about this. Never heard such a thing. Well, one step-daddy, but the mother killed him. I think you ought to run again."

That afternoon, a small side-wheeler appeared, and passage was arranged for "as far upstream as the ol' girl would go."

They went. Joining them were Junebug and a very mellow Dr. Thomason, with two worn suitcases and his medical bag.

CHAPTER THIRTY-SIX

The stern-wheeler groaned and rumbled as she reversed engines near the bank. Fetterman saw the dozen or so Union infantrymen, Springfield rifles at the ready, watching for an ambush. "I'm alone and unarmed," he yelled. As if they could hear him.

Crewmembers were lowering the footbridge before the boat shuddered to a halt, yards from the muddy bank. Someone with a hailer blared from the wheelhouse, "Come aboard, long as you can work or pay. And want to go south."

"Pinkertons, huh? I heard of you, but ain't ever met one before. Well, you called for me. What can I do for you?" Fetterman stared back at the two well-dressed men, seated at the dining table of the boat. Both wore revolvers under their waistcoats, and they had ordered everyone else out of the dining room.

"It's more like what we might do for you, Mister...?" The skinny short one spoke.

"Fetterman. Butch Fetterman. You gonna pay my fare? Save me from the engine room? Mister..."

"Maybe. That just might be the case. I'm Smith, he's Jones." He nodded at the tall heavy lidded man behind him.

"Y'all ain't no more Smith and Jones than I'm the President, but what's your deal?"

"We're looking for some folks. There's a reward on 'em, and we can even pay for information. Good information, mind you. Some now, more after we confirm it, but maybe enough now to get you where you're going. Which is?"

"Look here. I'm a marshal. I was after some folks myself, and my horse threw me and bolted. Lost my gun, food, some teeth, and most of my money. Right now I'm looking for a dentist, then a horse and a gun. So who're you looking for?"

"Town marshal, or Federal?"

"Town. Mason's Landing, a few miles back upriver."

"No dentist there? You was heading away."

"There's one, but I need a sober one, with gas. Now, you gonna give me a shot at that money, or not?"

Smith looked at Jones, who shrugged. "All right. We ain't sure who we're looking for. Three soldiers disappeared with ah, some army money. May have stole it, may have been murdered and robbed. Army found three burned bodies. Might be them, might be some sort of half-nigger family that owned the place that was burned down on 'em. There was also a couple of Rebs seen nearby, heading for New Orleans."

Smith stood and walked to a sideboard where he poured a mug of coffee, giving Fetterman a moment to digest his racing thoughts. *It's them for sure. Rebs and them breeds and niggers must've taken out a army payroll. Must be real money in this. I ought to go along with these two, use 'em to help me find them bastard Rebs. Or maybe not.*

Smith held up a flask. "You like a little touch, Marshal? You think of anything you seen, might help us?"

Fetterman nodded and reached for the spiked coffee as he made up his mind. "Yes sir. Thankee. I think I seen exactly who you're looking for. Big sidewheeler was through Mason's Landing, maybe a week ago. Name of the 'Bernice Ann,' I think. Let off some travelers and bought some pigs. Now, they was trying to lay low, but I seen a couple of Rebs with a wagon, had them a couple of niggers and some women. One of 'em coulda been a breed or quadroon. They didn't get off the boat, but the mate said they was bound for New Orleans, and was all together. Said they was real close-mouthed and nervous."

"Damn." Smith sat up and banged the table with his fist. "Got to be them. Don't you think, Jones? Listen, Marshal, we need you to travel with us, since you can spot 'em."

"Wisht I could, but I'm duty-bound to finish my own pursuit. Hell, you can't miss 'em. Make this boat go like hell, and you'll overtake 'em for sure, since they's stopping for every little town along the river. Now, is that good enough to get me some traveling money? I need to get doctored, armed, mounted and back after my own bandits."

Smith looked at Jones again. "I don't know. We ain't sure it's them, and we sure ain't caught 'em. They get to New Orleans ahead of us, they'll be hell to find."

Fetterman shrugged. "Well, give me what you can. You know where I live. If you do catch 'em, you can bring me my fair share on your way back north. I trust you."

Like hell I do. And I ain't splitting that payroll with you two yokels, neither.

Chapter
Thirty-seven

For most of their lives, the boat trip would remain the most relaxed period that any of them ever experienced. "Like a furlough," said Dobey.

The *Blue Cat* chugged on, north and west, through the twists of the Arkansas River. The travelers lazed on deck during the day and got to know each other better each night.

Bear and Big William slept in the wagon. The Watsons slept in or under theirs. Marie-Louise and Honey shared a cabin, as did Dobey and Melton. Unlike the *Memphis Belle,* the *Blue Cat* was a happy boat, with an honest crew and captain. Dr. John and Junebug slept with the crew, in different senses of the word.

They learned that Big William went to war with his master on a Rebel gunship, cooking for him, cleaning and loading his guns, til the master died from bad water. Put ashore to bury him, Big William did that, then walked down river until he landed a job in a riverboat engine room. He survived several disasters: fires, groundings, sinkings, and shelling by Yankee gunboats. Engine room men were always needed, and pay for Negro engine room men ranged from little to none. Just prior to working on the *Memphis Belle,* he served on a

Yankee gunboat, until it hit a torpedo and sank in shallow water.

Jimmy decided that Big William was dependable, and pulled Dobey's old Spencer carbine from the wagon's false bottom and trained Big William with it. Or tried to. It became apparent that Big William couldn't shoot well enough with the carbine to hit oak trees at thirty yards. Large, stationary oak trees. Jimmy began calling him Blind William.

"You drank that damn whiskey, din't you?"

"Nossuh," William smiled. "Just I gets a fog on my eyes, do I try to look too far."

Reluctantly, Jimmy gave him the Colt shotgun to try. At thirty yards, no one could miss with it, not even Big William. When Dobey asked where it was, Jimmy said that he was tired of it rubbing his back. "Blind-assed Big William might need it, we fetch some Indians," he added. Dobey's old Spencer was retired again, but only until Bear pushed for it to be "loaned" to Buck.

✳ ✳ ✳

Near Fort Smith, a massive tornado crossed the river in front of them. The boat captain saw it coming and reversed engines, then turned the boat to be ready for an escape back downstream.

The monster missed them by less than a mile, raining branches, dead birds, and one live polecat onto the boat. When they crossed the path of the storm, both riverbanks looked as if they had been pounded by artillery. Dazed animals wandered along the shores.

"A few things about the Great West I ain't missed so much," Jimmy observed. "Back in '54, I found a dead horse in a tree after one of these." Honey and Marie-Louise thought he was teasing them; Bear believed anything that Jimmy said; Dobey and Big William knew he was telling the truth.

* * *

On a hair pin curve of the Canadian, three days after leaving Fort Smith, they ran firmly aground on a shifting bar. On the bow, the ship's captain gave hand signals to his first mate up in the wheelhouse, backing one paddle, then the other, trying to ease her off.

"I fear I've come too far upstream," he opined. "I been past here before, but it do get tricky from here on." The second mate handed him a mug of coffee.

Dobey nodded his understanding, just as a bullet thudded into the second mate's chest. The mate fell on his butt, then scrambled aft, moaning and pouring blood.

About twenty-five Indians opened fire from the south bank, raining musket fire on the *Blue Cat*. Less than forty yards of water separated them, and that was dangerously shallow.

"Stay below the gunnels and get inside," the captain shouted. Looking at Dobey, he added, "Your men return fire."

Dobey, crouched behind the gunwale, fired steadily with his two long Colts, which slowed the Indians' fire. Jimmy scurried up to his captain and handed him his Henry, then opened up with his own Spencer. Within two minutes, Bear and Big William were blazing away, too, from the stern. Dobey said, "Where the hell are the Watsons?" Jimmy told him he had ordered them to watch the other side of the river.

By the time that Big William emptied the five chambers of his shotgun, Dobey fired thirteen aimed shots from the Henry. Bear and Jimmy each emptied their Spencers and reloaded.

On the beach were three dead Indians wearing gray uniforms, and five dying ponies. Perhaps seven other Indians were wounded and crawled or were dragged away. The astounded 'war party' backed away, having never seen such firepower before. Armed only with muzzle-loading shotguns, single shot Mississippi rifles, and a few Sharps, they were no match for the repeaters on the boat.

As it turned out, Buck quickly decided that there was no threat from the north bank and ignored Jimmy's order. He arrived on the port side in time to fire three rounds from his Spencer and take a splinter in the face from a musket ball that hit the gunwale in front of him. A ball passed through Big William's shirt under his left arm, lacerating the arm and his side; Jimmy stitched him up, as Dr. John had not yet sobered up from the previous night.

Among the *Blue Cat's* crew, the second mate was gravely hurt, coughing blood. The first mate had glass slivers in his hand and neck from a ball through the wheelhouse window, and one engine room hand, having run on deck to see the action, took a ball in his thigh to satisfy his curiosity. The first mate cut it out and poured rum on it, as well as on all the other injuries. He gave the rest of the rum to the dying second mate.

Jimmy reported to Dobey that he'd posted guards on both sides, and told everyone to reload.

"You seen some of them was wearing Confederate gray?" Jimmy was fired up. "Prob'ly took 'em off our boys they'd ambushed. Maybe scalped 'em, too. By God, you cover me, Cap'n, and I'll go ashore and scalp those three dead ones."

"This might be something entire different," interrupted the boat's captain. "Last year, Confederate Cherokees took and captured a steamboat back a ways on the Arkansas River. Might be that same bunch, or some like 'em. They been fighting all over this area for three years. Hell, you might have just defeated your own men."

Ten minutes later, they were hailed from the south bank. "Hallooo, the boat. Hold fire. We parley. You hear me good?"

"We hear you just fine," shouted Dobey. "We'll hold fire." He pulled on his jacket and cap, and showed himself.

A well-built Indian in the uniform of a Confederate officer rode out onto the beach and stared, surprised at Dobey.

Jimmy shouted, "You kill the men that was wearing those uniforms?"

"No. These are our uniforms. What are you doing on a Yankee boat? Did you change sides? Are you the ones who shot my men?" He was as hot as Jimmy.

Dobey put his hands out in a calming gesture. "We shot 'cause you attacked us. And you hit some of us, too. And this is not a Yankee boat. War's over. We're just catching a ride toward home in Texas. Who are you?"

"War ain't over, here. I'm Captain John Ridges, First Cherokee Mounted Rifles. Who are you?"

"Captain Thomas Walls, Eighth Texas Cavalry. This here's Sergeant Major Melton. There's no Yankees on this boat, and it ain't military. We paid to ride it."

"You won't ride no further upstream. It's full of logs from a storm. Damn, this is bad business. My colonel is back with the wounded. Told me to tell you to surrender and stop the killing, and we wouldn't burn your boat. But he don't know we was fighting with other Rebels. He damn sure don't know the war's over. You better come talk to him."

The Indian turned back toward the embankment and shouted, "Jimmy." Jimmy Melton, pulling on his gray jacket, almost answered the imperial summons, but realized Captain Ridges was not speaking to him. A young Cherokee, wearing sergeant's chevrons, trotted up to the captain, and they talked briefly.

Turning back to the boat, Captain Ridges shouted, "This here is Sergeant Jimmy Ridges. He's my baby brother. He'll come on board as a hostage, and you ride his horse back there with me. You want him to leave his guns here?"

Dobey shouted back, "If I can wear mine, he can keep his. Come on out. It's most shallow up front here." He handed Jimmy Melton his Henry, and said, "You hold on to this."

"Damn, Cap'n, I don't know about all this."

Dobey turned to the boat captain and asked, "You got any advice?"

"I think you'll be all right. They didn't burn that other boat, nor murder anyone. Ransomed the boat and prisoners, after stripping 'em of goods. They's got maybe six hundred men."

"Six hundred?"

"Oh, yes. Two regiments. Mostly Cherokee, but some Seminoles and Osage too. Commander is named General Stand Watie. Been beating the stuffing out of the Yankee Regulars and Indians 'round here."

The two Cherokees had ridden close to the bow of the boat, and the young sergeant dismounted. Dobey vaulted over the side into thigh deep water, and was caught and stabilized by Sergeant Ridges, who then handed Dobey his reins. Big William leaned over, and pulled up the slender Indian, who held up a bandaged arm, smiled and said, "You fellows shoot good. Glad you ain't Yankees."

Jimmy Melton shook his hand and said, "Y'all ain't bad yourselves." He pointed to William and Buck, who showed their injuries. "I'm pretty good at stitching. Lemme look at that arm."

From the river, Captain Ridges shouted again. "I want to recover my dead, and finish off those horses. Maybe butcher 'em?"

Jimmy Melton shouted back, "Thanks for warning us. We won't be startled now. Listen, you got my cap'n. We ain't gonna fire on you, and we ain't going no where, even if this boat does suddenly float. Go 'head on and talk." He saluted, and added, "Sir."

Captain Ridges returned the salute and they rode away.

☆ ☆ ☆

As their horses jogged up the embankment from the sandbar, Dobey saw at least a dozen gray-clad Indians behind cover, rifles trained on the *Blue Cat*. Captain Ridges nodded to them, and said, "What we've got here is the headquarters company of First Regiment. We should have waited til one of the line companies got here." He frowned. "But then, you and I might not be talking now."

"Glad you didn't wait. Couple of hundred men, you'd have shot us to pieces."

"Sort of what I thought. Colonel wanted to try it, though. Outdo the general, you know."

"No. I mean, I don't know. This that General Watie I heard about?"

"Yep. He took a steamer on the Arkansas last June, but had the whole First Regiment with him."

"So, there's two regiments of you?"

"First and Second Cherokee Mounted Rifles, and three battalions of infantry; mixed Cherokee, Osage, and Seminole. I guess you'd call Stand Watie the Brigade, or maybe Division Commander. He's a good 'un."

In a grove a quarter mile from the boat, six wounded were being cared for by a small medical team. A tall thin man in the bloodstained uniform of a colonel moved to greet them. "Ho, John. I should have listened to you. Did they surrender? Damn, they fought good. Hit me in the rib. Who's this?"

"He's Captain Walls, Eighth Texas Cavalry. Captain, this here's Joshua Creek, colonel of the First Cherokees. You ain't gonna believe this, Colonel. That won't no Yankee boat. It was Captain Walls and his men we was fighting."

Dobey dismounted and shook hands with the astounded Colonel Creek; Dobey's opinion of him had risen sharply when he learned the colonel had led the assault on the *Blue Cat*, and with a small force. Some colonels wouldn't have done that. General Forrest, the Wizard, would have.

"But, but, you flew the Yankee colors. I saw it. I am sure."

"They're just American colors now, Colonel. We lost. War's over. Lee surrendered to Grant weeks ago. It really is not a Yankee boat. My party is the only passengers, and the boat captain was good to us. Thought highly of you, too."

Creek was immediately suspicious. "I doubt he knows me."

"Nossir. I meant your unit. He said y'all had whipped the Yankees all over these parts for years. I hope you'll let us unload here, and let him go. We're his only cargo."

Colonel Creek thought a moment, then slapped his leg. "Well, by Damn, we still ain't been beat by Yankees. I should have known. John, tell the wounded that we was shot up by other Rebels. They'll feel better, for sure."

Captain Ridges glanced at the wounded, and deadpan, said, "Yessir. Is it all right for them to cheer?"

"Hell, John, how was I to know? Did you? No, you didn't either, and accidents happen, so get on with it. Got to put the best light on it. You know I'm right."

John Ridges grunted and moved off. The colonel turned back to Dobey and asked, "How many men do you have? Or did you have—I know we hit some."

"There are seven men in my group, Sir, and four women. Oh, and a sort of doctor and his, uh, female helper. Then there's the boat crew. You hit two of my men, and three of the crew. One's probably dead. Turned out pretty even, seeing as you attacked over open ground and we were behind some cover."

Colonel Creek was flabbergasted. "Seven? No. It's not possible. There was too much fire. Must have been twenty people shooting."

"Five of us had repeaters, Sir. Captured from Yankees. Five men can shoot like twenty." Dobey let Colonel Creek digest that for a moment. "If y'all don't surrender soon, you'll be facing entire regiments armed with repeaters."

"Maybe we'll just kill 'em, and take their guns, like you did. Anyhow, that's up to the general. Let's go get your men off that boat. I want to see those guns."

Sixteen year old Sergeant Jimmy Ridges was lithe, about 5'8", one hundred sixty pounds, and very handsome, or so thought Amanda Watson. She leaned over Jimmy Melton's shoulder to watch as he worked to dig out the ball lodged in the Cherokee's left forearm. Melton used a rum-soaked thin bladed stiletto he had borrowed from the first mate, as his own blade was too big.

He paused now, wiped away some blood and poured rum on the wound. The young man jumped and said "Durn," smiling at Mandy.

"Indians ain't supposed to flinch," said Melton, as he started back in with the knife.

"I mean to work on that, but it does smart."

"Maybe a lot of Indians ain't had whiskey poured in open wounds," offered Mandy in his defense.

They determined with some confidence that Jimmy Ridges had been on the receiving end of one of Big William's shotgun blasts. His horse went down with several hits to its neck and chest, and at the same moment, a ball passed through the leather sling on Ridges' rifle, and imbedded in his arm.

"Buckshot," said Jimmy Melton. "Rifle ball would have gone right on through your arm, smashed the bone. This one used up its force punching through that leather sling. Lucky."

Ridges frowned. "If I was lucky, I'd have been riding with my uncle today, instead of with my brother. My horse would still live, and my arm would not have an English pouring rum on it and cutting it."

"I ain't English, and I wish all of you had been off riding with your uncle, wherever the hell he is. And what I meant was, you're lucky you had your sleeve rolled up. There ain't no cloth pushed up in this wound. There, see? It's a buckshot." He handed it to the boy.

Jimmy Ridges held it up for the others to see, grinning. "Thank you. I will keep this as a great trophy. And I made joke; I know you are Texas, but a lot of our old people still call all of you English." He grimaced as Melton started to stitch him up. "Like you call all of us Indians."

"Ain't you?"

"He's Cherokee," said Mandy, proudly. *And brave,* she thought. *He didn't flinch much.*

"Yessir. Like I was Mandinka," said Big William.

Jimmy Melton's eyebrows shot up. "You telling me you're an Indian too?"

"Nossir," laughed Big William. "You're thinking of Mandan Indians. My mammy and pappy was from the Mandinka tribe, back in Africa. Man that owned me tole me so. Famous warriors, he said." He turned back to Ridges. "Sorry 'bout your arm and horse."

Ridges shrugged, then brightened. "I will say I was shot by a large African warrior. A Mandinka."

Big William smiled and said, "Sounds better than 'nigger,' don't it?"

Even Jimmy Melton laughed. As it died down, Marie-Louise offered another startling revelation. "Honey, she part Cherokee too."

It seemed that old Pop Weathers' Indian mother, one Mary Weathers, had been taken as a young woman in a raid on a Cherokee village around the turn of the century. Impregnated by one of her captors, she escaped and made it back to her tribe. The young half-breed bastard, Bob Weathers, was a misfit, though, and drifted west to Mississippi. He led a miserable life, so he told Marie-Louise, until he found her.

"Then he died, trying to save my baby, Honey-Marie, from those terrible Yankees."

"Then he died an honorable man," said Jimmy Ridges. "A Cherokee."

"Yassur," said Big William.

"Is true," added Honey. "But Mama, why you don't tole me before?"

"Some people in Mississippi, they still remember the fighting of Indians. Old Weathers, he din't tell nobody but me, so I keep to my own self. But now, I think is good for all to know." She solemnly nodded toward the Cherokees now approaching the shore with Dobey.

☆ ☆ ☆

"I am good," shouted Jimmy Ridges. "But how are you, Colonel?"

"I don't hurt much, Little Brother. We will take ropes and horses and pull the boat to shore, let people off, look after your arm. You're no longer hostage. I have given these people free passage." Dobey signaled his agreement.

Melton said, "I thought the other one was your brother. The captain."

"The captain is my real brother. The colonel is just speaking, uh…"

"Indian talk?"

"Cherokee talk."

"Sorry," muttered Melton. "I'll do better." Turning up to the wheelhouse, he shouted, "Captain Stafford—you better show us where to tie those ropes. Bear, you and Buck and this blind-assed Mandinka go help 'em. Ladies, better pack up. And wake up that drunk dentist." Big William grinned, saluted, and left.

"I'm quite awake, sir. Though somewhat confused." A half dressed Dr. John stood in a doorway, knife in his left hand, and an ivory-handled Colt Police Model in the other.

Four hours later, the wagons and livestock were ashore and connected, the hapless second mate buried, and Captain 'Boots' Stafford was ready to re-board his vessel and head back to Fort Smith. Dobey gave him ten dollars for the mate's family, and they were shaking hands, when he looked over Dobey's shoulder and whispered, "Saints preserve us."

Dobey turned. Hundreds of armed, gray-clad Cherokees lined the river embankment, while dozens rode slowly down onto the sandy beach following an impressive figure in the uniform of a Confederate general. Dobey's heart pounded like a drum, and the hair on his arm stiffened.

Melton said to no one in particular, "I got a chill. He some kind of a king or something?"

"That's my real uncle," said Jimmy Ridges.

CHAPTER
THIRTY-EIGHT

"This gives you free passage, from my men. I cannot speak for the bandit people north of the river." General Stand Watie folded the paper and handed it to Captain Stafford. "I cannot tell you what to do, but I would not fly that flag in this region. Not yet. Maybe not ever."

Captain Stafford thanked him, saluted, shook hands around, and fifteen minutes later, the *Blue Cat* steamed east, defiantly flying the American flag.

"Brave man," said the general. "Maybe not too smart."

"He won't no Yankee, General. He is just an American again now, as I guess we all are." Dobey sounded resigned to it.

Watie turned to stare at him, then sat on the ground abruptly, tossed his hat aside and called for tea.

"You rather have coffee, General?" asked Melton.

"I would almost forgive you for killing my men, if you had real coffee." Watie looked dubious.

"Gimme five minutes at that fire. Y'all go on and talk."

The general signaled Dobey and Colonel Creek to sit too. "I should not joke about my dead men. This is bad business, and my men are not happy. It is good you buried the one

English in front of them, and that my nephew saw the other wounded English on the boat." He paused. "But it is bad that you killed three of us, and hurt so many. And we lost horses. But you helped my nephew, even though you shot him. And one of you is Cherokee. We need to smoke on this."

As they lit up, a blood-spattered Dr. Thomason joined them and, without invitation, poured some coffee and sat. "Your medical team is quite good, Sir. I assisted in removing two cleverly placed bullets, and did one unusual suture." He stared hard at Melton. "I might have finished sooner, had someone not denied me a stabilizing brandy. I trust that I may have one now?"

"No one except condemned men drink in my camps," said General Watie.

"Too late anyhow," added Captain Ridges, as he joined them. He tossed a small, empty bottle to Melton. "He poured some on the wounds, and some in himself."

"Well, I'm certainly condemned. Abducted by a whore, confined on a boat with no decent bar, and about to be murdered by Indians for drinking in the afternoon. Certainly I qualify for a large glass now." He struggled to his feet and shouted, "It is a good time to die!"

Several nearby Cherokees, members of Watie's staff, nervously fingered their weapons and laughed, but the General said firmly, "Sit down, you old fool, and drink coffee."

As the dentist sat, huffing, Jimmy Melton asked, "What's a 'soocher'?"

"It is the sewing of a wound, Sergeant. It is an act I must frequently perform, in my primary duties as a dental surgeon. Frontiersmen seem to feel that they must knock each other's teeth out, almost as a daily ritual."

Jimmy turned to Dobey and laughed, "Hell, he just means stitching."

"Just a minute, there," inserted General Watie. "Did you say you're a dental doctor?"

"Charles John Thomason, at your service, Sir."

"Well, Doctor Thomason, you just look at my jaws here, and mayhaps you will see part of why I am so peevish."

As it turned out, Watie had an impacted molar. One hour later, the dazed general gazed at it in his palm. He croaked a dubious thanks, and asked when he could remove the hatchet from the top of his head. The dentist gave him a powder for the pain, and sarcastically suggested that he not take alcohol with it.

✽ ✽ ✽

Even as the dentist worked on the General, Junebug was filling in the women on the good Doctor John, with information pieced together from sober conversations and drunken ravings. Well educated, from a good family on the South Carolina coast, he had a successful dental practice by 1850. He also enjoyed gambling and women with little care about their marital state. As a result, he was called out several times. Hit twice, he still limped slightly, but was the clear winner of each duel.

He only killed three men. "Well," he'd say, "a goodly number more than that before I learned of disinfectants, but only three with pistols". Two of them richly deserved their ends, but the third was Doctor John's ruin. He was an eighteen-year-old with a gambling and drinking problem, the oldest son of a very wealthy planter. He was also the younger brother of the only woman to really interest the rowdy dentist, who decided to help the family and teach the boy a lesson, with pistols at dawn.

The boy felt that the dentist was beneath his sister, and meant to kill him. Chucky Jack, as Dr. John was then called, only meant to scare the boy, but hit him in the stomach. When he died, two agonizing days later, Dr. John's first career was finished, despite the fact that the dead boy's ball had broken Thomason's rib. "He moved," Dr. John would wail. "If only he hadn't tried to dodge. I meant only to break his damned arm."

As the general's pain dissipated, he became more forgiving. At that point, Jimmy Ridges approached and suggested that the Texans be given an escort, at least past Black Kettle's Cheyennes, or maybe on to their destination. In either case, he felt he would be the ideal leader for the escort, as he was a wounded veteran and General/Chief Watie's nephew. That latter fact was important, as no one in the Territories wanted to antagonize Stand Watie.

The general said he would smoke that over, and as it had grown late, he discontinued the conference until the next morning. When Dobey offered himself and his men for guard duty, Watie smiled approval of the offer, but declined.

When the women relayed the new information on Dr. John to Dobey and Jimmy Melton later, Jimmy's initial reaction was simply, "What kind of name is Chucky Jack?" Dobey explained that Colonel Charles John Sevier, a Patriot hero in the victory over the British at Kings Mountain, South Carolina, was called Chucky Jack. He was a profane scrapper.

Jimmy grunted. "I don't know about that. But if that skinny old man was winning gunfights fifteen years ago, maybe he's scrappy enough hisself to beat this likker thing."

☆ ☆ ☆

Unknown to Jimmy, Junebug had decided to help the scrappy old dentist herself. Explaining her problem to sympathetic Cherokee "medicine men," she obtained a powder that could be mixed with food to make alcohol repulsive. Dr. John owned a fair supply of a salve to deaden gums, a salve he could re-order. She traded enough of it to secure a goodly portion of the new powder, and put some in his soup that very same night.

The dentist startled everyone the next morning by showing up for the coffee gathering around the fire. He looked like death, warmed over.

"You all right, Doc, Honey?" Junebug asked sweetly.

"I have not slept. I am unable to hold down my liquor, despite my very best efforts. The moment I swallow, I have this gag reflex. It must be some vile illness I've contracted from these heathens. Perhaps I'll try coffee."

"Aw, Doc—I'm so sorry you feel bad. Try some of these johnnycakes. Them Indians give us some honey to go on 'em. Maybe it'll coat your stomach."

When small sips and nibbles stayed down, Junebug suggested he try to leave the liquor alone til the illness passed.

☆ ☆ ☆

As the officers waited for the General to restart the meeting, Jimmy Ridges and Bear talked.

"So, you Captain Walls' chief scout?"

Bear nodded. "Sort of. Maybe his only scout."

"Your sister is Cherokee, but you are not. You Mandinka too?"

"Mebbe. I don't know what my tribe was. What's a head-quarters company?"

"Scouts, mostly. My brother, the captain there, he's chief scout. General calls him the intelligence officer. But the company is also home for the colonel, the cooks, supply peoples, horse breakers and herders, messengers, medical peoples, like that. I have a section of scouts. Twenty of 'em."

General Watie soon called for the conference to resume, and was pleased when the Texans brought a pot of coffee. When it was shared around, Dobey asked if he could speak first.

"I've thought on this, and I have a proposal. We have some captured Yankee dollars, and we want to offer a wrongful death payment of twenty-five dollars to each of the dead men's families, and give five dollars to each wounded soldier."

The general nodded, his brow deeply furrowed. "Some men are wounded worse than others. My nephew there, Jimmy Ridges, and Colonel Creek, for them maybe five dollars is good. But one man's leg is broke, and another had his eye shot out."

"Maybe ten dollars for the worse wounds?" Dobey paused. "And maybe another ten to the men who lost horses?"

"Captain Walls, I think you are a fair man. Since most of the wounded also lost their horses, I think this will make them feel better. Colonel Creek, how does this plan sound to you?"

Creek smiled. "Be the first time I got paid to get shot. My men will understand, and will no longer grumble. It is good."

"Captain Ridges?"

"Hell, Uncle, we shot them first. They thought we was Kiowas or something, wearing captured uniforms. Yes, it is good. More than fair. If these won't captured dollars, I'd say we should not take them, but seeing as they is, well,...."

General Watie smiled and nodded again. "I am glad my officers think like I do. Perhaps I have taught something after all." Turning to Dobey, he said, "It is done, then. Give the dollars to Captain Ridges. Two of the dead men were brothers, the only members of their family to live through a Comanche raid. They were not married. We'll give their money to the family of the other dead man, as he had five children."

The other Cherokees murmured approval. Captain Ridges said, "When my wife hears of this, she may ask these Texans to kill me. Seventy-five dollars is a lot. But it is good."

Watie continued. "I have also decided to send a company, led by the new lieutenant, Jimmy Ridges, to go with you past Black Kettle's hunting grounds along the Washita. Some of his Cheyenne need watching, and there might be Yankee raiders from north of the Canadian who don't know the war is over. He will do some scouting for us that way, in case we are forced from our home grounds here."

"General, I am speechless. I was going to ask for a guide; this is more than we could expect. I have something for you, though." Dobey stood and signaled to Sergeant Melton, who waited twenty yards away. Melton approached, saluted the General, then handed a Spencer and a shot-tube to Dobey.

It was Dobey's old one, the one Buck had used on the boat. Dobey took it, and instructed Melton to go with Captain Ridges and pay him the agreed sum.

As Captain Ridges and Melton left, Dobey turned back to the General, and handed him the Spencer and spare ammunition. "I carried this, fought with it, for near on a year. I want you to have it, for your fair treatment of us."

The General stood, accepted it, and held it up for his staff to see, and got a hearty cheer in return. Unable to speak, he gripped Dobey's shoulder for a second, then turned and walked away.

✱ ✱ ✱

They rode west along the south bank of the Canadian at noon. The newly promoted Jimmy Ridges rode beside Dobey, his fifty Cherokee troopers riding ahead and on the flanks.

"That Spencer looks mighty familiar," said Dobey.

"Yes," smiled Jimmy Ridges. "My uncle gave it to me. Said it was meant to be in the hands of a fighter, not a tired old general. I hope you will show me how it works."

"Nice to have you and your men with us. Maybe you won't have to use it."

Jimmy Melton just snorted.

✱ ✱ ✱

Bear and Buck rode on the opposite side of the wagons from Dobey, Melton, and Ridges. Buck had Jimmy Melton's old Sharps carbine across his pommel.

"You mad about giving up that Spencer?"

"Naw. That Indian's got more experience than me, and the captain said we was on thin ice back there. If'n it helped get us this cavalry escort, Hell, I'm happy to let it go. 'Sides, Sergeant Melton says this Sharps is more powerful and served him well. Pretty fast, too."

Bear grunted. "That Boss, he knows guns." They rode a while. "Since I got this repeater, I'ma loan you one of my revolvers. Till you get you one. And I'ma ask that Jimmy Ridges can I ride some scout with his men, see can I learn how they read signs out here. Want to go?"

Buck Watson was astounded at the offer. Surprised that Bear would give up one of his Remingtons, but mainly aware of the implied acceptance of him as worthy of an important and dangerous task. "Hell yes. Yes I would. You think Boss will approve?"

"Let's ast him."

CHAPTER THIRTY-NINE

The pine forests and lakes of Arkansas gradually gave way to the scrub oaks and rocky gulleys of the Indian Territory as they plodded towards the grasslands. Possums became armadillos. As they moved westward, the men talked.

"She knows about the money yet?" Dobey asked, after making sure no one was within earshot.

"She knows," said Jimmy Melton. "Made her promise not to talk, though, not even to Honey. How 'bout Honey?"

"Oh, yeah. I did the same. Hard to keep that secret, when you're, ah, spending so much time with 'em. Think they'll keep it quiet?"

"Yeah, Cap'n, I do. I trust 'em." He picked his teeth with a straw for a minute, then continued, "You thought this out, beyond us getting to Canadian Fort? I mean, about us and them?"

Dobey took a deep breath. "Jimmy, I'm hooked. I mean to marry her. Told her already. Guess you know I ain't told her mother. Or Bear. Don't know how that'll go. How 'bout you?"

"Hell, Cap'n, we's already hitched, far as we're concerned. Ain't no chance of no church wedding for us nohow, even was they a church somewhere's out here. And don't worry about Bear, or Marie-Louise. They both likes you." He laughed, "Shoot, the trouble would be if you don't marry her."

"Good to hear. Well, beyond that, I thought we see about setting up with my stepfather, mother and brother, if they're still there. See if we can turn into storekeepers ourselves. Hoped you'd throw in with us."

"I'd like that. So would Marie-Louise. Who we be selling to, exactly?"

"Well, buffalo hunters. Lead, powder, knives, guns. Maybe some liquor. And food. Horses to the army. Take hides in trade, truck them down to Amarillo, or wherever there's a train."

"Jimmy Ridges says his men tell him there's all kind of longhorns running loose south of there. Might run some of them to the army, too."

Dobey thought. "Yes. Or maybe sell stuff to the ones that do herd 'em north. Canadian Fort used to be called Canadian Ford, til the army set up there briefly. It's probably an old buffalo crossing. Natural place for traffic. Jimmy, you realize we're about due south of old Vamoosa Station?"

"You reckon it's still there?"

Dobey looked north, as if he could see through the miles and years back to that place. "Hell, it's probably a school now."

Lieutenant Jimmy Ridges looked up to Bear in both senses of the term, wrongfully believing that the huge man had more combat experience than himself.

"What is this place you go to, Bear?"

"Boss Melton tole me it's called Canadian Fort, but ain't been no soldiers there for years. He thinks the captain's mama has a trading post there, with his stepfather and brother. We gone to throw in with 'em, build it up. See will it s'port seven or eight people."

"The Watsons—do they go with you?"

Bear grinned. "Thought you'd have ast Mandy that. Now, Buck, he wants to go with us, but his fambly, they's heading on to New Mexico. You ain't ast Mandy?"

"Mandy says she will go with me, but she can't. We don't keep women in fighting camps, and we're still fighting. I must go back and report my scout."

"Hell, Ridges, the war is over. Y'all gots to quit. If ain't nobody left fighting but y'all, the whole Yankee army will come against you."

Jimmy Ridges shrugged. "I know this. But I can't give over until my Uncle Stand gives over."

"That Mandy, she ain't gonna wanna hear that."

"Do you think she cares for me? Don't mess with me here, Bear. I'm all messed up over her. Captain Walls said she has been through a bad time, and might not be open to my attention now."

"He blind in love with my sister. Blind for sure, if he don't see that Mandy is watering up for you. Ever'body else knows it. What you gonna do?"

"I suppose I will come back and look for her, whenever Uncle gives over. Can you keep her from going on to New Mexico?"

"Me, I can try."

✶ ✶ ✶

May of 1865 was hot in the Territory. Jimmy Melton's horse kicked up spurts of dust as he trotted to Anne Marie's wagon, in response to a shout from Dr. John.

"What can I do for you, Chucky Jack?" Melton smiled. He knew the dentist had been in the agony of the retreat from the liquor for days now.

"I will tell you what you can do, you god-damned Cossack. You can get me out of this wagon. Let me borrow this saddle you've stashed here, and I will buy a horse from those Cherokees. I see they have several spares."

"Think you're ready for that?"

"My body has not let me have liquor for four days. I find I don't sleep so much, and even the swill you serve begins to have taste." He groaned as the wagon bumped over a rock. "Please, Melton. Help me regain my dignity. Let me ride."

"I dunno, Doc. What's a Cossack?"

☆ ☆ ☆

"Good to see the Doc bright-eyed, sort of, and on horseback," Dobey noted.

"Durn sure does, Cap'n," Buck responded. "Tried to buy that horse, but Lieutenant Ridges give it to him. 'Spect you recognize that saddle. Don't know what he'd accomplish with that little fancy Colt, though."

"Told me it's called a Police Model, Buck. .36 caliber, like mine, but smaller, five-shot. Not a bad gun. And he might surprise you with it. That old man was killing men with pistols 'fore you were born."

Buck stared at the dentist with new respect. "Wish we din't have to go on to New Mexico. Kind'a would like to stay on with y'all, once we gets to Texas."

"Why can't you?"

"Cap'n, I can't let my family go on without me to help look out for 'em. I know Mandy don't want to go. As she ain't needed for fighting, and Jimmy Ridges won't take her back with him, she might ast to stay on with y'all."

"Honey likes her. I'm sure that will be all right, if your Pa says so. You know how you're gonna get to New Mexico?"

"Nossir. We don't know much, 'cept it's West and South. Guess we'll ast questions as we go."

"You don't want to go Southwest from Canadian Fort, Buck—it's all right, for a ways, but then there's the Llano Estacado."

"Come again?"

"It means 'Staked Plain' in Spanish. It's so bad, old timers put stakes out there so's you could find your way across."

"Durn, Cap'n. What we gonna do? Daddy's got a cousin in Santa Fe, and he's set on going there."

"From Canadian Fort, the old buffalo trail goes north and crosses the Santa Fe trail. Should be traffic on that, summertime and the war's over. Maybe you could hitch up with a wagon train there. Some of us might go and wait with you, if you can wait til we get set up at the store."

✯ ✯ ✯

Jimmy Ridges poured another cup of coffee, and passed it to Melton as he sat by the fire. "Your men, Bear and Buck, have been riding with my lead scouts."

"Thanks, Lieutenant. I know. They asked me."

"Figured that. Well, my men say they are doing well. Buck picked up the track of that deer we are eating. One of my men missed it."

Dobey joined them. "Tell us about this Black Kettle we're heading for."

"Cheyenne," said Ridges. "Was loyal to the Yankees, up in Colorado. Six, maybe seven moons ago, Colorado militia attacked his camp at Sand Creek. Bunch of people killed on both sides, 'bout the same number of warriors for each, but the Cheyennes lost many women and children. Black Kettle says they was flying the Yankee flag and a white flag, and was where they was told to be, but it didn't do no good. Moved his camp down here on the Washita after that. Sort of an old woman. Don't want to fight no more. But he don't keep a tight rein on his young men, and we worry which way he'd jump."

"You mean, if he had to choose 'tween you and the Yankees?"

"'Tween us and the Yankees." Ridges put emphasis on the 'us' while drawing a little circle to include Dobey and Melton. "You're still in this, as you still wear the gray. Anyhow, a couple of days, I'll break out Uncle's flag and we'll show it as we get close. Nobody out here wants to be on Stand William Watie's bad side, 'specially no old woman Cheyenne chief."

Melton asked, "Speaking of old, what age is that tough old uncle of yours? He's got more sand than most men I've knowed."

"This will be his fifty-ninth summer."

✡ ✡ ✡

"Boss Melton, this little Fort we's going to. Is they something for me to do there, or does I go to Santa Fe with them Watsons?"

"Always work for a strong man, Big William, 'specially can he cook. Even if he is blind as a bat."

CHAPTER FORTY

And the women talked, too.

As they walked away from the fire, Mandy looked back at the men. "Says he wants me, but he can't take me now. Says we gotta wait til the war is over. I thought the war was over already."

"His war, it is not." Marie-Louise looked back, too, and unconsciously touched her own breast as her gaze lingered on Melton. "I think he is serious 'bout his work, your man, like my Jimmy Melton and Dobey."

"But they are taking you to meet Dobey's mother, to work with her, get married. How's that like my Jimmy? He's gonna take us to your damn old fort..."

"Is not really a fort, that place."

"Whatever it is, he's gonna leave us there, and go back to his brother and uncle, and maybe twenny Indian girls, and if I go on to New Mexico, I ain't gonna never see him again. I just know it."

"You mus' stop the crying, cher. We mus' think on this. Maybe that Santa Fe is too far. We will ask your mama to help. Maybe we get your Papa to let you stay with us in Canadian Fort. Maybe, if that is not so far, your Jimmy, he will come back. Did you, um, you know, did you yet? With him?"

"Nooo," Mandy wailed. "It's like he's scared to. He ain't even tried."

"Good. You don't need no baby yet."

✯ ✯ ✯

For several evenings, Lieutenant Jimmy Ridges put a section of scouts across the Canadian as pickets, while the main force of the convoy camped on the bluffs above the south side.

"Might have seen you down by the river last night." Honey was tentative. Though only a few years older, the whore Junebug was so worldly that she could be intimidating to almost anyone, though her nature seemed sweet. "You and Doc, that is."

"Seems a few folks is going down by the river," Junebug smiled. "What made you think you seen us?"

"Cherokees had a fire, cross the river. Dobey, he said he saw its reflection off of Doc's head. Maybe."

Junebug laughed out loud, as they walked back to the wagon from a toilet trip to the bushes. "Yeah, that's one time I won't let him wear that little hat he favors. And if we had a bed, I'd make him take his boots off, too."

"He seems to be doing some better now, since he, uh, he slowed down, you know."

"Honey, he's quit. Has to. He picks that bottle up again, it'll kill him, and I'll leave him first. I ain't nursing him no more. Now, lookit him. He's put on some weight, got some color, got some juice flowing again. Hellfire, he was like a young stallion last night. Only once, but you got to understand, I ain't been able to get a rise out of him til just lately."

"You kind of like him, don't you." It was more of a statement than a question.

"Yeah. And he needs someone to take care of him, but I got needs too."

"You have, or had, all those other men. You need more?"

"Honey, you think them customers had any interest in my needs? Not a damn one of 'em. But Doc is sweet, and last night was just fine." She turned, and raised her brows at Honey. "If you was close enough to see his bald noggin, you must've heard me. Couldn't you tell I had fun?"

Honey blushed. "I was surprised. Dobey, he asked me, why I don't ever make sounds like that."

Junebug stopped walking and grabbed Honey by both shoulders. "Oh, my stars. It's still all one-sided 'tween y'all. Honey, child, we got to talk."

✫ ✫ ✫

"Oh, I just don't know. My husband ain't never going to want to leave her nowhere, after he seen what happened to me back there." Hazel Watson glanced toward her husband.

"Ain't nothing we can do to change that, what happened, but maybe she can find a way to be happy." Marie-Louise kept her voice low as she walked with Mrs. Watson between the wagons.

Mrs. Watson sobbed, and, as was her habit, bit her thumb. "Mr. Watson ain't had nothing to do with me since it happened. Says he don't want to hurt me. Well, he is hurtin' me. Bad."

Marie-Louise murmured sympathetic noises while she digested that, but pressed her case anyhow. "Your baby, she has the same fears—that no man will want her. And she is feared that Santa Fe is too far, and that might keep him from returning for her. You see? She can stay with me and Honey, and our men. And Dobey's mother. And, cher, if this Jimmy Ridges don't come back for her, I will make the men bring her to Santa Fe."

"But what if he do come back, and marries her, won't I never see my baby again? Or my grandbabies?"

"Cher, if he comes back for her, she can make him take her to anyplace. Trust me on that, I guarantee."

"Maybe. I could try to convince her daddy to let her stay," she sniffed.

"And, cher, maybe you ask that girl, Junebug, maybe she could tell you some ways to get your husband back to doing right by you. You know?"

"Oh. Oh my." Mrs. Watson nodded, and smiled.

✲ ✲ ✲

"Honey-Marie, you seem very happy with your Dobey. He still don't be mean to you?"

"Oh, Mama, he wonderful. He make me so happy. He say, when we come to his mama's place, we can be marry, and have babies."

"But not now, cher, not on this trail. Non?"

"No, Mama. We careful. Mama, do you know he thinks you are like his mama?"

"No! Get away from here. He do?"

"Oh yes, Mama. He talk about his mama a lot. He told me once they was moving, and his baby sister was playing away from the wagon a little, and had her some fried chicken leg. Well, this ol' mean dog kind of animal come after it. There was barking and screaming, and what-all, and his mama, Miss Annette, she run out there right at it. She pulling up prairie grass and throwing it and yelling, 'I'll kill you! Get away from my baby!' Like a old she-bear, looking out for her cub. This animal, what do Dobey call it? Oh – coyote. That's it. Well, he snarling, but he back away. Then Dobey's papa, he a sergeant, he shoots it dead, and he say, 'Mama, you done good. I think he believed you!' And Dobey's mama, she say, 'I would have, too. Strangled him dead my ownself, did he touch one of my babies!'" Honey finally took a breath.

Marie-Louise mused. "I think I will like this woman. If we ever find her."

☆ ☆ ☆

Junebug squatted by the creek, then asked Marie-Louise to pass her a page from the catalogue.

"Well, that Jimmy Melton, I 'spect he's like a wild horse when he gets going, ain't he?"

"Oh, oui—very strong. Powerful."

"Ever' now and then you might just ride him like he was."

"Oh. You mean on top?"

"Yup. He won't dislike it, neither, specially when he sees how you like it."

Marie-Louise, thirty-two years old, mother of two, actually blushed. "Merci. I dunno. Maybe, this I will try. I dunno. Merci."

CHAPTER FORTY-ONE

Buck lowered the lever on the Sharps slightly, and checked the chamber for the third time. It was still loaded. He laid it across the ancient, rock-hard driftwood log, drew the Remington, checked the caps, and laid it on the ground beside the Sharps' cartridge pouch. He was ready. Corporal William Jumper had told him to be.

Jumper himself was fifteen yards in front of him, crawling to get a better view of the party of Indians butchering a deer downhill from them, on the riverbank. "Wait here, and be ready to cover me, if they ain't friendly Cheyenne," Jumper had whispered.

They cut the trail of nine ponies one hour earlier; the party had crossed the Canadian and turned west. Jumper said that seven of them carried riders, probably Cheyenne, but certainly Indians as they were unshod. Probably Cheyenne, because they were heading toward Black Kettle's camp too.

Bear and Sergeant Strong Branch were scouting about a half-mile south of the river, on a parallel course. Buck wished they were here. His mouth was as dry as sand. He put a pebble in his mouth, and cocked the Sharps as quietly as he could. The snap-click sounded like a cannon.

Jumper looked back aghast, signaled to be quiet, and turned back toward the seven Cheyenne. They were staring up the bank toward the brushy area where he hid.

Jumper shouted something that Buck didn't understand, then stood, holding his short Enfield over his head with both hands. It looked to Buck like a sign of peace. Buck sighed in relief, and started to stand up.

He was then amazed to see Corporal Jumper's hat sail back toward him, past him. There was an arrow in it. Jumper dropped to one knee and shot one of the Cheyenne, before scrambling back toward Buck. There was an arrow in his left arm, too.

The .577 caliber minie ball from the Enfield knocked the Cheyenne over the deer's carcass. Buck spit out the pebble, shot at a second Cheyenne who had started to charge up the slope, levered open his breech, shoved in another paper cartridge and re-cocked. When he raised up to look for another target, an arrow spranged off the petrified log a foot from his head. He fired at some movement downhill, and ducked to load again.

Jumper slid in beside him, gasping for breath, and started the drill to reload the Enfield: pull a paper cartridge, bite the bullet, pour the powder down the barrel, thumb-press in the bullet, draw the rammer, ram the charge, finger a primer cap from the pouch on your belt, prime the rifle, look for a target. Awkward, lying behind a log. Just regular damn-all fun, with an arrow through your left forearm.

By the time he'd finished, Buck had fired a third time, and reloaded. It was suddenly quiet.

"Keep a lookout. I will try to pull this arrow on through." Jumper grunted in pain, but couldn't budge it. He drew an old Paterson revolver and whispered to Buck, "Have your pistol ready for a charge."

"We gonna charge them? They's five or six left."

"No, but they might charge us. Slide around here on my other side, and saw off the tip of this arrow. Try to pull it back through, same way it came in. I'll watch. Keep your head down." Another arrow thunked against the log.

Buck sawed off the eight inches of arrow protruding from Jumper's arm. Jumper grabbed that piece, put it between his teeth, and said "Now, yank it back out. Put your feet on my arm, and use both hands. I will empty my pistol to keep them back." He bit down on the piece of arrow, and opened fire.

Buck did as he said, and by Jumper's fourth shot, the arrow pulled clear. There was a lot of blood, but no spurting. Buck pulled off his kerchief, and tied it over the wound. Hearing horses thundering up behind them, he grabbed the Remington and spun around. It was Bear and Strong Branch. They dismounted twenty yards from the rim, and crouched forward. Ten yards out, Bear stood up and let fly with his Spencer, four shots rapid fire. As the Cheyenne broke cover to run for their ponies, Strong Branch carefully shot one with his Sharps. Buck saw blood fly off the Cheyenne boy's head as he was hit.

"Let the others go," said Strong Branch. He looked at Jumper's arm, and changed the kerchief bandage into a tourniquet as he talked.

"This was just a Cheyenne hunting party. Young boys. Did you fire on them first?"

"No, Sergeant. I stood, made the peace sign and said 'Hello, Brothers' to them. They shot their arrows into my hat and my arm, so we fired back."

"You spoke in English to them?"

"No, of course not. I spoke in Cherokee."

"And you thought they would understand that?"

"I do not speak Cheyenne. They shot me before I could make any more signs."

"Listen, Sergeant, it wasn't his fault," Buck defended his companion. "It happened just like he said, and it's a wonder he ain't dead."

Bear came back from checking the downed Indians. "Both dead. Might've hit one or two more, but there's so much blood from the deer, I ain't sure. Some of their horses didn't go with 'em."

"Let's get the horses and the deer meat, and go report. We still don't know how close we are to Black Kettle's camp. He has many men, and they may come against us."

"We need to do that, but if we do, Lieutenant Ridges or Cap'n Dobey is gonna send us right back to find that camp." Bear was careful not to offend the old Cherokee sergeant. "Maybe we could send Buck and Jumper back with the horses and meat to report, and you and me, we could follow those scared boys right to their camp."

Strong Branch nodded. "That is a good plan. Ridges will like that." He smiled. "Give us your pistols, and get busy. Take the horses, and go fast. Leave the meat. Plenty more deer around here. Tell the lieutenant that when we find the camp one of us will stay and watch, and one will come back to report."

✵ ✵ ✵

Lieutenant Jimmy Ridges asked Doctor John to look at Corporal Jumper's arm, thanked the men for a good report and signaled Dobey to ease his horse away from the others.

"We could set up a perimeter here and wait. But since the Cheyenne ran west, I think we should keep moving, with flankers out, but close to the river. Maybe pick up those two dead Cheyenne, treat them with respect, take them to our meeting with Black Kettle. I do not think he will attack us, but he has many warriors, many more than us."

Dobey mused a moment. "Yeah. Good plan. He does come at us, we can set up below the high bank, have the river at our back. They come down the river, they're channeled, and we'd slaughter them. And they sure don't want to cross that river at us, under fire. They got many guns?"

"Some. Not enough to face us. I think they'll mill around, have conferences, wait for us. Black Kettle don't want to fight. He tried to negotiate with the Yankees last year at Sand Creek, while they was shooting at him. Maybe, when we get close, we'll spread out like regular cavalry on line, try to scare him a little. Then we'll talk." He looked to Dobey for approval.

"Lieutenant Ridges, I don't think you need any help at all. It's a better plan than mine would have been. I'd have never thought about taking those bodies in. That's a great idea. When we rejoin your sergeants, I'm gonna make sure they know this was your plan, that you were just being courteous to me as a captain."

Ridges beamed.

CHAPTER
FORTY-TWO

"Perhaps it is because I cannot keep liquor down, and perhaps it is because I have run out of cigars, but your cooking is a tonic to me. I must have gained seven pounds. My clothes actually fit. I'm sleeping well, despite that meddling wench's insistence on attention." Doctor John shifted in his saddle, to smile and wave to Junebug over in the other wagon.

"Yassuh." Big William clicked his tongue, to encourage the mule to pull Marie-Louise's wagon on through the shallow creek and up the slight bank. He liked to listen to the dentist, even when he was contentious, and just now he was being complimentary.

"Perhaps it is merely a miracle, but nevertheless, I choose to give your culinary skills full credit. My mother had a large Negress, Flossie, who was a magician in the kitchen, a goddamned magician I tell you, producing meal after incredible meal, and your cooking reminds me of hers. And she had a full staff, a full pantry, utensils from Europe, while you, sir, are working with scat."

"Sir?"

"Mere scat. Animal droppings."

"No suh! Ain't never cooked with no droppings, I promise."

"No, no, no, William. I meant your equipment, your few resources. A few pots and pans, almost no condiments, yet you too are a magician. If we ever reach some semblance of civilization again, I shall hire you away from those two Cossacks, and we shall open an eating establishment. Maybe whores and gambling on the side."

"Yassuh. What's a Cossack?"

✲ ✲ ✲

Jimmy Melton trotted back to the wagons, and shouted, "Stay awake, now. We're close to the place they fought. See them buzzards?"

Doc nodded and waved. "Hand me one of those shotguns, please, Big William."

Marie-Louise reached back into the wagon bed, took one of the long guns and handed it to Big William, and put the other over her lap.

Big William handed the gun to Doc. "Can't see no buzzards, myself."

"My God, William, they can't be a half mile up the river. Surely you are not older than I—when were you born? Or do you know?"

"My master, he said I was born in 1820." Big William smiled to hide his resentment. "I s'pose you didn't think an old darky would know something like that."

"Well, I'll certainly be damned. You are five years older than I am. You don't look it. And I did not mean to be condescending about your knowledge. It's simply that most men, people, out here, aren't aware of their birth year." He checked the caps on the shotgun. "Nevertheless, at forty-five years, I'm surprised at your loss of vision. Can you see up close, make out words?"

"Yassuh. I can read. Just can't see too far, not small things, like birds. Boss Melton, he calls me Blind William." He shrugged and grinned.

"Well, I may have something for you. I'll be right back." He trotted over to the other wagon.

Melton rode back to join them again. "That's the place. Scouts found the bodies. Corporal Jumper and Buck took 'em right to it." He smiled at Marie-Louise, who was obviously apprehensive.

"Ever'thing, she is all right, cher?"

"Yeah. All clear. They had to chase off a big damn bear, but that means there ain't nobody else around."

"Not our Bear?"

"No, Marie. Our Bear's on up there somewhere, tracking them Indians, 'scuse me, them Cheyennes."

"Boss Melton, that Doctor John says you and Cap'n Dobey was Russian cavalrymen. Just tole us that. Didn't he, Miz Marie-Louise?" Big William seemed concerned and confused.

"Yeah, well, we ain't no Cossacks. And never was, neither. He just means it as a insult. Says they's the most meanest cavalry in the world. Wait til he goes up against Comanche or Kiowa, he'll see what 'mean' is. Worse yet, Apache."

Doc rejoined them, and handed his medical bag to Marie-Louise, seated beside Big William.

"In the bottom there, you'll find several sets of spectacles. I took them from people who didn't survive my medical assistance. Some are just reading glasses, but some are for distant vision. Help him try some on."

With the fifth pair, Big William said, "Oh my sweet Jesus, Doctor, I can see them birds."

Melton snorted, "I guess you can. They ain't but five feet across the wings, and less'n a hundred yards away."

"Nossir, Boss. Not them buzzards. I mean them two pigeons, just took off across the river."

Doctor John gave Melton a smile of incredible smugness. "Damned Cossack."

Melton flared. "Bold talk, for a skinny old bald man. I s'pose it helps that you got a twin barrel shotgun pointing in my general direction."

Doc carefully handed the shotgun back to Big William, who had halted the wagon. "I spit in your general direction, sir." And to Melton's astonishment, he did. And in the blink of an eye, that little Colt Police Model was out, cocked, pointing at Jimmy Melton's chest.

Melton, later, could not remember seeing him draw it. It was suddenly just there.

"Easy, Doc, Boss, y'all ain't enemies here," said Big William.

"I know that, Goddammit. The Cossack does not."

Melton focused on Doc's eyes, watching for a flinch, any opening. He saw none.

Doc abruptly de-cocked the Colt, still staring at Melton. "You are the last man I know that I would pick a fight with. You, or your captain, either. Junebug saw your performance in Mason's Landing, and told me. Warned me, as if I were blind, unable to see how dangerous you are. That's what 'cossack' means: dangerous, tough, mean. But as you see, I am not helpless. Finally. Again."

Melton let out his breath. "Yeah. I did see that. I don't think even the cap'n is that fast." He was embarrassed.

Doc said quietly, "It was not an insult, Melton. You are helping me get my life back. You, the captain, Big William, that evil slut Junebug, all of you. I'm grateful. It's as if I've been sleepwalking for fifteen years. But I cannot accept a slight." In a louder voice then, for all to hear, "But even if I got off the first shot, there's an excellent chance that you would have still killed me. Everyone here knows that."

Melton muttered, "You talk too much," and rode to find Dobey.

✳ ✳ ✳

As the scouts finished lashing the two dead Cheyenne on horses, Jimmy Ridges turned to Dobey and Melton. "These Cheyenne, they were lucky."

"I'm not sure how that works," Dobey answered. Jimmy Melton just stared as if the lieutenant was insane.

"Lucky that the bear got here first. He kept the other scavengers away and he began to eat the deer first. It was already butchered part ways, and not wearing smelly clothes, so he had not yet chewed on these men."

"Yeah," said Melton. "Pretty damn lucky. Where's the deer?"

"The bear took it in his mouth and ran across the river with it when our men came close. The deer was bigger than either of these dead boys, also lucky for them. He took the biggest kill."

"If you're saying these boys 'bout used up their luck, I'd agree with you."

"Yes," Ridges smiled, happy that Melton agreed with him. The big Texan was intimidating to everyone. "We'll go on a ways before we camp. All this blood will draw other animals here, and the two boys are bled out, so they won't trail us."

"Lucky."

Shouting caused them to scramble back up the embankment, in time to see Bear ride in.

✳ ✳ ✳

Old Ben stepped out of the privy as he pulled up his pants and re-shouldered his suspenders. Mason's Landing was quiet most mornings, and especially right at dawn. A couple of yards away, a rooster crowed away with great determination.

"Wastin' your breath," muttered Ben. "Whole town's made up of sporting ladies and drinking men. If'n you does wake 'em up this early, they liable to kill you. Go make some eggs or something." He threw a stick at the bird, then opened the back door of the jail.

"Ol' fool nigger," he said to himself, "you knowed they wasn't no way them white folks was gonna keep you as marshal. You just lucky you got this ol' jail to sleep in. Now the war's over, you needs to just get you a job on one a' them down-river boats, where they is regular food. Get on back to Baton Rouge. Yessir, that's what you needs to do."

As he stepped from the cell corridor into the office, the smell of cigar smoke brought him up sharp out of his reverie. A familiar face sat at the desk. A dreaded familiar face.

"Morning, Rastus. No, no, no, now, don't even think about leaving. No sir. I don't want to turn this scattergun loose on your legs, least not afore we have a good talk. Just turn around there and let's cuff your wrists to them jail bars. That's right, face right up against 'em. Hands up high, Rastus."

Ben felt the cold cuffs snap onto one wrist, then the other. "I, I'se never done nothing to you, Boss," he stammered. A knife nicked his back as his shirt was cut away.

"Oh, I seen you grin when that sumbitch knocked my teeth out, Rastus. Now, you just tell me all you heard about them Rebels, and where they was going, and how, and so on."

"Boss Fetterman, I don't know nothing about that. You think them white folks told me nothing?"

The knife nicked his buttocks this time, as his rope belt was cut and the blade was used to push his pants down.

"Spread them legs, nigger. Let's see do this help you remember."

Ben felt the cold steel on the inside of his thigh before he realized what was coming next. He began to scream.

CHAPTER
FORTY-THREE

When Bear reported that Black Kettle was less than twenty miles west, right on the Canadian, Lieutenant Ridges decided to cook at the sight of the fight, and press on to a dark camp afterward. Bear had picked a spot, eight miles farther on, that he thought was defendable. He ate and drank slowly and thought about each answer, as Jimmy Ridges and Dobey questioned him.

There were thirty-six lodges, so maybe one hundred and fifty people in camp, but lots of coming and going from the southwest so there might be other camps out there, Bear thought. *Didn't seem like enough young men, so they might be away hunting or raiding. Lots of horses; they stirred up too much dust to be counted, but over two hundred. There was a lot of agitation among the Cheyenne, but mostly they seemed to be having meetings. When they would start to shout, an old black haired-man would calm them.* When Bear mentioned that, Jimmy Ridges said that the old man was probably Black Kettle.

Bear finished his report. "Anyhow, we move now, and we can make that camp 'fore dark. We gonna strike 'em in the morning, or try to talk to 'em?"

Ridges said "We'll leave the wagons, women, and spare horses nearby and move on 'em 'fore daybreak. Line up, ready to charge 'em, with the sun rising behind us. Then we'll hold up our guns and see if they won't parley."

"Good luck with that," whispered Corporal Jumper. Buck coughed to suppress a giggle.

Ridges turned to glare at them, then smiled. "I know. You tried it and were almost wiped out. But their wind is up now. They don't know who we are. Everyone will put on their gray jackets tomorrow, even though it is too hot. Black Kettle should not want to fight Stand Watie's men, but he has us outnumbered maybe three to one. We may have to kill him." There was a murmur of approval from the Cherokee sergeants. "Finish eating quick. Bear will lead us."

✫ ✫ ✫

Doc cleaned his plate with sand, stuck it in his saddlebag, and helped Junebug up into the Watson's wagon. "Doc, honey, can I ask you a big favor?" She grabbed his hand as he squeezed her bottom.

"Why, almost anything, Lass. You're my savioress."

"I worry sick about you. There's so much danger here already." She paused. "Please, Doc, don't take the Lord's name in vain so much."

Doc looked at her, stunned. "Sweet God in Heaven, am I to have a whore chastise me on my language? Jesus Christ, Junebug, I am trying my very best..."

"See, Doc, there you go again. It scares me. Indians don't kill you, or a snake, then a lightning bolt will. Please, Doc, just try."

Doc mounted and rode, for once in his life at a loss for words.

When he caught up with Marie-Louise's wagon, he slowed to a walk, and spoke to Big William. "That cook, Flossie, she used to serve us cool tea. It was sweetened, sugar or honey, I don't know, and crushed mint always, but there was something else. Could it have been the juice of oranges?"

"Yassuh—sure could have been. I've fixed that myself. Sure wish we had some oranges. Cut up a mess of 'em, squeeze 'em, put 'em inside a pig on the spit. Maybe little cuts 'tween the ribs, so's that juice mixes in with the meat. Ummm-um! Make your tongue slap the top of your mouth. Yassuh."

Doc rubbed his face. "I would kill for a God-d..., a, uh, an orange, just one, right now. Big William, I despair that I will ever see one again."

In the dark camp, Bear squatted beside Dobey as he checked his revolvers. "Myself, I still don't know have I killed someone yet. Maybe a Cherokee at the boat fight," he shrugged, as he looked at the caps on his Remington.

"Don't think I'd claim that one," smiled Dobey.

"No. But Cap'n, those fights, this one and back at the boat, they were sudden. No time to think. Now, I must think about the morning, no?" He paused. "That time, in Mason's Landing. Did you know you was gonna shoot them deputies, before you got down from the horse? Did you already know?"

"No, Bear. I meant to disarm them. But when that one went for his pistol, there was no more time for talking. Turned out they were scum, anyhow."

"What will it be like in the morning?"

"We'll try to scare 'em, get 'em to talk. But you have one or two picked out. If they charge, or open fire, you start killing. And don't let up."

✼ ✼ ✼

Not very far away, Black Kettle was trying to wrap up his war conference. He sent for two of the survivors of the 'deer fight,' and addressed the other leaders at the fire.

"I think we must be careful here. I know our Dog Soldiers will not take a slight laying down, but maybe these young men of ours gave the slight."

The two young warriors approached the conference fire nervously, nodding to the older men.

"Tell us again of how this fight happened. You have had time to think and remember. What you say will help us find the right path now."

Striker started to speak, but the younger Tree Bender cut him off. "We followed the Osage party for two days, and stole two of their ponies. Then we saw the deer..."

An old fighting chief, Weasel, laughed. "Why don't you start with your birth?"

The laughter at Tree Bender's expense eased the tension. Black Kettle put on a serious face. "Just start with the appearance of the enemy fighters. When did you see them? What did they say, and do, and look like? How many?"

Tree Bender was too embarrassed to talk, so Striker began. "We were down on the river flat, butchering the deer that Tree Bender dropped. The first enemy stood up on the bank above us, and said something. He held his rifle over his head."

"With both hands? Like this?" Weasel demonstrated with his Hall carbine. "That means 'parley.'"

"Yes, Weasel. There were others, I don't know how many, maybe five or six, but we could not see them. Yet."

"And how did this fighter look, and how did he sneak up on you?"

Tree Bender, even more embarrassed, responded. "We were making noise, happy for the good raid, happy for the kill. We were in our land, this side of the river."

"You thought you were safe. Good lessons are often expensive."

"Yes, Grandfather." He held up his bandaged arm, and gave the older men a rueful smile. "The first fighter was not white. I think maybe a Cherokee, and he wore a gray uniform, with a yellow marks, some stripes like a tipi on his arms, but upside down."

"Gray. Not Blue. You are sure?" There was much muttering around the fire.

Tree Bender nodded, and Striker spoke. "He's right. Squirrel Killer was surprised and shot two arrows at the Gray Man very fast. He shot off his hat and hit him in the arm. The enemy fired one shot, then ran away. I think he killed Squirrel Killer."

"Yes. I looked at Squirrel Killer before we left, and he was gone. But the Gray Man didn't run far. He joined some other men behind a rock log, and they poured heavy gunfire at us. That's when I was hit."

"And then some more fighters came," added Striker. "One was a giant Black Man. He had a short rifle that fired many times, without reloading. And at least one more Gray Man. I think he had a Sharps. He killed Black Feather."

"You know this to be true? I would not like to think my son was left wounded." Spotted Pony spoke for the first time. He was a famous fighter but had been crippled in the attack at Sand Creek the year before.

"He was aiming his arrow at Black Man, and the second Gray Man shot him in the head. He did not suffer." Tree Bender nodded agreement, and Spotted Pony grunted thanks for the assurance. "And then we ran away."

"And left three ponies and two dead men," said Weasel.

Striker stared at him, eye to eye. "They had guns. We did not. I think there were more of them than us. I think they wanted to talk, and we made them angry."

Black Kettle struggled to his feet. "Enough. I have decided, for me. I believe these were Stand Watie's men, the Gray Cherokee Riders. He has never attacked us, though he could roll over us like a flood. He has more men than there are trees along this river. I think that, in the morning, we should send riders to try to make peace. Just say our young men were startled, and thought the Gray Men wanted their deer. And we should move the camp tomorrow farther away from Stand Watie's hunting grounds, to the Lodge Pole River, toward the setting sun. That's what I think. And you young men, you go back and bring us the bodies of those two boys."

The Cherokee Scouts moved out about 0400 hours, with Bear leading. An hour later, Bear found Sergeant Strong Branch in the rocky stand of trees they'd agreed upon, and the little army dismounted and moved forward, leaving one man from every five as horse holders. They moved to a low ridge above the camp, where they spread out and lay down on the reverse slope to wait for sunrise.

Lieutenant Ridges sent Dobey, Melton, Bear and two Cherokees with Paterson revolving carbines on their horses to the right of the line, near the river. They were to take the Cheyenne under enfilading fire if they charged the Cherokee line.

At the first green flash of daybreak, Ridges and his flag bearer mounted and rode into view on the ridge line, and his thirty-five riflemen silently stood up. As he raised his weapon overhead, so did his men, and Dobey with his four riders trotted out and lifted theirs, too. It was almost a minute before they were noticed.

An old Osage woman, a slave sent to re-kindle the cook fire was first. She noticed a dog growling, and turned to find why. Staring into the rising sun, it took another ten seconds for her sleep-numbed brain to register what she was looking at: a two hundred yard long line of gray-clad men, holding rifles over their heads. She screamed, turned, stepped in the fire, and screamed again. The village erupted like a kicked anthill.

Fortunately for all, Black Kettle himself was the second person in the village to see the Cherokees. Up early to make water, he had just stepped out of his tipi when the woman screamed. As his warriors boiled out of their tipis, he was already shouting, "Do not shoot! Do not fire! Tell everyone! No shooting!" Others picked up the call, and soon a line of seventy armed men stood behind Black Kettle as he waved a white flag on a pole.

Another ten Cheyenne mounted and faced Dobey's mounted party. They put on a small sideshow, pirouetting their ponies, doing bounding dismounts and remounts, and flourishing their weapons.

"Damn good horsemen," observed Jimmy Melton.

At that moment, Big William lumbered up bareback on a mule with a rope harness. He pulled up beside Melton.

"Look like you's outnumbered, Boss," William gave Melton his biggest smile.

"Thought I tole you to stay with the wagons."

"Yassuh. But Miz Marie-Louise, she walked up top and looked down to here. Then she came back and said, 'You take your black ass and that Avenging Angel,'" Big William patted the Colt shotgun, "'and go help Bear and Boss Melton.' That's what she said."

Melton actually blushed. It was somehow frightening.

Lieutenant Jimmy Ridges rode forward thirty yards and shouted in Cherokee, "I come from my Uncle, Chief Stand Watie, to talk to Black Kettle." The flag-bearer rode out with him; he was an old Creek named Speak Easy, who could converse in all the dialects of the Southern Plains. He repeated everything in Cheyenne.

A handsome black-haired warrior of maybe sixty years stepped forward. "I am Black Kettle. My Chiefs and I have talked, and thought you might be coming. How is Chief Watie?"

"He is well, thank you, Chief. He is still undefeated. I have two of your warriors, who died when they attacked my men, a half day's ride down river." He lowered his carbine, and signaled Buck and Jumper forward. "I am returning them to you, with their horses. I would have brought their deer, but a bear took it away. Can we lower our guns, and have a smoke?"

✳ ✳ ✳

As Ridges, Dobey and Melton joined Black Kettle's parley, the Cherokee scouts formed a defensive perimeter on the ridge line around the wagons. Fires were started, and breakfast served.

Doc picked up a canteen that had been emptied to make coffee. "William, you fill that with coffee, and I'll walk it down with some cups for the captain and that God-da...that damned Cossack Melton."

"'Speck that they could use some. I'll walk with you," Bear finished a corn dodger and picked up his Spencer.

"Thank you. But why don't you give that repeater to Buck here, in case we have to run back up this hill? Borrow Big William's Colt scattergun instead. I believe it would serve better down there, in those close quarters."

"Good. You think good, Doctor John. Are we taking your medicine bag, too? I think we hit some more of them."

"Yes. Good thinking yourself. If you sling that shotgun, they might not think you're the Archangel coming for them, and you can carry my bag."

As they walked up to the conference fire, Speak Easy stopped talking and looked at them expectantly. Bear said, "Go 'head on. We just bringing some coffee to the bosses here."

Speak Easy explained that many white men had to have the 'black water' to wake up, which drew some laughter. He then asked Dobey to explain where they were going.

"There's a ford, on this river, the Canadian. Used to be a small fort there. Some call it Canadian Ford, some Canadian Fort. It's on a trail coming from the north, off the Santa Fe Trail."

Weasel said, "There is a trading post there. Old white woman and a crippled man run it. We trade with 'em some. They're honest."

"That's probably my mother and brother. Wonder what happened to my step dad? Anyhow, we're going to help them, make the business bigger, now the war's over. I hope you'll keep trading there. We'll want horses, skins, salt. You'll have to tell us what you want."

When translated, Dobey's simple statement left the conference in shambles for ten minutes. These were staggering facts. The war was over. Who had won? Were the blue coats gone for good? Did this mean more white men? Fewer? More would be good for trade, since there were plenty of buffalo just to the west. Maybe the whites would all go on to Santa Fe, and fight the Apaches. Or the Mexicans, again. What's a step dad?

At a break in the questioning, Dobey and Melton thanked Bear for the coffee, and were told it had been the Doc's idea.

Melton looked at him hard, and said, "Well. You ain't half bad, for a Goddamned bald old drunk."

"Best not let Junebug hear that language. She might cut you." He looked back to Dobey and Lieutenant Ridges. "Speaking of cutting. Shall I offer my services, or will that offend?"

Ridges nodded to Speak Easy, who had heard the exchange. In Cheyenne, Speak Easy said, "That older one who looks like he's been scalped, he's our medicine man. He doesn't wish to offend your medicine men, but if they need help because of this fight, Lieutenant Ridges offers it. His specialties are teeth and venereal disease."

Chaos reigned again. One warrior stood and exposed his infected member, while others crowded in to show Dr. Thomason their teeth. An English-speaking captive was found to translate, and Doc was led away to hold sick-call elsewhere. Melton signaled Bear to go with him.

Finally, Black Kettle knocked the ashes out of his pipe and stood. "Well, I am pleased that Chief Stand Watie does not choose to go on the warpath against us over this misunderstanding. We have always been friends. And you have honored us by bringing us the bodies of our dead warriors, who started this, and their horses. And you didn't let that bear eat them. I'm going to give you four fresh horses, for your Chief. And I'm going to move toward the headwaters of the Lodge Pole, nearer to Canadian Fort, so that we may trade with your friends here, and maybe look over them for you. If your Chief Watie would like that."

"He would consider that a most important gift."

"We will move today. You may ride with us, so there'll be no more trouble with other Dog Soldier camps in these grasslands."

Dobey's group returned to the Confederate perimeter and were astounded at the speed with which the Cheyenne camp was dismantled. In less than an hour, the lead travois headed west, and one hour later the campsite was lost in the haze behind them; a haze caused by the movement of hundreds of Cheyenne horses, which had been kept out of sight, up river.

At noon of the second day, Black Kettle rode up to Dobey and Jimmy Ridges. "South, there, one half day's ride, is the Lodge Pole River. We go there. For you, that post is two more days slow riding up this river. Ridges, if you wish now to go back to Watie's camp, I will send Dog Soldiers to escort your friends to the post."

"Thank you, Chief. My uncle said to take them there, so I will. But I will tell him of your generosity, your hospitality, when I give him the horses. I wish you good hunting."

CHAPTER
FORTY-FOUR

The Texas Panhandle was almost always hot in June, but this was unbearable, and not yet seven in the morning. No wonder the corn had died.

Annette Walls Balliett felt every one of her forty-five years, as she headed back from the outhouse. Her joints ached, her back hurt, reading gave her a headache. Though she didn't drink, having lived with the side effects of alcohol forever, there were times like this morning when she almost wanted a stout one.

She didn't stock the demon rum, though. That was a sure way to speed your trip to your reward. Indians who traded honestly with you would kill you for the stuff. Soldiers or Mexicans or drifters, nice as you please sober, would tear a place up, shoot you dead or worse, and feel bad about it later, if they even remembered it. Nosir. She hadn't survived thirty years out here, two dead husbands, one crippled son and one probably dead in the war, just to piss it away for some quick profits on liquor sales. Though God only knew what they'd do if things didn't get better soon. Never mind soon—it was already too late.

The U.S. Army kept a small camp here, off and on, in the '50s, though it never earned the name "fort" that folks allowed it now. They left for good in '61, and things went downhill from there.

Her first husband was a hard-drinking, hard-fighting, lovable Irish first sergeant, 'Big Mac' Walls. He was killed by Kiowas in '52, in Colorado, near Fort Motte. Left with a daughter and two young boys, Thomas and Thadeus, and forced to leave her quarters, she was saved by the post sutler, who'd been smitten with her for two years. She and the children moved in, and Timothy Balliett was more than a Godsend.

Balliett, the son of an Irish Army brat and a French trader, grew up in a trading post in the Territory, before enlisting for the Mexican War in '48. Medically discharged in 1849 with a mangled hand and leg, he returned "to the trade," became the sutler at Fort Motte in 1850, and fell in love. Thirty-year-old Annette Walls was in love as well—with her husband. When he was killed, Three Fingers Balliett finally had his chance. Never very handsome, he was quick-witted and hard-working. He became a good second father to the boys.

It was in his trading post at Fort Motte in the winter of '53 that they withstood the great Kiowa raid. Tad's leg was smashed, but he, young Thomas, Annette, and Balliett killed a bunch of warriors before the Kiowa withdrew. Some of them had been killed by gunfire from the barracks, seventy yards away, but the fort's commander gave them credit for at least nine.

For his "conspicuous bravery," young Thomas was also recommended for West Point by the major commanding the fort, who may have been influenced by the fact that Tom's father died taking a lance meant for him. The major was a lean intelligent German named Hamburger. Tom thought that Major Hamburger had hung the moon.

When Fort Motte was abandoned in '58, Balliett decided that Canadian Fort was an ideal site for a trading post, and moved the family there, minus their West Point cadet. They built a sturdy adobe store which doubled as their home, then added a corral and barn. They slowly built up a decent business in horses and buffalo hides, and Balliett hired a young Mexican vaquero, Tomaso, to find and break horses for sale to the hunters and army.

With the secession of Texas from the Union, the blue-coats left in '61. Worried about a pick-up in activity from the Comanche to their west, Balliett, Tad, and Tomaso dug a deep trench from the store to the barn, and hid two shotguns and ammunition out there, in case an Indian raid caught them away from the store. The real trouble didn't come from that quarter.

In '63 a small patrol of bluecoat Colorado Volunteers rode in one afternoon, asked after Rebels and Indians, then proceeded to get drunk. One of them baited Tomaso as a "Greaser," and Balliett told them to pay up and move on. As the soldiers mounted up, one said, "I ain't being ordered to leave over no damn Mexican," and shot Tomaso. Balliett rushed the killer with an axe, but was shot down by the others. Tad bolted the doors, and he and his mother scuttled through the trench to the barn. The soldiers emptied their pistols through the store windows, and finally rode away. Balliett and Tomaso both died that night.

That was over two years ago. They had been in survival mode since then, as most folks were on the frontier. A year ago, Tomaso's family came north looking for him. Ignacio Gomez had already lost four sons and most recently, his wife. With two daughters, Carmela, fifteen, and Manuela, twelve, he pegged his last hopes on his last son. The news of Tomaso's murder almost killed him.

Annette and Tad were as gentle as they could be, but Ignacio could not, would not comprehend until they took him to the grave. There, his face contorted, he grabbed his left arm, and collapsed. Annette finally revived him, but he remained partially paralyzed.

The Gomez family brought two pigs and a goat with them, and there was some seed corn in the two-wheeled dog-cart, pulled by a burro. Every little bit helped.

The girls could cook, tend the garden, and fetch water, so Annette employed them in the kitchen, and Tad and Ignacio added a covered porch with tables for serving food. When that was finished, Ignacio showed Tad how to add a smithy to their enterprise, and then became the only one-armed black-smith within a hundred miles. Six months later, Tad took Carmela as his wife. She was the one bright light in his mea-ger existence.

Balliett's Post was now a full-service establishment. There was a restaurant, gunpowder, lead, meat, hides, limited clothing, condiments, tobacco, coffee, lots of beans, horses, horseshoes, wagon wheel rims and repairs, a mail drop. All it lacked were liquor, whores, medical care, regular paying cus-tomers, rainfall, and safety. Some of that just had to change. The war had stopped virtually all traffic to and from the Santa Fe Trail.

As Annette approached the store, she made the decision she had dreaded facing for years. They would leave.

Inside, her little family moved lethargically to put to-gether another breakfast. She clapped her hands and said, "Listen up. There's gonna be a change. We're finished here. We're heading south and east, soon as we load up. Maybe Fort Worth, I don't know. I just know it ain't no good like it is."

✳ ✳ ✳

Three hours later, the wagon was loaded, as well as the dog-cart. Annette took a last look around. "Nacio, get your burro watered and hooked up, then help Tad with the mules. I've got to leave another note."

Ignacio stared past her out the open door, then pointed. "Comanches."

☆ ☆ ☆

Dobey had a terrible feeling of déjà vu as he looked down on the community of Canadian Fort. There was a large adobe building, a lean-to shed on each end, a barn, outhouse, and corrals. A small garden and cornfield, all brown and withered from the heat. No cook smoke. No dogs or chickens. No horses or milk cows. No people.

Well, not exactly. There were five people on the ground around the adobe and the barn. Even from this distance it was apparent that they were dead. They wore little or no clothing. Several had long black hair and the bodies were sun-darkened, as though they'd lain there for some time. It wouldn't need to be long in this heat. Not yet noon, it was already scalding hot.

Dobey couldn't hear the flies yet nor pick up the smell of death, but he knew it was there, waiting for him to come a little closer. He was in no hurry now.

Dobey's throat constricted. He hadn't seen his family in years. Years of fighting, and years of school before that, and finally this long trip 'home'. For most of that time, he hadn't even known where his family was. And now this. He couldn't breathe.

They'd heard the gunfire rolling over the plains more than two hours ago. At first, they thought it to be a distant thunder, but then realized that the skies were cloudless forever. They'd come on fast, but there had been no shots for quite awhile now. As they'd crested the ridge above the outpost, Melton thought he'd seen figures pushing some livestock into the trees along the river, heading away.

The river was half a mile further downhill to the right, beyond the barn. As he rode slowly down past the outhouse, Dobey could see the barn doors were standing open. Melton and Bear rode with him, pistols drawn, twenty yards out to either side, on full alert. The others waited atop the low ridge with the Cherokee scouts.

Melton and Bear spread out some, walking their horses slowly to check out the bodies. Bear halted and said, "Dead goat here. Three arrows. They ain't Cheyenne."

"Prob'ly Comanche, or Kiowa." Melton stood in the stirrups for a better look around. "Might be better we look these folks over, Dobey. You go on to the store. You might not want to see this."

Now Dobey fought the rising bile. Between the privy and the main building, his horse danced a little, then jumped a deep trench. It ran from some bushes behind the store to the back of the corral, then angled toward the back of the barn.

Dobey nudged his horse closer to the store and found that the trench began at a small door below ground level behind the bushes. Maybe it was secure. He couldn't tell. He looked back to his right toward Bear.

"Watch out for this ditch, Bear." With sagebush growing along it, it wasn't apparent until it was almost underfoot.

"Done crossed it, Cap'n. Empty back here. Anything in it there?"

Dobey shook his head and eased his horse past the store.

The far side of the adobe was the front. As he rounded to that side, Dobey was surprised to find a wagon and dogcart standing in a circle of debris with empty harnesses. When no one answered his call, he started to dismount.

The arrow came from the lean-to on his left. It went through the back muscle under his left arm and thudded into his saddle. As his horse danced sideways, dragging him, Dobey clamped his arm down on the arrow and twisted, breaking the shaft and freeing him from the spooked mount. He went down on his butt as another arrow sailed over his head.

One huge Comanche was ten feet away now, screaming and charging with a tomahawk. A second warrior was in the shed trying to notch a third arrow. Dobey shot them both twice, but the bigger one loomed over him. The warrior started the chopping stroke when his chest exploded in a spray of blood and he fell on Dobey.

Dobey pushed him off and struggled to his feet. Beyond the shed, Bear had dismounted and was reloading his Spencer after killing Dobey's assailant. Dobey shot the second Indian again for good measure.

Three mounted warriors burst from the barn and charged them, brandishing lances and clubs. Bear's horse bolted.

Bear deliberately shot the three Indian ponies, dropping them twenty yards away. As the first warrior jumped clear, Dobey drew a second pistol and opened up ,hitting him with a couple of shots and knocking him down.

Hearing gunfire behind him, Dobey spun to find Melton kneeling by the right end of the store, firing his Spencer at the attackers who'd come from the barn. From the shadows of the smithy behind Melton, a skulking Comanche stood and rushed forward with an axe.

Dobey yelled, "Jimmy!" He got off a shot and hit the Indian in the shoulder. The man dropped his axe but fell on Melton, screaming and biting. Dobey turned back toward the barn to see Bear drop the last of those fighters with a carbine shot. He then ran toward Melton and his attacker as they grunted, yelled, and twisted in the dirt. Melton had drawn a pistol but lost it, and now the big warrior had gotten behind him and locked him in a stranglehold while trying to draw his knife. Dobey pointed the pistol at the Indian's head from two feet away and snapped on an empty cylinder. The man's head disintegrated anyhow.

Twenty feet away, Bear stood with a smoking Spencer. Melton pushed off the dead man and glared at Bear. "Cut that pretty close, didn't you?" He picked up his own carbine and stood, looking around.

Bear shrugged and said, "Them other bodies? They're all Comanche. How 'bout the ones on your side, Boss?"

Melton said, "Yeah, mine too. Let's look inside."

The door stood open in a shattered frame.

"Prob'ly used that same damn axe," said Melton.

"Probably. But there's a little door 'around back too, could have been open." Dobey was having trouble talking. They stepped in, Dobey swinging right, Bear covering left.

The building was empty. Except for an old buffalo rug in the middle of the floor it was almost clean. No bodies. No blood. There were not even cobwebs.

"Maybe they got out through that ditch to the barn," said Dobey, almost choking.

"Them three mounted Comanche was in the barn, Cap'n. I'll go check," Bear went out, then turned back. "But maybe they was taken, Cap'n. Ain't no blood in here. Let's get them Cherokees down here and go after 'em."

Melton came in, his boots and spurs clattering on the wooden floor, the noise echoing on bare walls. "You find another note?"

Dobey shook his head, not trusting his voice. His eyes fogged a little, causing him to trip on the rug as he started back out.

Melton caught him as he stumbled, then pointed at the floor and whispered, "Dobey."

Dobey's spur had jumbled the rug and exposed a rope handle on a section of the floor. Melton motioned for Bear to come in and pointed it out to him too. Bear looked at Dobey and mouthed, "Open it?"

Bear grabbed the handle, but Melton stopped him. "Hold on—go slow, now," he whispered, then turned to Dobey. "I don't know what we'll find here, Cap'n, but you may not want to look. Let us go first. You stand over there." He nodded to Bear, who yanked the trapdoor open and peered down.

There were screams, followed by a shotgun blast. The screams gave Bear just enough time to spin away from the gunfire. Splinters flew from the ceiling.

Dobey found his voice and yelled, "Godalmighty, Bear, be careful. Son of a bitch! Are you hit?"

Ears ringing from the blast, they all still heard the next voice. "Thomas McDougall Walls, is that you up there? Using that language in front of your mother?"

☆ ☆ ☆

"We was leaving, Thomas. This very morning, leaving this lonely place. Going to find some civilization. I done my best to make it work, 'cause my Timothy thought this would be a good place. It just ain't." Annette Walls finally let go and began sobbing. "I only stayed so long 'cause I didn't want to leave him."

"Where is he, Ma?" Dobey stroked her arms.

"Oh, Thomas, you must have ain't got none of my letters. He's up on the hill out there, with Tomaso. Drunk soldiers kilt 'em, some years ago."

"Tomaso?" Dobey looked around. Tad and Bear had brought some chairs in from the debris-strewn yard.

"Nacio's boy." She nodded toward Ignacio and his daughters. "Their brother. Our horsebreaker." She sniffled, wiped her nose with a rag that Manuela handed her, then heaved a deep sigh. "Oh, yes. Done left Becky back at Fort Motte, but

I put a marker for her on the hill with Timothy and Tomaso. Visit 'em every day. Ain't much else to do."

"I got one letter from you after West Point, Ma. From Fort Motte. I went there looking for you before the war. Jimmy Melton here was with me. We found your note, but that's the last I heard 'til this April. We came straight here."

Annette squeezed his hand, eyes still glistening. "Oh, Thomas, I have been so scared you was dead too. Didn't want to put up another marker for another empty grave." She bit her fist and stared out the door at the hill. She sobbed again. "And I really, really didn't want to leave Becky again."

"Then don't, Ma. The Cherokees have gone after those Comanche raiders. I expect they'll get back your, uh, our livestock, or some of it. War's over, Ma. Things will start flowing again. I brought help and a lot of money and stuff, Ma. A lot. Maybe we can make a go of it now."

Melton had been sitting a few feet away as Doc worked on his bitten ear. He pushed Doc away and stood beside Dobey. "Make a go of it? Forget about making a go of it." The usually taciturn Ranger had excitement in his voice. "Miz Balliett, I been riding with your boy for over seven years. He's been dying to find you, or at least people been dying that got in his way. Now listen – it ain't about just making a go of it. We got all we need to build a real town here."

Doc snorted. "For a damned Cossack, you sure run off at the mouth."

Annette Walls Balliett smiled at the Doc, and said, "Well, I hope he will." She turned back to Melton and touched his arm. "Sergeant Major Melton, I don't know what you went through getting my boy back to me, but I want to hear every word of it."

THE END

ACKNOWLEDGMENTS

This work is classified as historical fiction, which means I've mixed in a few factual events and real people, with a lot of imagination. The classification also allowed me to play loosely with the facts. In many cases, I've replaced someone's heroic ancestor with one of my fictional friends, or put imagined words in the mouth of a real person.

The Eighth Texas Cavalry, Terry's Texas Rangers, were very real. Their record was superb. Fort Pillow, and the events I've described there, were real. In subsequent hearings and investigations, Terry's Rangers were singled out as the one Confederate unit that tried to stop the slaughter, and as the unit that took most of the prisoners. A great source book, *River Run Red*, by Andrew Ward, Viking, is available on that event. Alexander Shannon and his Raiders also were factual, as were their mission and results. The Rangers really did make the first and final charges of the Army of Tennessee. For more on the Rangers, see *Terry Texas Ranger Trilogy*, State House Press, P.O. Box 15247, Austin TX, 78761.

As far as I know, there was never a Mason's Landing at the site to which I've ascribed it.

General Stand Watie, his Cherokee Mounted Rifles, and their performance were essentially as I've portrayed them.

They did capture a riverboat on the Arkansas. Having chosen the losing side, they were relocated after the war, to obviously worthless lands in the Territory. On top of huge reservoirs of black goo, but that's another story.

Fort Motte, Colorado, did not exist, nor did Canadian Fort (or Ford). There is, however, a remarkable little town named Canadian there in the Panhandle, not far from the factual Adobe Walls.

Black Kettle and the Dog Soldiers were also real. Unfortunately, so was Lieutenant Colonel Custer. Again, another story.

Primary thanks go to the two ladies who share my home; my wife, Mary Skipper Long, and mom, Mildred Page Long. They've nurtured, listened, and encouraged me far beyond the call of duty.

At my office, special thanks go to two other ladies, Brenda Loner and Susan Yaeger, for typing the early drafts and all the corrections, and for attempting to show me how to get things done via computer. They were not successful. As they will confirm, I am a dinosaur, baffled by technology, other than that of guns. This work was handwritten, in a furious doctor-like scribble.

Because of that, we finally shifted to a medical transcription service, Transcript-USA, of Columbia, SC. Great people, there. Thanks, y'all.

Thanks also to J. Lee Butts, prolific author of action-packed Westerns. Jimmy Lee tried his best to get me to do right with my writing. I fear I disappointed him, but I did learn a lot.

Another productive writer, John W. Huffman, steered me through the final stages of publication, with his tireless wife Misty doing most of the work.

Special thanks to Bryan Penberthy for editing this work, and to Editor Ellie Davis of Presque, Charleston, SC, for steering me to Bryan.

I wish to mention my primary source documents, *The Blackpowder Annual*, a longstanding publication from Dixie Gun Works (Pioneer Press, PO Box 684 Gunpowder Lane, Union City, TN, 38281; phone 731 885-0374). Unfortunately, it is no longer published. Apparently distributors were not willing to assign it shelf space as an annual. I encourage you to call or write them to obtain back issues, before they're all gone. I did. I will really miss the *Annual*. Get just one copy and you'll see why.

Finally, thanks to all the family and friends who loaned me their names, vignettes, and encouragement for this effort, and to my partners in the South Carolina Writer's Workshop, who worked with me through the editing and continue to help me with the sequel. It's been fun.